Heart Stopper

R J Samuel

To Jesse, Hamish, Clio, and the rest of the menagerie, past and present. Love is not a strong enough word.

Author's Note

While some of the technologies mentioned obviously exist, the author has exercised broad license in altering them and creating new imaginary ones.

This novel is entirely a work of fiction. The names, characters, and incidents portrayed in it are fictional and the work of the author's imagination. Any resemblance to actual persons, living or dead, events, or companies is purely coincidental.

www.RJSamuel.com
Twitter: @R_J_Samuel

ACKNOWLEDGEMENTS

Thanks to all my readers, especially those who have given feedback. Thanks to Maeve Healy and Felicia (Flish) McCarthy for pushing the boat off the shore and keeping an eye on it during the journey, with a steadying hand and encouraging words. Thanks to Mary McGann, Bernadette White, Yvonne McEvaddy, and Evelyn Parsons, my early readers who provided excellent feedback and helped me to continue and to finish. And to Susan Millar DuMars, for her thoughtful and very helpful critique. Thanks to the members of the Kujowriters group who patiently listened to the early chapters at Java's (where one can find the best 'vegetarian' chicken Panini).

My research into pacemakers took me to many websites where I found a lot of technical information but I am also grateful for the human stories that influenced my approach to the technical aspects of the novel.

R J SAMUEL

PROLOGUE

Fairer Hall, New York
June 1974

Daniel Fairer the Third (or Three as his mother called him in her rare moments of levity regarding matters of the family) crouched behind the bulk of the couch in his grandfather's study. He was nine years old. The sound of his mother crying cut through him bringing out tears of his own. He strained to hear her as she spoke, her voice filtered through the dust-laden sunlight that streaked its lines from the arched windows to the wooden floor. He could see the rocking horse his grandfather had carved for him hugging the paneled wall.

"You know this isn't fair, he's *my* son. Just because you didn't have a son, that doesn't give you the right to take mine from me."

"I'm not forcing you to do anything." His grandfather's voice was only marginally louder than his mother's was but the words carried farther and clearer.

"But you're leaving me no choice!"

"You always have a choice. You can walk out of here with Daniel and try to make it on your own. It was your choice to get pregnant out of wedlock, your choice to have him. Your choice not to marry his father. And now you're repeating your mistakes."

"If it was all that bad why do you want him all to yourself now? Why can't you help me for once and just let me take him with me?"

"He is still my flesh and blood; he will do what you would not. I will make sure of that. Catherine, these are *your* decisions. You can portray me as a villain all you want but I am doing, as always, what is right for this family. If you're going to insist on leaving, on following these, these...barbaric people..."

"Father! They are not barbaric. I love Leo and he feels the same. He's going to be really famous one day, as a *true* healer."

"Those are your choices, Catherine, you take Daniel with you and bring him up in that pack of heathens, no money, no inheritance, no medical education, no chance to be what he is destined to be; or you leave him with me and he will have everything he could possibly need and he will *be* a Fairer."

"I can't leave him and you shouldn't be punishing him for this."

"Then take him, it is not my decision to punish him, it is yours."

Daniel heard his mother's footsteps walk past to the door of the study and then echo through the grand hallway.

"Daniel!" Her voice was shaky but determined.

Daniel crept out from behind the couch and walked over to his grandfather who was sitting at the antique desk, head in his hands, eyes closed. He touched his grandfather on the shoulder and the man raised his head to look at him.

"So, my boy, you were here the whole time, were you? What did I tell you about the nasty things that happen to little boys who eavesdrop?"

"Sorry, Sir."

"Then you heard your mother. She has gone to find you. You had better get packed."

"I'm not going to go with her, Sir." Daniel rushed on when he saw his grandfather's eyebrows rise slightly. "I want to stay here. You said I'm a Fairer, I'm Daniel Fairer the Third and I'm going to be a world famous cardiologist, just like you." His back was straight but his lower lip was trembling. "Why can't Mother stay?"

"Daniel, it is not my decision. She will be leaving today and if you don't go with her you probably won't see her for a very long time."

"But if I go with her I'll be a barbari like you said..."

His mother's voice was sharp as she spoke from the door to the study. "Daniel! I've been looking everywhere for you. Go and pack your things, we're leaving."

"I'm not going Mother, I'm staying here with Grandfather." He glanced at his grandfather and then raising his chin he turned to face her. "Why don't you stay, please?"

His mother's shocked face made him feel nauseous and the tears started running down his face freely.

"I have to go, and you're coming with me, you'll see, you'll be happier."

"No, Mother, I'm staying here, please don't make me go with them."

He saw her face go white and then a flush of red crept onto its surface and she glared at the man sitting beside him. Her lips moved but he heard no sound and she turned and walked out of the study.

An hour later, he heard the gravel sounds of her car as it coughed out of the long circular driveway.

∞

Daniel listened for her every day and night until he left for medical school at the age of eighteen.

1 CHAPTER ONE

Galway, Ireland
Saturday, July 9, 2011

Priya didn't want to open her eyes but the air felt different. Chilly, slight scent of aftershave. Both strange as her heating normally came on and warmed her bedroom in the morning, whatever the Galway weather outside. And she certainly never wore aftershave. Whatever she was lying on also seemed different, softer.

She opened her eyes. She was on her side so the first thing she saw was a door that she didn't have. Her doors were oak stain-painted pine that looked like painted pine; this door actually did seem to be oak. The curvy blue and green glass handle glistened. She let her eyes wander closer, a bedside table with a large green-shaded lamp. Her phone and keys lay beside the lamp. She reached out for her phone and was suddenly aware that she was naked except for her underwear.

She turned around quickly but there was no one in the double bed with her. The covers on the other side were not neat but right now, there was no one there. She checked the time on her phone, 5:08 a.m. It felt later, the light falling in through the skylight above the bed made it seem later but then Ireland was like that in the summer, gently lit by 5 a.m. and not switched off until 11 p.m. It didn't help her scattered sleep patterns.

She had left the pub last night with a woman, an interesting woman, American, intense. Actually that was all she could remember about the woman. About the rest of the night. She didn't think she had drunk that much.

Whatever was on the other side of the door beyond the bedroom was quiet. There was an open door on the far side of the room and it looked like it led into an en-suite bathroom. No sounds from that direction either.

She had woken up in a few strange apartments in the last few months but never empty ones. She was always the one who left early.

Priya felt the sudden urge to pee. She sat up and her head thumped in protest. She swung her legs over the side of the bed. The deep carpet welcomed her feet and cuddled them all the way to the door of what she had rightly assumed was the bathroom. Priya pushed the door open and rushed to the toilet. She raised her face and sighed in relief as she peed, there was a skylight here too but the Egyptian marble tiles absorbed and diffused the sunlight into soft terracotta warmth.

She looked around the bathroom. It was neat, almost hotel-like. There was a modern version of a Victorian bathtub at the far end, teetering on its claw feet. She washed her hands in the ornately tapped sink and examined her reflection. A bit worse for wear but she usually wore the minimum of makeup when she went on a night out and the only damage was a slight smudging of the kohl she had penciled around her eyes. The advantages of a brown complexion and good skin; she grimaced at the mirror; wouldn't last much longer at this rate.

Priya went back into the bedroom. She looked around for her clothes and was relieved to see them draped over a stool in front of the dressing table. She dragged on her black silk trousers. Everything else she'd worn the night before was there, lacy black long-sleeved top, black sandals. Except for her jacket. With her keys and cards and money. And her ID. She grabbed her phone off the bedside table. It showed the time as 5.16 a.m.

She felt the smooth glass heaviness of the door handle against her palm as the door opened inward soundlessly. It opened onto a large airy living room. White walls. Skylights everywhere. A wall of glass proudly displayed a view of the Atlantic Ocean. The dawn red glinted over the flat sea calm. There were closed doors on the other side of the living room. The chrome and wood galley kitchen was visible.

Her jacket lay purple across the arm of a cream leather couch. Purple leather. Summer in Galway, unpredictable and a nightmare for wardrobe choices. She was certainly not going to be fading into the background.

She was parched, the lining of her throat felt like she had been sanding it for hours. She walked towards the kitchen and noticed one of the closed doors on the other side of the room was actually open a few inches. She found a glass and gulped down the cold tap water, washing the glass after in the empty kitchen sink and putting it back where she'd found it.

The silence in the apartment was tiptoeing into the folds of her clothes. She wanted to get out of here. But as she passed the open door to what she presumed was another bedroom she found herself drawn to it. And she was curious. The apartment seemed to give off a male energy. The vague scent of antiseptic cleaners mixed with the strands of aftershave and something else, something that reminded her of open drains on a wet day.

The bottom of the door stroked the carpet as she nudged it open and peered in. There was a skylight here too and the brightening dawn creeping in fought against the dark room but she didn't need to switch on the lights to see. The body was dead. It was male and pale. He was sitting on the floor facing her, his eyes open and still, his hairless torso propped up against the bed. Priya screamed. Or thought she did, no sound came out. His mouth was open and she tried to scream again, still no success. Priya knew him. Knew enough of him to feel the shock of difference between her energy-filled charismatic boss and this slack-jawed empty shell of skin.

∞

The apartment was still. The only sound was her breath struggling against the bile rising in her throat. Priya took a step back, away from the room.

Her body made the decision. She turned and ran.

She prayed for the streets to be deserted as she grabbed her jacket and raced for the front door. She grasped at the handle. It was locked. Sobbing, she pulled at it helplessly until she discovered it was easily released by the knob below the handle.

The hallway outside was deserted. Priya slipped out of the door. The elevator was directly in front of her. She pressed the Down button. *What was she doing?* She could hear the lift ascending and polished the button frantically with her jacket, then with her sleeve. She realized she was moaning softly as she did this. The door to the stairwell was only a few yards down the hallway. Making up her mind, she turned and ran to it, grateful for the carpet in the hall dampening the sound of her shoes. The door swished open and she pushed through. It fell back into place and she rested the back of her head against it, catching her breath, listening.

The stairwell was dark, illuminated only by the greenish yellow glow of fire exit signs. No carpet here, just painted concrete, dully reflecting the dim light. Not meant for anything except for emergencies. Well this was an emergency. Why hadn't she called the ambulance then, or the police? Ambulance wouldn't have done Daniel any good. And the police, she didn't want to think about why.

The sound of the lift opening. Then she heard a voice. Whispered, muffled.

She ran. Her footsteps echoed and bounced off the walls of the stairwell, down five shadowed flights of zigzag stairs. . She was running on instinct now. And her instinct screamed *Michael, alibi* though she knew she'd done nothing wrong, well, nothing violent. That she could remember. And she couldn't explain to anyone what she was doing there anyway, least of all to herself.

Priya reached the ground floor and flung open the heavy exit door to the outside. Dawn was almost fully dressed. She slipped on the neatly laid white stones as she ran between the manicured laurel bushes eying each other across the path that led out from the walled courtyard to a circular cul-de-sac. She scanned the cars parked there, but they were expensive ones awaiting their expensive owners. The tree-lined street was empty. It led out from the cul-de-sac and she could see where a larger street dissected it. She didn't remember ever being in this part of Galway before. The black engraving on the grey stone at the entrance to the circular cluster of apartment buildings informed her that she was leaving 'Seaview Close'.

The smell of the sea hit her before she saw it. The downward tilt of street ended at the sea, crossed by the main road that lined the Salthill promenade. There were quieter streets she could use but she decided to follow the main road that ran most of the way into town. She didn't want to be seen but the thought of walking the little back streets did not appeal.

She reached the main road that traced the edges of the Atlantic Ocean. The breeze tugged at the sea, sending up tiny waves that reflected the dying dawn in white shards. The aging resort, catching up on its beauty sleep before the afternoon onslaught of both locals and tourists, did not spare her a glance.

The walk to Michael's apartment took a very long 20 minutes. She worried past the housing estates full of B&Bs,

mindful of holidaymakers having their early morning breakfasts, gazing out the window planning their sights for the day. Michael lived in the arty part of Galway. Near the Spanish Arch. The banners and posters prepared for the coming two weeks of the Galway Arts Festival. There was no one on the streets and apart from two homeless guys sleeping on the stone benches by the river, she saw no one and more importantly, she thought, no one saw her.

∞

Priya could see that Michael was struggling to keep his face calm when he opened his door to her. His normally wavy hair was sticking straight up, his pajama bottoms on inside out, the label sticking into the tiny roll of hair-covered middle that he tried so hard to exercise away. She had called him from the street outside his building, afraid that knocking on his door would awaken the neighbors. He'd answered after five rings, sounding groggy and tired. And hadn't questioned her. Yet.

She edged past him as he eyed her clothes, her uncombed hair. He held her chin in his hand and examined the kohl-stained despair in her eyes. She pushed the door shut behind her and he hugged her.

"Hey, girl, bad night?" His voice was soothing. She was a whole foot and a half feet shorter than him and his voice whispered into her hair.

"It's not what you think, Daniel is dead. I found him. *Jesus*, Michael, I found him, and I left him. I ran. I don't know why I ran. But there was someone there. More than one, I don't know how many."

He had released her as she spoke, trying to hear the words muffled in his chest.

"What? Daniel? Did you say Daniel? Priya!" He shook her. "Stop for a second, you're making no sense."

Priya sank down onto the floor and he knelt beside her, rubbing her arms. He took her jacket from her hands.

"Could you put that in the washing machine, please? And this." She flailed at her clothes pulling the lace blouse off and starting to unbutton the trousers.

"Whoa, whoa... Priya! What's going on? Talk to me." He picked up her blouse and laid it across her chest, draping the arms over her shoulders and down her back.

"You've seen it all before, you prude." She laughed, and then covered her mouth in surprise.

"You're in shock." He raised her chin again. "Just tell me again, slowly this time."

She told him. Every detail she remembered. Which was only from the moment she'd opened her eyes and checked the phone clock at 5:08 a.m. She remembered the exact time for some reason but only a vague outline of the night before, or at least the evening before.

"And last night?"

"I remember leaving Massimo. No, actually, I remember going into Massimo. I remember a woman. That she was American. There was something about her, intense or dark. But she was cute. I think. Well, not exactly cute, more attractive than cute, interesting."

"Priya! This is surely not some weird dream brought on by drink and your endless search for the wrong woman! Jeez, that description...if you were one of my witnesses I'd never let you up on the stand."

"I'm trying! And no, it was not a dream. If it were, I'd be waking up nice and comfy in my own bed right now! Not sitting on your very hard floor half-naked."

"I'm going to call the Guards." Michael got to his feet.

"No!" Priya slipped on the floor as she tried to stand up. Michael caught her by the hand and she winced.

"Please, Michael, no cops."

They stared at each other. She was clutching her blouse to her chest with one hand, her other hand hanging loosely in his.

"I think a cup of tea might be in order, come on." Michael turned and led her towards the kitchen. The relief spread through her but she knew she would have to explain her reasons to him, at least some of them anyway.

"You and your tea, I need a strong coffee or, preferably, a strong brandy."

"I think I can manage both. Why don't you go and wash up and I'll get everything sorted here. I need to think."

∞

She came back out a half hour later, her hair wrapped up in a fresh clean towel of his. She was wearing his sweatpants, the legs rolled up into two big tires of blue cloth, bumping off each other as she walked. His old UCG college sweatshirt snuggled around her chest but almost reached her knees.

They'd gotten their college sweatshirts at the same time. That's how they'd met, bumping into each outside the college shop. He was a country lad from County Mayo, transplanted the hour away to the 'big city' to attend law school. He had that Irish complexion that reddened in a puff of wind. He was tall and lanky and had unruly hair the color of the brown gold gorse in the field behind her house. He wouldn't have been much use on his family's farm, his wrists too delicate, his nose permanently stuck in books on mythology and myth, Irish, Greek, Arabic.

She had taken him to the Science Ball with her. He'd been so proud to accompany her, the trousers legs and jacket sleeves of his black rented tuxedo only an inch too short. She wore a pink satin dress that contrasted so well against her brown skin that both glowed. He wore a pink cummerbund and bow tie. She left him for a minute to collect their posed photo taken by one of the many official photographers who hung around the grand hallway of the Great Southern Hotel when the various student Balls were held. The photographer showed her the Polaroid that he'd taken and remarked, "How did this Irish sod manage to catch an exotic beauty like you?" He leered at her "Guess I might have a chance then." Michael never asked why she held on to the Polaroid only and never picked up the portrait that would have been prepared from the professional camera and probably sat awaiting them in the studio pile. He had framed the Polaroid and it leant casually on his French oak sideboard.

She forced lightness into her voice, "What did you do with my stuff? I thought I'd left some here."

He handed her a small glass of brandy. "I gave it all away to the charity shop." He grinned at her shocked expression. "Ok, I put it in the hallway closet. Didn't want my many women to think I had another woman living with me, did I now?"

"Huh! Like you'd bring a woman through those doors without my prior approval." She gulped the brandy down and snorted most of it back out through her nose. "Damn! I hate that stuff! Adds to the shock." She grabbed a neatly placed dishtowel off the oven rail and wiped the brandy off her nose. "That hurts!"

"Priya! There's kitchen towel there, don't use my dishcloth!"

∞

They sat in Michael's living room, Priya swaddled in a quilt on his couch gripping a mug of coffee; Michael perched beside her on his Moroccan pouf. She knew the questions would need to be answered but her head still hurt and she just wanted to close her eyes and sleep and wake up to another day, a day without dead bodies in it.

Michael's apartment was on the first floor of a medieval building converted into five apartments, each on its own floor. He had spent months decorating it, painting the walls with terracotta, he and Priya struggling with the over-sized brown leather couch and armchairs up the narrow twisty stairs. He had bought exquisite blue and green silk tapestries from India and red and black rugs from Turkey and had them shipped to Galway.

"He didn't have any wounds on him, nothing, no marks on him at all." Her voice was low and muffled as she spoke from the depths of the quilt.

The image of Daniel's body, slumped against the bed, slammed into her mind. Daniel had always projected the right image for his setting, he had been the ultimate chameleon, smiled at the right times, said just the right things to the right people. He had worked out a lot but his suits, made for him, covered his physique and he managed to look elegant in his clothes; he never looked out of place wherever he was. Many times, she had seen the shift of colors in him as he started to reflect his surroundings; leaving the routine of their research, the crumples disappearing to be replaced by softer folds as he charmed a patient, the smoothened edges for the funding agencies. But he was constantly tugging at the stray cowlick on his head that refused to be tamed, the only part of his appearance he couldn't control especially in death. She felt like reaching out and smoothing it down in her mental picture.

"I need to ask you, why didn't you just call for an ambulance and the cops?" Michael's voice was a gentle intrusion and her hand jerked spilling coffee on the quilt.

"I panicked! What would you do if you woke up in a strange apartment and found your boss lying dead? Ok, ok, don't answer that, you'd never end up in that situation, would you? Just me, the screw-up."

She swiped at the small stain of coffee and Michael got up, talking as he went into the kitchen.

"I'm not even going to dignify that... Do you want me to call the Guards now? We could say you panicked, or that you were still drunk. Are you sure he was dead? Could he have been passed out drunk or -" Michael walked back from the kitchen where he had retrieved the kitchen towel.

"He was dead." She raised her head from the mug. "Definitely."

He handed her a sheet of kitchen paper and sat down again.

"There's more to this, Priya. You're keeping something from me. We could still extricate you at this stage, it's risky but possible. Why won't you let me call the cops? The worst they could get you for is obstruction of justice but if you ran because you were scared for your life and you called them now, there shouldn't be any problem."

"The eternal lawyer, nothing slips by, does it?" She shifted her position, shrinking further into the warm cave of the quilt.

"Well...?"

She gulped down her coffee and handed him the mug. He looked exasperated but got up to get her more.

The day outside was waking up and she could hear the street noises drift in through the open window, the aroma of the different coffee brands brewed in the cafes below mingling with her own freshly ground coffee. She enjoyed annoying Michael by getting him to make an espresso in his specialty machine that occupied pride of place in his kitchen and then dumping the espresso into a large misshapen mug she had made in an unsuccessful experiment with evening classes in pottery. She had given him the mug as a present, chuckling inside at his polite but reserved enthusiasm.

"He hurt me." She spoke through the hiss of the machine and Michael didn't react. He finished making the coffee her way, walked back over, and handed her the steaming mug. She stared at him and he said, "Sorry, did you say something?"

"Daniel tried it on."

"With *you*? But he knows you're gay! When? Why didn't you tell me? What happened?"

"You remember the night of my birthday last year? You were in Mayo so I went out with the crowd from work. Stuff happened and well, he gave me a lift home." She stopped. Her hands gripped the mug tighter, its roughness soothing.

"And...?"

"I was drunk, he wasn't. He got the wrong idea. It isn't that straightforward."

"Did he, you know...?"

"No. But I got hurt."

"And you didn't report him?"

Priya looked away from Michael, the street was starting to come to life, cutlery being sorted and laid out on pavement tables, chairs unstacked to await the early morning people-watchers.

"Priya…? Why didn't you report him?" Michael sat down on the pouf and leaned in to pry one of her hands off the mug and hold it between his own. She still didn't meet his eyes.

"Because it was my fault," she said.

His hands stopped their gentle rubbing motion.

"The Guards got involved. That was fun. Having to tell them that I let him take me home, that I'm gay and had no ulterior motive. That I was so drunk that I didn't see the danger. Actually, I couldn't even tell them the truth."

"Why? What do you mean? What was the truth?"

Priya looked away from the window and straight at him. "I can't tell you, I don't like to even think about it. It was stupid, unbelievably stupid. Valerie was there, it was my birthday, I had gotten the call from my dad a few days before, I drank a lot that night and I wasn't used to doing that at the time..."

"Valerie Helion? I should have known she'd be involved somehow." His hands were gripping hers.

"She was just her usual self. And I...well, I should have known better."

"You've never known better when it comes to that woman. I can't believe you hooked up with her again."

"I didn't. She was flirting with Daniel in front of me and I..." She slipped her hand out of his and slid down further on the couch.

"I don't want to talk about that night." Her voice was low but firm.

"So you went to the cops, what did they do?" There was a tremble in his voice.

"I didn't go to them. They came to me. What do you think they did about it? He's an important man. Fair play to them, they questioned him," her mouth twisted, "very discreetly. Do you know how much money Daniel had invested in Galway, in Ireland?"

"I'm totally confused, Priya. They came to you? But they didn't take it any further?" Michael's fists were clenched; his eyes had watered. "Why didn't you tell me? I could have done something." He got up and then sat down again.

"There was nothing to take further. And I hadn't even been in the job a year; besides, that was just after dad had called from India to say mum was sick. He still managed to slip in how proud he was of me for getting the job, of making a go of it. That's why I got so drunk that night, I was too busy burying my head in the sand to see anything. It just didn't seem to matter after that when things got worse with mum. I hated Daniel for a while because the whole thing delayed me going to India. And then when she died, I just…" Priya looked at him and the emptiness had crept back into her eyes and settled into its comfortable nest, its home for the last three years.

Michael rested his hand on her feet through the quilt. "You know Priya, at some point you are going to have to accept help. You were always your own knight in shining armor but this is crazy. If you won't accept it from me at least talk to someone, you know, in a professional capacity."

"Armor was a bit tarnished after that I have to say."

Michael was looking at her with that mixture of concern and exasperation.

"Michael, I just freaked out when I ended up there looking at him, like that. It was his apartment, or I least I assume it was. I know he lives in Seaview Close. I don't know how I ended up in his apartment. I was in the guest room, I think. Come to think of it, the bedroom looked more like a hotel room than someone's home. That's why it didn't make sense; it was off, you know…? I just reacted."

She continued, "Look, I know I drive you crazy and I disrupt your life and I mess everything up. I don't want to be involved in this. I just want it all to go back to normal, or at least, some semblance of normality. If I tell the cops now they're sure to bring up the stuff that happened last October and they're going to want to know what I was doing there and they're not going to believe I don't know and that I didn't have anything to do with it. If we don't say anything, someone will find him, they probably already have. I mean, why was anybody there at that hour?"

"Priya, slow down… I don't know. I still think you should go to the Guards."

"I can't. I can't go through that again. I didn't do anything but they'll make it out that I did. I thought you'd understand."

Michael was silent for a few minutes then he took in a deep breath and sighed.

He said, "I do understand. I understand that you're carrying around so much guilt for all sorts of things and it doesn't matter how many times I tell you that you weren't responsible. I just think you're making a mistake and you'll regret it. But I won't say anymore about it, for now. Let's wait and see what happened, how he died. If there's anything suspicious or anything you could clear up for them then I'd like you to tell the cops. I'll stand by you."

Priya had shrunken into the quilt as he spoke. She lay quiet and then eventually nodded, the movement of her head against the fabric ringing loud in her ears.

"Can I stay here for a little bit?"

"Yes you can stay here; of course you can stay here. Why don't you try and get some sleep." He got up and took the empty mug from her hands. "If you don't want me to say anything, I won't."

She looked up at him. "I need you to say something if you're asked… I need you to say I was here all night, well, at least from the time I'd have left Massimo." He didn't reply and she rushed in. "If we're lucky, no-one will ask. Please

Michael, it's going to be so much of a mess anyway, with Daniel dead, just let me stay out of the way on it. I'm going to have to get through this weekend and go to the clinic on Monday and pretend like nothing's happened."

He looked at her for a long moment and then nodded and went into the kitchen to wash the mug. She'd never needed to beg him for anything before and it felt strange.

2 CHAPTER TWO

Sunday, July 10, 2011

The diplomat didn't say much. Lay on the bed and stared at the white walls. Hid his pale flabbiness under the clinic gown. Smiled at the young nurse who didn't speak his language and who smiled back as she shaved his graying chest hairs. He tried to hold in his stomach as she ran the razor under his collarbone. The procedure was quick and mostly painless, just the jab of the local anesthetic. But he didn't like the feeling. The thought of wires being pushed through his veins. The doctor had explained it to him and he knew he wouldn't actually feel the leads but the gray coils crawled through his mind on their way to his heart.

Afterwards the diplomat tapped the lump under his collarbone. Not hard. No. Just a light finger really. The man had reassured him it would work. It had to work though he knew deep inside that he was expendable, to them. His wife wouldn't agree, or least he hoped she wouldn't. The kids, who knew? These days, with their grown up ways, he wondered whether they would notice.

He wondered whether to write a Will. Despite the reassurances given by the man, he thought he would. It would be the responsible thing to do, just in case it all went wrong. August 1. He had 21 days.

He hoped the Will would not be needed.

3 CHAPTER THREE

Monday, July 11, 2011

Priya sat in her car, her heart thumping, and stared at the building in front of her. The green glass walls of the clinic dripped rain. The sign above the sliding doors were in elegant script and read 'Fairer Cardiology Clinic'. The walk to the front door was short but she was going to get wet. She never carried an umbrella despite the vagaries of the Irish weather.

She was delaying but she knew she would have to go in soon. Make it look like she was coming in for an ordinary day at work. She had slept badly for the last two nights. Several times, she'd thought of calling the Guards but she'd made no phone calls, and received none. Telling Michael she wanted to be alone, she'd returned to her house after a few hours crashed out on his couch. She spent the weekend lying in bed, alternating between long periods of sleep and long periods of tears. Loud jagged bouts of crying that surprised her with their intensity. She hadn't cried like that even at her mother's funeral. Then, she had held herself together and gone through the necessary movements, holding everything together for her father. Now, seven months later, she was falling apart. And outside, the July storms, heavy and gusting, had alternated with cool bright sunshine that gently baked the house.

The rain was falling harder as a car pulled in sharply beside hers. Aidan Lynch drove a midnight blue BMW that he'd had for a year but he was still like a little boy with a new toy. He was looking at Priya with curiosity so she made hand gestures to indicate she didn't want to get wet. He reached back between the cream leather seats of the car and grabbed an umbrella.

"You'll be late if you sit there waiting for this rain to stop." He had opened her door. He held the umbrella for her and kept his hand on her elbow ducking his head to keep them both covered as they walked into the clinic.

∞

It was obvious there was something wrong the moment they walked into the plush reception of the clinic. The normally immaculately made up receptionist, Clodagh, was sitting dazed at her desk, her eye makeup smeared, and her nose red. She looked up at them and said, "Dr. Dan's dead. They're waiting for ye in the boardroom."

Priya slumped down on one of the upholstered chairs in the little arrangement laid out in the reception area like a piece of art. She didn't need to fake a reaction; her legs had felt weak as soon as Clodagh said the words.

Aidan said, "Daniel's dead? What happened? When?"

"They're going to tell us in there I think, the others are already here, I was just waiting for ye, we'd better hurry." Clodagh came around the desk to Priya. "Are you okay, Priya? Do you need anything?" She got a cup of water from the water dispenser and handed it to Priya.

Priya gulped down the drink. "Thanks, yes. Sorry. We'd better go in." She had to keep calm. There was no way anyone here could have known about her experience on Saturday morning but she felt like they could read every guilty emotion on her face. Aidan and Clodagh were both looking at her face and she realized they were noticing her eyes that were swollen from the weekend of crying.

"I had a flu, in bed most of the weekend. I hate getting flus, I'm a terrible patient." She rubbed at her nose that was redder than Clodagh's.

"You poor thing. Don't give it to me though, I hate it too," Clodagh said.

Aidan held out his arm for Priya and she leaned on it grateful for the support. Clodagh grabbed his other arm and led him down the glass-lined corridor to the boardroom, Priya in tow.

∞

The other members of staff were in the boardroom, all but one sitting solemnly around the large table. The clinical staff of two doctors, four nurses, and Priya's closest colleague, and the other electrophysiology technician, Tara McFadden, were there as well as the two secretaries. One of the two doctors in the room, Dr. James Reddington, was also one of the co-founders of the clinic, Daniel being the other. James was standing at the window of the boardroom when Priya and the others trailed into the room. He looked tense and drawn, his thin face breaking into a frown when he saw them but he just inclined his head in greeting. The three latecomers hastily grabbed a chair each and nodded greetings around the silent table. James moved to take his seat at the head of the table.

"You have all probably heard the news by now. Daniel is dead. He was found in his apartment by his mother on Sunday afternoon."

The buzz around the room sounded like bees in Priya's head. Sean Brady, the other doctor, asked, "What did he die of?"

"Myocardial infarction. Ironic, isn't it?" James rubbed his eyes. "He's one of the leading cardiologists in the world, he saves people's lives on a daily basis, and he dies at 45 of a heart attack."

Priya felt a queasy sense of relief. The niggling worry at the back of her mind all weekend that she might have had something to do with Daniel's death now seemed unwarranted.

"Who found him?" Sheila Hughes, a nurse at the clinic since it opened, was a small dynamo of a woman; but this morning she seemed drained of her usual excess.

"His mother." James looked irritated at having to repeat himself. "She was visiting him; as usual it seems, for Sunday lunch. She found him, called the ambulance, who in turn called his GP. The GP signed it off as a heart attack. Daniel seems to have been there for the weekend. I just found out late last night when she called me. I thought it would be better to wait till this morning when you were all in and tell you together."

Tara blurted out, "That's why he didn't turn up for my birthday on Friday night." She put her hand over her mouth when James looked at her.

"Daniel's body is going to be flown back to New York in the next few days. The Fairers are arranging to have him buried in the family plot. Anyone who wants to go to the funeral will be accommodated obviously." James looked around the table. "I'll be meeting his mother later today and I'll have more details for you tomorrow but I think with all the arrangements that have to be made, the funeral will probably be at the end of the week. We have patients who are already booked in for pacemaker implants and programmer checks over this week and I don't think Daniel would have wanted us to cancel anyone without proper notice."

James continued through the murmurs of assent from around the table, "However, I think we can arrange it so that the clinic is closed from Thursday. I will be going to New York for the funeral obviously and I will arrange to meet with Daniel's grandfather a bit later on to discuss the future of the clinic. I don't think it will be appropriate to disturb him at this difficult time but I know you will all want some idea of what is going to happen."

James got up from his chair. "Aidan, will you come to my office. We need to prepare a press release and get it out as soon as possible. The rest of you, it is going to be a very tough day and if you don't have any patients in you are welcome to leave. Priya, obviously the research work will be stopped completely until further notice; we'll need to meet the team at Research as soon as possible." He muttered to himself, "I need to talk to Gerry and Valerie again," and then sought out his secretary. "Mary, will you come in to me too, we need to draw up a list of people I need to call before the press release goes out."

The noise level in the room went up immediately the door closed behind James, all the staff expressing their shock in repeated meaningless expressions that seemed to Priya to rub on every exposed nerve in her body. She nodded her head in the right places all the while desperately waiting for the right amount of time to pass before she could escape to the relative isolation of the office she shared with Tara. She knew some of the staff were looking at her curiously but it seemed inappropriate to mention her flu again. She knew they were wondering whether she had been as close to Daniel as the rumors suggested. The atmosphere was starting to weigh heavily on her and she excused herself and rushed to her office.

∞

Priya sat at her desk feeling the nausea hit her in waves. She could hear the murmur of conversation continuing to roll around the clinic as people wandered back to their offices. She heard footsteps outside the room and Tara walked in shutting the door behind her.

"You don't look good, girl." Her short blond hair tousled, her pale pretty face now rubbed clean of make-up Tara didn't look too good herself, but Priya didn't feel like pointing that out.

"Are you going to go to New York for the funeral?" Tara asked.

Priya nodded. She had just made up her mind. She needed to see this through. She had a sense that she was missing something.

Tara said, "Did Daniel seem sick to you? It's strange; he was so into all that healthy living stuff, exercising all the time. And he ate healthy too, do you remember that time at the French restaurant when he would only eat the salad, none of that cream sauce he said. Seems a bit weird to me, having a heart attack at his age, and he never smoked, didn't drink much. And look at me, drinking all the time, smoking. At least I eat healthy and the Pilates has been great." She smoothed down her knee-length skirt and patted her stomach. "Priya, you're really not looking good. Why don't you go home, do you have any patients in for checks, do you want me to do yours?"

Priya shook her head. "I've got Jacintha coming in, I need to be here."

"Hmm… yeah, you'd better do her check. Wouldn't want to upset the old biddy again."

"You know, one day one of the patients is going to hear you calling them names and report you."

"Nah, my patients love me too much. It's just your Jacintha that prefers the exotic brown *Doctor* Joseph to do her programmer checks. Funny how she trusts you in a medical capacity but would probably cross the street otherwise. And she doesn't realize you've got a PhD not a medical degree."

Priya smiled. "You know she wouldn't, you're too hard on her, she's just old-fashioned. But she loves hearing an Irish accent coming out of an Indian looking woman. Besides I prefer her to the ones that say one thing but look like they'd rather not have me near them."

"I probably doesn't help that her son had a heart attack right there when *I* do her check, I mean, why couldn't that happen when *you're* doing it. Now she crosses herself when I pass her."

Priya stared at Tara, her eyes pensive, and said, "I worked with Daniel on Thursday and he was fine. A bit quiet but that was more like he was thinking about things, not sick. But he's been quiet like that for a few weeks now. Not his usual self."

Priya hadn't told anyone in the clinic about the night of her birthday or the subsequent humiliating experience with the Guards. So she couldn't tell Tara that the last four or five weeks had been almost as bad as the months following the episode last October. The tense and hostile silence after it had been broken by her mother's death in December. She had needed leave and Daniel had been surprisingly supportive and, despite their history, she had developed a wary sense of kinship with him when she returned to work in January. They had never spoken of that night again but the quality of their silence together had been different. Till a month ago.

Tara said, "You've been pretty quiet yourself. Was there a problem with the new Controller?"

The Program Controller Home was the third version of the machines they used in the clinic during the regular checks to communicate with implanted pacemakers. This version was being developed for home use. Priya had worked on the Controllers when she was doing the research for her PhD; the pacemaker it controlled, the Mark I pacemaker, had been Daniel's personal project with his research company that had commenced prior to the opening of the clinic. Priya spent part of her time consulting on the coding, and the other part carrying out the regular checks on the programming of the pacemakers installed by the clinic.

Priya said, "We got the figures back about a month ago. There was no problem with the Controller Home. Daniel took the figures with him; he just gave them to me two weeks ago. I haven't even had a chance to look at them properly. I'd better look at them after I do Jacintha's check."

Priya suddenly felt uneasy, she didn't want Tara to know she'd taken the papers home. Along with the papers on the Controller II, which Daniel had also given her for some reason. There were strict rules in this very secretive business.

Priya said, "Talking of Jacintha, I'd better go, she's probably chatting Aidan up as we speak if the poor lad is anywhere near the waiting room. But then, she's not the only middle-aged woman who'd like a bit of that boy, is she?" Priya had to laugh at Tara's face.

Tara said, "I am *not* middle-aged, unless you think I'm only going to live till I'm 60! By the way, I wouldn't start anything if I were you; I haven't even *mentioned* your Friday night adventures. I like how it's *my* 30th birthday and *you* get the present." Tara stopped. "Hey, you okay?"

Priya's stomach had clenched at the mention of Friday night and her face had obviously reflected the sudden rush of adrenaline. She got up and rifled through the filing cabinet searching for Jacintha Whelan's file. Priya hated being at a disadvantage, at not remembering the night. She hated anyone knowing more about what she had done than she did. She was about to swallow her pride and ask Tara when Clodagh opened the door and popped her head into the office.

"Priya, Ms. Whelan is waiting in Room 3. I had to put her in there to give poor Aidan a break."

Priya grabbed the thin file and hurried out of the office and down the hallway to the room she used for the pacemaker checks. She tried to gather her thoughts, to focus on the patient awaiting her.

∞

Priya used the room for her research as well as the routine pacemaker checks so there were different versions of the Controllers on trolleys lined up alongside one wall.

"I'm so sorry, Jacintha, things are a bit in a state at the moment here." Priya placed the file down on one of the trolleys.

Jacintha Whelan put her teeth back into her mouth and smiled at Priya. She sat up straight in the chair. Jacintha's son, Liam was seated in his usual place at her side.

"Good morning Dr. Joseph, you're looking a bit better since I saw you in March." Jacintha turned to Liam. "Isn't she? Sure, she was so thin then I thought we wouldn't be able to see her after a while." She adjusted her glass and stared through them at Priya. "Bit better, but still not as good as before."

"You know how to make a person feel good, Mam." Liam had his usual look of apology for his mother's forthrightness but Priya was used to it.

Jacintha continued with a short pause for breath, "Isn't it awful, dear, about Dr. Fairer. Scared me when Clodagh said it, it did so. He looked so healthy. Such a handsome man, you know, with that lovely tan and those white white teeth. You know, the Americans always seem to have such lovely teeth. Not like yours Liam, my fault that." She patted Liam's thigh.

Priya rolled the trolley with the Controller II on it up to Jacintha's side using the movement to hide her smile at Liam's expression. He had stained teeth from his mother taking medication when she was pregnant. He was forty and he still lived with his mother and brought her to every clinic check. Now he had to come for his own checks at the clinic and his mother accompanied him but sat out in the waiting room while he was seen, the girls joked that Jacintha did that to keep an eye out for Aidan.

Priya asked, "When's your next check, Liam?"

He was Tara's patient, which seemed fitting considering he had had his heart attack in the room while Tara had been carrying out the check on Jacintha when Priya was on leave following her mother's death. Jacintha was Priya's patient; Priya had carried out Jacintha's monthly checks for the two months post-op.

Liam said, "I had mine in June; Mam's was delayed so we couldn't have it on same day as usual."

Priya said, "Sorry, I think that's my fault. I was out for a week and somebody here didn't want to have her check done by Tara for some reason." Priya smiled at Jacintha. "You know, she's very good at her job, Liam will tell you that too."

Jacintha spoke over Liam's assent. "Sure, she might be good but I'm happy with you and I just *couldn't*, you know, after what happened. It was awful! I thought he was gone. All I can say is Thank God we were in here. Trust Liam to have a heart attack in the best heart clinic, he was always such an obliging boy. They had him taken care of so fast. He's fine now, aren't you, Liam? One of those pacemaker things in, just like your mother."

Liam had given up trying to find a gap in which to speak. He just nodded.

Jacintha stopped talking as well while Priya started the check. She used the Controller II that was designed for checks in a clinical setting and worked using wireless technology.

She set up the frequency of the controller to match the frequency transmitted by the pacemaker. Priya rolled the trolley as close as possible to Jacintha's side and held the programmer wand over Jacintha's collarbone. There was a beep and the LED display on the wand showed that the controller and the pacemaker were locked onto the same signal frequency.

The controller started the communication by sending an auto-identification sequence to the implanted device that resulted in an identical response from the implanted device detailing its serial and model numbers. The controller then sent an interrogation command that elicited more information from the device including Jacintha's name, diagnosis and other medical details.

The controller requested information from the pacemaker on any untoward incidents recorded since the last check. It checked on battery power remaining in the lithium battery. Although the device ran on a patented self-sustaining form of energy, the smaller than normal battery was installed in the device as a backup.

That was strange. Priya examined the readings for the battery power. The normal range was between 95% and 100%. Jacintha's readings showed the remaining power at 90.28%. She repeated the communication but the result was the same.

She checked Jacintha's folder. The summary results of the controller readings for battery power for all the previous checks were listed as 'Within Normal Range'. The actual receipt-shaped printouts were stapled to a card at the back of the folder. Each sheet had a line for remaining battery power. Priya was conscious that Jacintha was waiting and decided to examine the figures in more detail later. The battery lasted 6 years so there was no risk but it should not have been utilized at all. She continued with her routine.

Priya said, "We'll soon have the new version of this controller on the market. Then you'll be able to do the checks at home and just send in the readings."

Jacintha said, "I like coming in here, do we have to use the home one?"

"Well, your checks are going to go to 6 monthly after this one and it would be better if you had the home controller in between times. You can come in with Liam on his 1-year check in December and hopefully we'll be able to send ye home with the new controller then. And we'll see you 6 months later anyway. Don't worry; I'll keep an eye out on Aidan for you."

Jacintha giggled. "Sure that boy is a bit young for me, more your age I'd say. Ye'd be a good match, you with your lovely skin. You Indians girls are so pretty and that boy with his blonde hair, he's like one of those gods, you know, the ones from ancient times, not the Irish ones, Liam, where are they from?"

"You mean Vikings, Mam?"

"Yes, Liam, Vikings. That Aidan looks like a Viking."

All the rest of the data was normal and Priya re-set the device. "I think we'd better talk about something else. Must keep your heart rate down while we do this check. Your pacemaker is screaming at me." Priya laughed. "Just joking Jacintha, we're done. Everything is normal here."

4 CHAPTER FOUR

Wednesday, July 13, 2011

The handheld device beeped as the technician held it over his collarbone. She wrinkled her forehead as she concentrated on the digital readout. The diplomat waited for her to finish setting it up. She would soon explain how he was to use the device. He needed to concentrate; he had never been that good with technology. He managed all right with his PC but that was the limit of his computer experience. He had watched his grandchildren play with the Wii and marveled at their comfort. He envied that, as well as the ease with which his children and his colleagues at the embassy used their Smartphones and the other gadgets of a modern age that he felt was passing him by. His eldest son had promised him an iPad thing for his sixtieth birthday in a few months. They'd be able to face each other then or something like that. If that involved seeing his sons and the grandkids more often than the one annual visit, then he would gladly learn to use it.

But that was less important than learning to use this device. Even though it was just a precursor to the real one. He had 19 days left.

5 CHAPTER FIVE

Thursday, July 14, 2011

The black suits wandered towards the gravesite, crows' feet shuffling along a telephone wire. Priya tagged herself on to the end of the single file procession following the priest threading through the neat rows of headstones, bedraggled flowers snuggled against them, wilting in the evening heat. She smoothed out her suit. She didn't fit. She'd ironed the trousers and they looked slightly more worn than the jacket that had been hanging up in her closet for years and aired out for her formal interview with Daniel. The interview. Daniel. His lifeless stare. She was starting to sweat again. The heat and humidity of New York had hit her like a wall of wet when she'd come out of the airport this afternoon.

The Fairer family had kept the funeral small, choosing a small chapel and an exclusive cemetery in the Long Island suburbs. They had provided plane tickets for the six clinic staff who had decided to attend, to fly from Shannon to New York on the afternoon of the funeral. James was there, as was Sean, Sheila, Clodagh and Mary. Along with Priya, they were the original staff having been there since the opening of the clinic just over a year ago. Valerie and Gerry

Lynch, who had co-founded the Fairer Research Company with Daniel, were there somewhere further up the rows, she hadn't seen them come in, they had travelled separately.

The staff had lined up in the back row of the chapel, dazed and jetlagged and listened to the priest extol the virtues of their late boss, and his family. None of the family had spoken; she'd glimpsed their rigid black backs in the front row of the chapel. Priya only knew of his family from the occasional remarks Daniel had made. She'd gathered that his mother lived in Connemara and had heard him on the phone to her. His sister worked for the company too, she thought, in some sort of financial capacity. His calls to her had been less frequent. And the grandfather, Daniel Fairer II; she'd looked him up on the internet. What she probably should have done last year when she had gotten the job at the clinic but she had never gotten around to it at the time, caught up in the excitement, the energy that seemed to surround Daniel. She wished her father were here instead of in India on what was now going to be an annual medical pilgrimage. He should have been here anyway; he knew the Fairers better than she did. She had booked a hotel; she didn't want to spend the night alone at the house.

They had reached the hole in the ground. The line of mourners circled the open grave and she got her first proper look at the family as they stood directly across from her. The tall white-haired figure of Daniel's grandfather, shoulders stooped inside his black suit. The internet pictures had shown a middle-aged man, strong, tall, important, shaking hands with dignitaries. Most of the photos included Priya's father. Daniel had mentioned to her once in passing that his grandfather was the most active 85 year old that he'd ever known. The man now looked much older than his years.

Mother and daughter, she couldn't make out which was which at first look. Both wore black veils. She saw a glimpse of gray hair peeking out from under a hat. The mother was surprisingly sleek. That was the only word Priya could think of to describe her. Very different from the impression she'd gotten from the overheard phone calls. Her black suit was beautifully cut, Priya knew nothing of fashion, but it seemed to sit so well on her slim frame. Priya rubbed at her own ill-fitting suit. She looked at the sister. Dark, dark hair. She searched for her features through the dark shield. The woman was staring right at her. Priya dropped her gaze immediately, her sudden fright too obvious, her own veil non-existent.

A woman, American, intense. *No!* Priya's eyes jerked back up. The woman was still staring at her through the veil. The mother turned and spoke into her daughter's ear and the stare was broken.

The priest raised his hands.

∞

Priya stole frequent looks at Daniel's sister as the priest droned out his lines. *What was her name? Rain?* She remembered Daniel calling her that on the phone. At the time, she had thought it was such a New Age hippy type name for a financier. Each time she looked at Rain, she was caught. Her mind fidgeted with the permutations. Rain was definitely the woman she'd met in Massimo; she had to be. And from the glares she was receiving, felt even through the veil, Priya was at a disadvantage. Priya didn't remember what she'd done, Rain obviously did.

The graveside ceremony seemed to drag on for hours, but twenty minutes after they'd arrived at the cemetery, the priest said the final words as the coffin was covered with dirt.

∞

"It's Reyna actually." The woman's grip was firm, the palm dry and cool.

Priya felt the heat in her face and cursed the two red spots that she knew were now appearing on her cheeks. Reyna was only about 6 inches taller than Priya but seemed to tower over her.

"Sorry, I've heard Daniel on the phone to you before and he called you Rain, I remember because I was thinking at the time that it was such a hipp…" She stopped and felt her cheeks burn harder.

"He liked to make fun of the name Leo and my mother decided to give me, Rain, I changed it legally a few years ago, it's now Reyna, R-E-Y-N-A. Perhaps you might remember that for a better reason?"

Priya couldn't see if the eyes behind the black glasses were smiling or not. She stared at the features of the face, which were striking in their sharpness. She looked down and realized her hand was still in Reyna's. She snatched it back. And this time there was a slight curve to Reyna's lips.

"I really must go and express my condolences to your mother." Priya looked around the study of the Fairer mansion. The mourners had been conveyed to a very expensive area of New York, the houses hidden behind high walls and reached by long driveways. The rest of the staff were at the buffet table in the adjoining room. While the funeral itself had been kept small, the gathering afterwards at the family home was packed. Daniel's mother was at the other end of the study, in conversation with a couple, her head bent attentively.

Priya started to turn but Reyna placed a hand on her shoulder and stopped her. Priya felt the hiss of air in her ear as Reyna leaned in and whispered, "So, was it quick? Painless? Were you enjoying yourself with your boyfriend when he died?"

"What?" Priya turned and found herself just a few inches away from Reyna's face. The mirrored glasses reflected the whites of Priya's eyes. "He wasn't my boyfriend." Her voice came out a lot higher than she wanted. She lowered it. "Why on earth would you think that?"

"I left you at his apartment. My mother finds him dead the next day. She thinks a woman had been in his bed with him. You never mention it to anyone that you were there."

"*You* never mentioned that *you* were there! Look, I was never in bed with him. I found him there. I know I shouldn't have left like that but he was dead and I just panicked. I know I made a mistake. And he wasn't my boyfriend!"

"That's not what he told me."

"What are you two talking about?" The voice interrupting was soft but Priya jerked back in surprise. "I didn't realize you knew each other."

Reyna turned slowly to face her mother. "I've heard so much about her I just had to introduce myself."

The slim gray haired woman held out her hand to Priya. "My daughter has terrible manners. I'm Catherine, Daniel's mother."

Priya's hand shook as she accepted the proffered hand. "Priya Joseph. I work at the clinic in Galway."

"Joseph… so you're Joe, sorry, P.T. Joseph's daughter?" Catherine's eyes were warm and she smiled as she spoke.

"Yes. Actually, that's how I first met Daniel."

"Don't you mean that's how you got the job?" Reyna cut in.

"Rain!" Catherine glared at her daughter. "Priya, I'm so sorry. Rain is not dealing very well with Daniel's death."

"Mother, its Reyna. And yes, I'm not '*dealing*' as you say. I'm surprised you are." Reyna turned to Priya. "Excuse me, I must go and talk to my grandfather. *He's* not dealing very well either." She turned abruptly and walked away from the two women leaving Priya staring after her in shock.

Catherine placed her hand on Priya's arm. "Why don't we go and get a drink dear?"

∞

Priya allowed Catherine to lead her on a slow amble towards the bar built into one wall of the study. Their passage through the guests was hindered by condolences offered every few feet. People stopped Catherine to shake her hand, introducing themselves, their names usually prefaced by Doctor. Priya wondered at their curious looks at

Catherine, who seemed to sail oblivious through them, her course firmly set.

"Brandy, my dear?" Catherine was already pouring herself a Hennessey, the smooth golden liquid settling into the full curves of the beautifully delicate brandy glass. Catherine held up the glass to the light, the broken light bouncing and sparkling in her eyes. "Waterford Crystal," she said, "Only the best for the Fairers."

"Actually, I don't like brandy." Priya scanned the bottles on the thick wood counter. "Perhaps a port...?"

Catherine poured the drink into an equally beautiful glass and handed it to Priya.

"Slainté." She clinked her glass off Priya's and took a tiny sip. "So, Priya, what did you make of my daughter?" Priya could see now that Catherine's eyes were slightly glazed, the pupils wide, but her voice was steady.

Unlike Priya's. There was a quiver in Priya's voice when she spoke. "She's obviously upset at what's happened."

"And have you two met before today?"

Priya gulped down some port. *Should she admit to meeting Reyna that night in Massimo? How much did Catherine know of her daughter's movements?*

Catherine seemed to take pity on Priya. She said, "Reyna was staying with me in Connemara when she came to Ireland. She was supposed to meet Daniel at the pub on Friday night. Perhaps you met her there. Daniel mentioned he had to go to somebody's birthday party there, somebody from the clinic. I assume you would have been there for that."

Priya felt her face go hot again. She was grateful for the air-conditioning without which she would probably have been sweating profusely. As it was, she could feel a light sheen on her face.

"Yes, it was Tara's birthday. And Daniel didn't turn up; he was supposed to be there. I might have seen Reyna there. She did seem familiar when I saw her today." *Was she babbling? Could Catherine see through her feeble words?*

"I guess he must have been dead by that stage." Catherine took a long swallow of the brandy emptying the glass. She poured some more out for herself. "My son, the world-famous cardiologist, dies from a heart attack. He wanted to be a famous doctor so much; he wanted to be just like his grandfather." Another sip. "Not like his father. He didn't want to be like his father. Though who could blame him. Leo was too different for all of them. The Fairers." Catherine almost spat the last word out. Then her tiny burst of anger seemed to fade and she mumbled, "But I was wrong, wasn't I." She brushed at a wisp of silver that had escaped from her neatly styled hair.

Priya glanced around the room. Nobody seemed to be listening. She wanted to be back home, in her little cocoon. She looked for Reyna but there was no sign of her or her grandfather. Priya felt a jolt in her stomach, *what had happened with that woman?*

"She's probably with her grandfather sorting out the rest of the day, and the week, and probably the next few months."

Priya brought her attention back to Catherine immediately. "I wasn't looking for her." She was annoyed with herself for stammering. *What was wrong with her?* "I was just admiring the room; it's quite lovely, isn't it?"

"Yes, it is. But you'd be surprised at the things that have happened in this room." Catherine looked around the room as if seeing for the first time. "He was standing right there." She pointed to the antique desk that they could just see through the crowd. Priya noticed a dark wood rocking horse under the desk. The light darted off the intricate saddle on the rocking horse, the mute sheen of its rosewood body blending into the paneled landscape.

"Daniel?" Priya asked.

"Yes, my 9 year old boy. My beautiful baby boy. He chose to stay here, with his grandfather. I had to leave him. I had to go. I was pregnant with Rain, Leo was going." Catherine's eyes were focused on the rocking horse. Its one visible carved eye stared into the distance. "Leo was going, with or without me. Tell me Priya, how is your father doing?"

The sudden change of topic threw Priya off her train of thought. "He's fine." She hesitated when she saw the question in Catherine's eyes. "Well, not really. He's doing his duty in India at the moment; he's going to go there for a month every year to help out at a clinic there." Priya's face tensed. "He's trying to work through his guilt I think. My mother was treated at that clinic and they screwed up. It had nothing to do with him; they were only on holiday there. And he didn't want to offend the 'great' doctor that ran the clinic. He questioned him, but not enough. So she died. And I was too busy getting my act together in Ireland with the new job and … other stuff. Wanted to prove everyone wrong. Didn't realize how serious it was." She stopped. "I can't believe I'm talking about this to you, today. I haven't spoken to anyone about it."

Catherine took Priya's hand and squeezed it. "I may not look like it right now," she grinned and the grin turned her face into that of a child, "But I'm a healer." She smiled at Priya's expression. "Yes, I know. I broke with the family tradition. They don't mention it much. But you'd understand that."

Catherine looked around before leaning in to whisper, "I found Daniel, you know."

Priya nodded. Her throat felt swollen.

Catherine continued in a whisper, "The GP said it was a heart attack. I'm not too sure."

Priya could smell the brandy coming from Catherine's breath. She would forever associate that smell with death she thought. She remained silent. What was she supposed to say to this woman?

Catherine said, "There was someone there with him. A woman. In his bed. I know it."

Priya felt a wave of panic. She couldn't understand why she was feeling guilty again. She *knew* she hadn't been in bed with Daniel. But she *had* found him. And left him.

Catherine's voice was still quiet but she wasn't whispering any more. "I am not going to just leave it like that. Daniel was my son. If there was some woman involved I am going to find out."

Priya stayed silent, aware of the thudding of her heart in her chest.

Catherine said, "You're going to help me. You knew Daniel well. He spoke about you a lot. He liked you."

Priya said, "I really didn't know him too well. I don't think I'd be much use." She looked around the room, hoping someone would come and rescue her but people were absorbed in their own conversations.

"You'd be more able to find out those kinds of things." Catherine sighed deeply. "I have to mingle; these people need to tell me how sorry they are for my loss. I'd better let them." She looked at Priya as if seeing her for the first time. "I've really enjoyed meeting you. I would really like it if you would come and stay with me in Connemara for a little while. I have a little healing center there." Catherine nodded almost to herself. "Yes, my dear, I'll see you there. We'll discuss it more; find out together what happened to Daniel. I'll send you the details, it's not very accessible, I keep it private. I don't want to steal anyone's thunder."

∞

Priya felt shell-shocked as she went into the other room to join the staff from the clinic. James and Sean were speaking with a few of the other doctors there; from the snippets of conversation, she gathered they were mostly cardiologists as well. Priya was silent as she stood beside the three women from the clinic.

Clodagh looked even smaller than she usually did perched on her raised office chair. "This place is grand, isn't it?" Her voice was hushed. "Did you see the way all that silver is laid out on the table? I knew they were rich but this is something else."

Sheila and Mary were both gripping saucers, the delicate china cups they held giving out a scent of chamomile tea. Mary had chosen to wear a brown suit and she looked as faded and uncomfortable as the rough fabric outfit.

"Did you see the spread?" Clodagh asked. "I wish Aidan could have come with us, you know how he likes all these things."

"Speaking of the Lynches, there's the odd couple." Sheila was trying to point with her chin.

"Sheila! Don't let them hear you," Mary said. Their voices were low and Valerie and Gerry Lynch were in the other room heading their way but Sheila and Mary still looked like two middle-aged schoolgirls caught copying homework.

Priya watched their approach. She wasn't sure she could handle seeing Valerie now. Gerry was a step behind Valerie as usual; his hand resting on the small of her back as if to reassure himself that she was still within reach. Valerie was wearing a black suit, its blackness setting off her dark blonde hair with its restless bronze highlights swaying as she walked under the light fall from the chandelier. Gerry's business suits were dark but he always wore ties that he seemed to pick for their unusual patterns. Today, his tie was probably the most somber one he could find in his collection but it had swirls of red and gold shimmering from its black base.

Priya did not feel that familiar rush of adrenaline as she looked up to meet Valerie's eyes. The usual challenge was there in those shaded brown eyes, the flecks of gold that had fascinated Priya as they had lain together guilty and sweat-ridden, were now just objects of beauty that could be admired as she would the dance of light in a rolling colored marble. She felt a sense of relief that the rush was gone, the hold loosened, maybe lost.

"Hello all." Valerie looked around the room and spotted James and Sean still in their deep conversation. "Did they fly the whole clinic out here?" she asked. *Damn*, her voice still had that throaty quality that seemed to rasp ever so lightly at Priya's chest, a gentle note that made her wish again, for just one second, Valerie was not the woman Priya knew she was.

"Only the ones that were there with Daniel from the beginning," Sheila said, her hackles raised.

"Yes, I guess that one year you knew him must make it very hard for you." Valerie glanced down at the hand Gerry placed on her forearm and then back at the women. "It's a tough time for us all. Daniel said a lot of good things about his staff, he was very proud of all of you. Gerry, why don't you stay here with the girls and I'll just go in to give my condolences to Daniel's grandfather. The poor man must be in a state." Valerie nodded to them as she left and headed towards the door Priya had seen Reyna and her grandfather disappear through earlier.

"So, ladies, you're all looking very well, I must say." Gerry Lynch offered a tight smile at the group. He was good looking in an average way, no distinguishing features but an overall pleasant effect. Slightly thicker than slim, fleshy over firm physique of a man who used to frequent the gym regularly in his thirties but finds his attendance slipping as life over forty gets in the way. The gray showed through, sharp and precise, lined around the edges of his short styled black hair and the red on the tips of his ears and the back of his neck were always patchy on his pale complexion. Today, there was a matching red rim around his eyes.

"Hello Dr. Lynch, isn't it awful?" Sheila placed her hand on Gerry's arm smiling up into his eyes. "Would you like something to drink; they seem to have everything here. No alcohol, I know. Don't you sometimes wish you drank, at times like these? You must be devastated; you've known Daniel for so long."

"They were all in NUIG together for their Cardiology Fellowship. That's how all of this started, isn't it? The research company, the Mark I pacemaker, the controllers. You were pioneers, Gerry," Priya said in a rush. She had always admired Gerry's research work; he had been her mentor and friend when she had done her PhD research through the company. This had made her guilt all the harder to deal with.

"I was adding up the years and we've known…Daniel and I knew each other since 1999. That's 12 years. Twelve amazing years." Gerry shook his head and looked around the room, "Aidan didn't make it?"

Clodagh piped up "I was just saying how he would have loved it here, well not loved it you know, being a funeral and all that, but…"

"You're right Clodagh, he would have loved it here. Now, how about we all go and refresh your glasses and I'll grab a coffee."

∞

Priya didn't see Reyna for the rest of the evening. She seemed to have disappeared with Daniel's grandfather. After about a half hour, Valerie had come back on her own, and she and Gerry had left the reception a few minutes later. Priya stayed and left with the rest of the staff from the clinic. Priya spent the night at a hotel in New York and took the overnight flight for Shannon the next afternoon. The others were staying on for a few days in New York but she wanted to put the events of the last week behind her and get back to the safety of home.

6 CHAPTER SIX

Friday, July 15, 2011

The diplomat sat at his desk and stared at the device lying in front of him. The controller. For his pacemaker. He hadn't realized the adjustment it would take, to accept that there was something alien in him. But it had only been five days; he assumed his acceptance would grow over time.

He prodded the device, sliding it a few inches across the rough paper of his thought pad, as he liked to call it, the leather-sided rectangle of paper that rested on the desk. His scrawls now covered over half the surface of the paper, doodles, scribbles, endlessly repeating sketches of cartoon heart shapes.

What punishment would he face, if he survived? Nobody would know anything, except him. And the man. The diplomat had sent his wife away to stay with her sister until the middle of August. She would need to be told that he'd had a pacemaker put in; he'd deal with that then. He had persuaded her that she needed a break, that he would be so busy carrying out his embassy duties he would have no time. But he had promised her time, after.

He had 17 days.

7 CHAPTER SEVEN

Saturday, July 16, 2011

Priya let herself into her house. She lived in what was now a very expensive area of Galway. Barna village was on the west coast of Ireland. It had started out as a satellite of Galway city, deserted in the winter, roads jam-packed in the summer as the Galwegians made a dash for the sea at the first sign of sun. Her parents had bought the house when they moved to Galway in the eighties and Priya was ten. Priya remained in the house when her parents left for New York in 1993. She was 18, doing a Science degree in NUIG; it would have been too much of an upheaval. So she stayed, and ended up staying. After 26 years here, she was as Irish now as the Irish would let her be. Despite having been born in New York and spending her early years in India with her grandparents, her main memories were now of Ireland, as was her passport.

The house was silent. She had left it in a mess, in a hurry. The front of the house was dark, even on sunny afternoons. The kitchen at the back was bright, opening out onto a deck she had built herself so that she could sit out in the evening and soak in the panoramic view of the blue green and grey Atlantic.

She picked up the junk mail off the floor. She'd only been gone two days but there was a pile of the stuff. Businesses desperate for customers were offering whatever they could to a population that refused to spend now that they had spent their full during the years of the Celtic Tiger. The paint on the hallway wall was peeling in a few places. She just didn't feel like touching it up. She added it to the list of tasks she had to get around to at some point. Since January, she had just gone to work in the morning, come back home in the evening, grabbed a glass of wine, and sat out on the deck absorbing the alcohol along with the sea salt air. She didn't work on her on-going paintings or start new ones; her little studio in the box room waited but the colors never flowed. She'd also never finished the last remaining credits for the Open University course on Art Therapy she had been doing. Some evenings she called to see Michael but mostly he came to her place if he wanted to see her. She knew he wanted to see her but she didn't want to see anyone. And most weekends she went out, searching for her pain, to drown it with alcohol and the occasional woman.

She dropped her suitcase on the floor of the gloomy front room, shoved the junk mail onto the bookshelf and walked straight to the bright kitchen. She poured out a juice for herself and went out to the deck. The sun was on one of its rare early morning trips to Galway. On many occasions during the hour and a half drive from Shannon to Galway, she had found herself nodding off and only a determined effort and loud music on some station that played the classic hits of the 70s and 80s had kept her awake. As she drove through, Galway seemed to be slumbering, gearing itself up for the second week of its festival. She hadn't slept on the overnight flight; the tourists on the full flight had not seemed as disturbed by the intermittent yelps of a protesting child in the row behind her. And now she didn't want to sleep. She was restless. She settled in to the deckchair, glass of juice in hand.

Something was wrong. The vague sense strengthened to the point that she couldn't lie there. Sighing, she placed the glass down on the deck and walked back into the house. Nothing seemed out of place in the kitchen. She re-traced her steps into the living room. Her suitcase had fallen over and was lying on its side. She looked around the room. It was even darker after the dazzling sun sparkle off the waves. The paintings she had done over the past ten years were stacked in the living room, their bright faces resting against the wall. The two small windows looked out onto a tired front garden contained by a low stone wall that separated her from the road. It was the main road from Galway to Connemara, but it was narrow; hemmed in by hedges and bracken intermittently punctuated by the entrance to a house.

The furniture in the room had been purchased ten years ago and was showing signs of wear. The newer IKEA bookcase held her large collection of novels, an eclectic mix, as well as her textbooks for work. And that's where she noticed what had set off the ripple in her mind. She always organized her books by author. She was disorganized in almost every other aspect of her life but in this, she was pernickety. Books organized by author, and then by title, all alphabetically. She needed the comfort of her well-worn friends, of knowing where exactly to reach for the words that would take her out of her world, cheer her up, or at least accompany her on her despair. She saw now that the authors in 'K' were switched with the authors in 'L'. Ludlum should be after King but he wasn't. She quickly scanned the rest of the shelf, all the others were in order, Roy coming after Picoult, Coben after Binchy, even her DIY books were still in alphabetical order.

She rang Michael's mobile. It was Saturday morning, exactly one week after she'd woken up with a dead man.

Michael answered, "Hi, how was your trip?" He sounded chirpy. He was usually irritatingly happy in the mornings, she hated mornings.

"Michael, did you call into my house while I was away by any chance?"

"No hon, sorry, did you want me to? I thought since you were only going for a couple of days..."

"No, no, I didn't need you to, I was just wondering. Look, there's something weird. It's tiny but it's weird. You're sure, you're not kidding around, are you? Just tell me if you are, I'm too tired and it's been a weird week."

"Priya, I have no idea what you're talking about."

"Ludlum is before King. Well, one of Ludlum's is actually in the middle of King's."

"Priya, you don't think this OCD thing with your books might just have gone a little teeny bit too far?"

"Michael! You know me and my books. Someone was here. I was hoping it was you."

"Why would I want to go through your books? I'm more than happy with mine, dry and boring as they might be to you." He paused. "Okay, look through the rest of the house; see if anything else has been disturbed. You're sure there's no-one there?"

"Oh great, no I'm not sure, but I don't get the feeling there's anyone here. I haven't been upstairs yet though." She glanced at the stairs in the hall through the open living room door.

"Wait for me. Don't go upstairs. I know there's probably no one there but just hang on until I get there. You'd probably be better equipped to deal with anyone than I would be though, just get that baseball bat out."

Priya knew he was trying to lighten the tension but he was probably right. He wouldn't have been much good in a physical altercation. Even at her 5 foot 2 inches to his 6 foot 6 inches, it had been Priya who had stood up to the drunken debaters turned pushy in the college bar. Though usually because she'd started the trouble in the first place, annoyed by the alcohol-induced stupidity as she called it from her high moral ground of sobriety. She'd never actually gotten into a physical fight though.

Priya whispered into her phone, "Hurry up then. I'm going to get the bat. Actually no, I can't, it's upstairs by the bed! Okay, I'm going to go outside to the back and wait for you. Two weaklings should be better than one."

The field at the back of her house was an acre of grass with brown gorse tufting out of the scattered rocks of varying sizes from pebbles to boulders. It ended at a 6-foot drop to the sea. Her own personal cliff. She picked her way carefully through the uneven ground, carrying the glass of juice in one hand and a kitchen knife in the other. She sat halfway down the field facing the house with her back against a large rock, feeling its warm solidity steady her nerves. The sound of the waves crashing against the stony reef soothed, its restless energy sapping hers. It was a long half hour.

There was no movement in the house. The upstairs windows were empty. She didn't have curtains in her bedroom preferring to be able to stare at the sea from her bed, or to sit on the windowsill dangling her legs over the short drop to the deck. Someone had been in her house, had gone through her things, and had touched her books. The thought galled her. It couldn't have been a burglar. There were items downstairs that a burglar would have taken. Most of her stuff was of sentimental value, pieces gathered by her parents on their many trips to locations all over the world. But there were some commercially valuable things too. *So if it wasn't a burglar, who was snooping around her house?*

With a fright, she saw a movement at her bedroom window. And then it opened and Michael stuck his head out. He smiled when he saw her, back up against the rock clutching the glass and the knife, frowning at him.

"All clear," he yelled.

She scrambled up. "I thought we were going to check together! Since when did you get so macho?"

"Not macho, chivalrous. Now come up here and see if there's anything else out of place."

∞

They sat together on the deck, she in her usual chair, and he in his. Like a married couple. Looking at him, she wished for the hundredth time she could have felt it. That almost desperate love he seemed to feel for her. They'd dated for two years while they were in college. It had actually been while she was in the relationship with him that she'd fallen for the first time for a woman, surprising her as much as it had shocked him. She'd had to make a choice, the security of Michael and his certain love versus the intensity and excitement of her emotions for a fellow student in the IT postgraduate program she'd done after her Science Masters degree. And she'd chosen Michael. But that had lasted just two more months, something irretrievably lost in the shuffle. She was glad she hadn't left him at the time for a woman. Not because he wouldn't have been able to deal with it, though she suspected he would have been crushed tighter by that, but because they were able to remain close friends, working through the end of their relationship, working out their commitment to each other that didn't need a 'boyfriend/girlfriend' tag to validate its importance to them individually.

They had searched the house and found nothing else out of place. Priya told Michael about meeting Reyna and Catherine, mostly Reyna. The woman's contempt burned in Priya's memory.

Priya said, "Catherine thought there was a woman in the apartment with Daniel. She said she was going to find this woman no matter what."

Michael said, "Does she think this woman had something to do with Daniel's death? I thought you said the GP said it was a heart attack?"

"Yes, he did."

"Then what…? Does she think Daniel and this woman were, you know, having sex or something?"

"I don't know, Catherine didn't come out and say it. Though Reyna thought I was the woman with him and she *did* pretty much come out and say it, that we'd been having sex and he died and I left him." Priya's voice faltered. "Reyna was pretty disgusted with me."

"Priya, you wouldn't have been in the apartment if she hadn't brought you there. I know she didn't know that you had some kind of unpleasant history with Daniel but still, she could have put you in danger."

"I guess from her point of view I must look like a real bitch. I mean, she thinks I'm Daniel's girlfriend, I must have flirted with her, she has to take care of me as I'm too drunk to get home, she leaves me in her brother's apartment, my boyfriend's, and then her mother finds him dead and says there was a woman with him, in his bed. Jeez, Michael, when it's put like that! And now her mother is going to keep digging to find out who was there."

Priya put her face in her hands and lay back on the deckchair and let the sun beat down onto her skin

"Valerie and Gerry were there too." Priya said through her fingers after a few minutes. .

"Well they knew Daniel really well." Michael swung his legs over the side of his deckchair and sat up. "I wish you didn't have to see that woman ever again."

"It was okay. *I* was okay. I think what happened on the night of my birthday sort of loosened her hold on me you know."

"You still haven't told me what happened that night."

"And I still don't want to talk about it. Michael, I couldn't bear to see the look in your eyes. I know you think I shouldn't feel guilty about what happened but I can't help it."

"And when are you going to talk about what happened with Kathy?"

Priya remained silent.

"You know Priya you're going to have to deal with this stuff. You've had a bad few years. And it all started with that bitch Valerie Helion or Lynch or whatever she is!"

"Talking about it is not going to bring Kathy back, or my mom for that matter," she said. "I'm not asking for help. I'm just trying to get through without hurting anybody."

"You mean, without letting yourself get hurt. You won't let anyone close now. For Christ's sake, Priya, you won't even get a dog! You're crazy about animals, in fact, you're the craziest person I know when it comes to animals, but you won't get a dog in case something happens to it."

"I've just come back from my boss's funeral and it's just been a week since I discovered his dead body, I've got his crazy mother searching for a woman in his bed, his crazier sister thinking I screwed him to death and you're giving me a lecture about dogs?"

"I'm sorry, I know, it's just been driving me crazy, especially for the last year, what you're doing to yourself. And this is just like you now. What happened to the Priya I knew, who'd stand up for herself, who'd take on anybody anywhere, who, God forbid, would be in a relationship? Who wanted a family?"

"You mean the one who thought everything in life was black and white till she got drowned in grey? Michael, I can't talk about it, not yet. Why can't you understand that I just want to get on with my life? Without thinking about what happened. You know, hold on to the job, and build some sort of career. Have you noticed how many people are losing their jobs? I can't afford that. I've now got a mortgage, Michael, I can't lose this house, it's the only thing I've got now, the only place left to call home."

Michael was clenching his fists. "It's been a seven months since your mom. And two years since Kathy. I don't mind that you're not talking about it yet. I wouldn't mind if you were still in a state, God knows you deserve to be. But what scares me is that you're not. On the outside anyway. You're acting as if nothing happened, like if you drink and screw around, you'll come back. And you won't. At least not the Priya I know," he relaxed his grip and patted her feet, "and love."

He got up and started pacing.

"Look, Priya, what you went through was not ordinary. You need to accept that those things happened and you need to heal after stuff like that. It wasn't your fault in either case."

"*Case*?! They're not just some cases like the ones you deal with in court. And, in a way, it was my fault. In both 'cases'."

"You went to her immediately something happened with Valerie. You did the right thing. *Hell*, you did the honorable thing. You had both agreed to split up, it's not your fault what happened, and that was months later."

"I should have listened. I was so caught up with my stuff with Valerie."

"Kathy wasn't well, Priya."

Priya had her head in her hands. She got up and she could see Michael shake his head as she walked away into the kitchen. That conversation was over as far as she was concerned.

∞

She came back out a few minutes later with two glasses, one of wine and the other, water. She handed him the glass of water and sat down beside him.

Priya asked, "So, meet anyone nice while I was in New York? You know, cat being away, you being the mouse and all that."

He ignored her attempt and changed the conversation anyway.

"So why would someone go through your things? Especially your books. I mean what were they hoping to find?" he asked.

"Certainly not the education on the medieval history of every last brick in Galway they would have gotten if they'd gone through *your* bookcase."

"Priya! I'm serious."

"Well, okay. They've probably gained an even greater understanding of the psychotic mind, the vain pumping of the self-help lobby, as well as the workings of the incredible Pacemaker Controller Mark II if they bothered to read through the boring research papers."

"Priya...!"

"No actually Michael..." Priya sat up, suddenly looking thoughtful. She swung her legs off the deckchair and put the glass down on the deck. "I need to check those papers, I forgot all about them. I shouldn't have brought them with me, I just wanted to figure out something that's been bugging me." She hurried into the house and straight to the pile of papers on the floor beside the bookcase. She'd shoved them in the corner between the bookcase and the wall in her last attempt to vacuum the floor.

The folder with the research material on the (very secret she groaned) pacemaker Controller II was still there. She thumbed through it; all the sheets seemed to be there. But she couldn't tell if someone had read them. Espionage was a common worry in the medical devices industry and she normally wouldn't have brought the files home. If this had happened a week ago, she would have had to face Daniel and own up to her stupidity. As it was, she now had another secret and the secrets were starting to weigh her down. She knew she would have to come clean on this one, whatever the consequences.

8 CHAPTER EIGHT

Monday, July 18, 2011

"You took research files *home?*" James Reddington was staring at her in disbelief. "And you *left* them there when you went to New York?"

"Something wasn't right and I wanted to be sure before I worried Daniel." She was trying to convince herself, she certainly didn't appear to be convincing James. It was Monday morning, she was really beginning to hate Mondays.

"Dr. Joseph." She cringed at his tone and the use of her title and surname. The clinic staff were used to being very informal with each other, an attitude encouraged by Daniel, but obviously not by James from now on. "This is an extremely serious matter. It is a breach of the security of this clinic, of our research partners, and most of all," he used a JR monogrammed handkerchief to wipe his brow, "of the strict security standards of TechMed Devices."

"It went right out of my head when I f..." she corrected herself quickly, "When Daniel died." She was discovering she really was no good at this business of secrets; she'd almost said *when I found Daniel.*

"I understand we have all been through an incredibly difficult time, in fact, are still going through it. But this happened before he died."

"James, sorry, Dr. Reddington, it was the first time I've ever done that. I couldn't explain what I felt was wrong with the figures and - ?"

"*Felt?*"

"Yes, I still can't really explain it. I didn't get a chance to go through the papers what with Tara's birthday and then Daniel..." She added, "And my flu over the weekend."

"*Felt*, Dr. Joseph?"

"I've always had this thing for figures and their order. It helps my coding. I see the numbers as pictures, images, paintings. There's a flow and an order that is really quite beautiful," she hurried on when she saw his expression, "well, I was looking at the code from the Program Controller II, and I felt this, this... bump... Like you've got a bit of blackberry seed stuck in between your teeth and your tongue seems to go to it no matter what you're doing..."

"Priya...!"

"Sorry, I need to look at the code again before I can say whether there is a concrete reason to worry. You can understand, can't you, why I couldn't go to Daniel without looking properly?"

"I certainly can if you were going to regale him with stories of blackberry misadventures." James almost smiled as he said it. Priya was relieved to see the slight thaw.

But he continued almost immediately, "However, we still have a major breach of security."

He planted his elbows on the desk and rested his face in his hands. He stared at the folder open in front of him. "Leave the files with me, I need to look through them and see what has been exposed." He looked up at her and she squirmed at the annoyance in his eyes. "You know I'm also going to have to tell Gerry and Valerie and see what they think should be done."

James frowned. "And Daniel's grandfather. I'm going to have to fill him in. I guess he's the one who'll take over Daniel's role."

Priya asked, "Can I have a copy of the file? I could look through it and see if I can find anything."

James looked at her for a long moment and then nodded. "Obviously, even I won't be able to save your job if you take the copy out of this building."

Priya said, "I'm really sorry, James, I've never done anything like this before and I definitely won't again."

"You may not have the chance to, Dr. Joseph. You may not have the chance." His voice was tired as he came round the desk to usher her out of his office.

∞

It was 8 p.m. and Priya was exhausted. Daniel sitting there dead, his unseeing gaze, Reyna's accusing stare, Catherine's questions, unknown hands violating her possessions, and now a possibly imploding career. The events of the past week were blurring into a haze of images, all bad. This didn't help her in her quest to analyze the figures from the study. She hadn't realized how reliant she was on the use of imagery that she'd described to James. And the numbers were just not cooperating. They seemed strangely reluctant to be painted onto the canvas. She sat twirling her pen, balancing its arc on her thumbnail.

She was staring at the jumble of numbers on the screen, when Aidan walked in. He hesitated when he saw her.

"Sorry, I was just looking for Tara," he said.

"She was off today. Can I help you?"

"No, no, it's okay. I'll catch her tomorrow."

Aidan walked over with just the hint of a swagger. He perched on the corner of her desk. She could smell his aftershave, a vaguely musky odor. He worked in the sales and marketing side of the clinic, a job he had gotten through his brother, Gerry. She looked up at him with a questioning look.

"So, did you enjoy Friday night?" His tone was neutral but his eyes and lips held a little smirk.

"Friday night?" She was blank for a moment. "Oh yes, Tara's do. I'd forgotten, what with everything that's happened since. I guess it was okay."

"And your 'friend'...? Did she enjoy the night?"

"My friend…?" She felt like a parrot. "Do you mean Tara?"

"No, Tara's my friend too." He was looking at her as if she was being as dim as she felt. "I mean the other one, you know, the one you spent half the night with," the smirk was now obvious, "the very attractive one."

So he had seen her with Reyna.

"Oh her..." Priya tried to be nonchalant. "She was a tourist. I was just being friendly; telling her what there was to do in Galway and stuff. Civic duty and all that."

"Did you show her the city on your ride home in her cool Merc?" He was trying not to laugh.

Damn, damn, damn. "I don't remember. I guess she was kind enough to get me to Michael's place."

Aidan looked like he was going to keep tormenting her so she looked at her screen and said, "I really have to get this stuff done, trying to catch up."

He got up, still grinning, and brushed down his suit trousers. "Well, have a good evening then."

He left her staring at the screen. Her mind was working feverishly. *Had he recognized Reyna? He hadn't been at the funeral; she'd never visited the clinic.* There was a good chance he had no idea who the woman was and had just been teasing her. For her own peace of mind, Priya decided it had just been his usual banter.

She forced her mind back to the readings in front of her.

So what was she seeing that was setting off her teeth? Priya looked again at the notes she had scribbled down. Parts of the Controller II code looked familiar. She did not have access to the Controller I code so she did not know what had been changed in the upgrade. But something that seemed out of place and she just couldn't put her finger on it. A section of the figures showed the readings from routine checks done in clinics around the world. The numbers showed the electrical activity recorded by the leads in the heart from the area around the SA Node. Priya wished she had a graphical representation of the figures. There were thousands of readings dating from 2007 when the Controller II had replaced the Controller I. She did not have the readings for the Controller I. Her initial mental translation of the numbers showed a peculiarity. There were dips in the voltages. She needed to figure out whether there was a pattern.

She looked at her watch. It was 8.15 p.m. She had been staring at these figures for almost eleven hours transcribing them, translating them, playing with them, and reverse engineering the code. She realized with a sense of loss that a few years ago the patterns of numbers would have danced to her command. Funny what stress and the willful destruction of a mind could do. She needed a break and the time to let her mind relax and absorb.

The clinic was quiet. She normally enjoyed this time when the rest of the staff had left and she could think better. Tonight, though, the silence felt heavy. It was still bright outside her window, the grey brightness of a summer that wasn't feeling sure of itself. She started to gather her hand-written notes into a pile to take home. Priya put the papers into her bag and tidied up her desk, feeling a strange reluctance to leave her office. She would *not* be taking home copies of the research figures this time but she had the important details in her notes. Maybe a look through them while she lay out on the deck would provide answers.

∞

The watery sunlight glowed green through the tinted glass of the clinic walls, the cedar wood frame of the building casting long thin shadows on the wood floors of the hallway as she clicked her way to the reception area. The car park was deserted apart from her sky blue Volkswagen Beetle, a car that she had finally purchased a month ago after weeks of deliberation. Cars in Ireland were so expensive, even secondhand ones, that she'd questioned the luxury but had impulsively taken on the car, and the loan. The finance company were happy to give her the loan based on her relatively well-paid job, relative to the many people that were now jobless in the dying screams of the Celtic Tiger. Trading in her much-used and much-loved 10-year-old car had been a wrench but she needed something reliable. She was good at DIY but not with cars.

She unlocked the car as she approached it and was reaching for the handle when she felt it. A shiver of dread, a feeling of being watched. She looked around the car park but she couldn't see anyone. She looked back at the clinic. It squatted in the dusk, no signs of movement within its bowels. The car park was edged by tall leafy trees on one side and the Corrib River on the other. The river flowed through the middle of Galway from its source at Lake Corrib and the campus of the university lined it on its course into Galway. The clinic had been built on private land further along the river from the grounds of the university, near the college's shiny new research facilities. The new building that had been built to hold the Research Company was on the same site, separated by part of the car park but it wasn't visible from the clinic. Daniel had obtained funding from the Irish government to pad out the considerable amount he and his grandfather had privately invested in the research company and the clinic. Both he and the government had been eager to share in the millions of euro that would flow from a successful product in the medical devices field and both had been delighted with the results.

Priya climbed into her car, the keys slipping through her fingers as she tried to get them into the ignition. She flipped the manual locking for the doors and grabbed a look at the backseat and the space behind her seat. Nothing there. *This is crazy.* She tried to calm her breathing and searched for the keys at her feet. The car started on the first attempt and she sighed with relief. Pulling out of the car park, she noticed a dark car moving up behind her in her rear view mirror. It must have been parked around the side of the clinic under the shade of the trees.

She turned right, crossing traffic stopped at the red lights, gestured through by the tired wave of a Galway commuter. The traffic was not as heavy at this time as it would have been a few hours earlier when it was usually backed up on the many roundabouts clotting the arteries supplying Galway. The city council was going to replace these roundabouts, themselves constructed at great expense and disturbance, with pedestrian crossings. Crossings that were going to cost another small fortune and cause even more chaos. But right now, she was grateful for the other cars on the road. She looked in the rear view mirror; the dark car had been let through the same gap and was behind her but not close enough for her to clearly see the single occupant.

Priya took the circuitous route home and the dark car was behind her the whole way. She pulled into the narrow entrance to her house but didn't get out of her car. She sat there looking in the rear view mirror, heart beating a little faster than normal, her stomach feeling queasy. He had been a hundred yards behind her, *where was he?* Just as she was about to get out she saw the car. It slowed down almost imperceptibly as the driver saw her car and then sped up to pass her house. *Damn, she should have gotten out; she would have had a better look at him.*

She hurried into her house, locking the door behind her, switching on the lights in the hallway, living room and kitchen as she went. She spent the next few hours sitting on the deck looking through her notes but every half hour she stood for a few minutes beside the small front room window peering out at the empty road. She gave up any pretence of study at eleven, deciding on a shower and bed.

∞

Priya turned the shower off. The bathroom was quiet, breathing in and out in time to the wind seeping through the open window. She tried to listen through the drips, her ears rang with the stubborn residue of a recent sound, a sound that wasn't water flowing, a sound that had cut through the swirl of water around her head. The bedroom through the closed door was silent. She turned the tap back on and the water rushed down over her. She rotated the temperature control, toward H, on and on, till her skin felt white hot.

She heard it again from under the stream of water, what sounded like the metallic screech of a cat's wail. This time she turned off the shower and stepped out of the stall, wet prints settling in her wake. Switching off the bathroom light she let her eyes adjust to the darkness outside before sidling to the window to stare out at the deck of the house and the field and sea beyond. She had forgotten to leave on the outdoor lights and the back of the house was drenched in its own shadow. She couldn't see the dirt track that ran beside the house from the road and down alongside the field.

The reflection of the moon on the ocean normally calmed her but tonight the trembling glints of light smiled vacant and aimless. She slowed her breathing listening and the sea strained to listen with her. The sniff of seaweed drifted through the moist air. She saw the flicker of a light in the shadow of the back door, for just a second, and then it disappeared gulped up by the darkness.

Goosebumps had poked up on her arms and the water on her skin and around her feet was drying. She grabbed a towel from the rail and hugged it to her, keeping her eyes fixed on the spot where the light had appeared. She waited and her eyes and ears adjusted but there was no further light or movement or sound from the deck.

She gave up her bathroom vigil after half an hour and crawled to bed. She got up four times during the night to go to the bathroom window and to the guest bedroom at the front to look out of the window there, before returning to bed. The night passed without any further sighting of the dark car and in silence apart from a restless sleep feathered with dreams of cats crying.

9 CHAPTER NINE

Tuesday, July 19, 2011

The diplomat was tired. The weekend had been long and lonely. He had rattled around in the house, trying not to think, but only thinking. Thinking while he ate his badly cooked meals, thinking while he practiced with the device, thinking while he took out the garbage. Thoughts of death. Not his. If everything went as planned, not his. Thoughts of a woman he met every year. A politician who was doing her job. Who felt so strongly about her country that she wanted to protect it from what she considered the grasping nature of other countries. So she championed a cause and she would be signing it into being the day after their meeting. Did she deserve to die for that? The diplomat's only answer was that he loved his country too, and it didn't deserve to die.

As the diplomat had lain in bed and tried not to think, he had realized his hand lay on his collarbone, a habit he had already formed after just 9 days.

He had 13 days.

10 CHAPTER TEN

Tuesday, July 19, 2011

It was 9.00 a.m. when Priya arrived at work but the clinic car park was full and most of the staff seemed to be around. Priya gave Clodagh a questioning look; the receptionist was on the phone but she covered the mouthpiece and whispered, "Meeting at 10 a.m. in the boardroom. Mary sent around an email. They've been in for ages, even before I came in." She gestured with her head towards James' office.

Priya found Tara already in their office. She was surrounded by folders and her hair looked like she'd been running her fingers through it.

"Morning, Tara."

"Hi. Check out your email quick. We've got a meeting with the bigwigs at 10."

"Bigwigs...?"

"Yup, someone from the Fairer crowd, I think the grandfather himself, and 'Dr. Reddington' of course." Tara pulled a face. "I'm trying to refresh my memory on my cases, not much point though. What do you think they're going to do about us?"

"I don't think they can close down just like that. We have patients and James is a good doctor, he has a great reputation now. So has Sean. You guys should be fine. The main problem is our research side. Daniel was brilliant at creating a vision. But Gerry and Valerie at Research are pretty smart too and I think they did most of the actual research and development."

Priya didn't want to contemplate losing the job. She'd taken out a mortgage on the house in Barna at the height of the boom in Ireland to buy it from her father. Her mortgage payments, the car payments, the ever-increasing utility bills; even working fulltime she just scraped by, the bulk of her salary eaten into by taxes and various stealth charges introduced by the government in a desperate attempt to save the failing economy.

"I'm sure it will be fine." It sounded like Tara was trying to comfort herself as well. "Daniel did a great job of setting up this place and I'm sure James won't want to lose the money that's coming in. He'll just have to work with Research himself. They'll be relying on you to fill them in on Daniel's thought processes though," she grinned at Priya, "cos you would have known what they were, wouldn't you...?"

"Tara! Don't you start on me. You *know* we didn't have anything going on."

"I know, I know." Tara was laughing now. "Wonder what Mary would think if she knew that all the rumors she started about you and Daniel were so way off," she crossed herself and lowered her voice, "because you're one of those 'perverts' whose souls she prays for every Sunday at mass?"

Priya couldn't help but laugh. Tara did a great imitation of Mary whose personality was a complete contrast to Tara's irreverent one.

∞

Priya and Tara filed into the boardroom with the rest of the staff. Just over a week on, the focus had already shifted from the news of Daniel's death to the tension surrounding the retention of their jobs. The chatter was subdued, the glances at the door frequent, as they waited for James and Daniel Fairer II.

At exactly 10 a.m., the door opened and James came in. His face had new lines and he had gained some gray hairs. Behind him, Reyna walked through the door. Priya could not control her face as her jaw dropped open. She quickly closed her mouth as James and Reyna took their seats at the head of the table. Reyna was wearing a deep blue trouser suit and her long thick brown hair hung in a ponytail.

James said, "This is Reyna Fairer, Daniel's sister."

There were muttered greetings from the staff. In the babble, Priya saw Aidan's face. He looked stunned; his reaction to Reyna's appearance making it obvious to Priya that he had recognized the woman from the pub. Priya could feel Tara's fingers digging at her side, *oh no, why had she been out with them when she'd made a fool of herself with Reyna.*

Priya's heart beat faster as Reyna scanned the people at the table nodding a greeting to them. Reyna's eyes flicked briefly over Priya's face with no noticeable change in her expression. Priya noticed now that Reyna's eyes were topaz-brown, clear and direct with crinkly lines set into their corners, in a face that was lean and full of straight lines. Straight jaw, long straight neck leading to a little hollow from which her collarbones curved. Her skin was tanned just a shade darker than the V-necked cream chemise she wore.

Reyna said, "I can understand you are all anxious to know what is going to happen to the clinic. My grandfather is not able to travel but it would probably not have been necessary anyway as Daniel's Will has handed over control of the clinic to me."

There was a collective intake of air around the table and Priya noticed again that slight almost undetectable quirk of Reyna's lips as she paused very slightly and then continued.

"I have had discussions with Dr. Reddington over the past few days and as I am not a clinician, in fact I have a business and finance background, I will be spending the next few weeks working closely with Dr. Reddington and discussing the employment of a clinician and researcher to take over the work that Daniel was carrying out. Daniel was a gifted clinician and researcher and he will be difficult to replace. But he worked hard to set up this clinic. I know what it meant to him and to the patients his work has benefited. And I know this work is important to all of you too. So I can assure you that I will do everything I can to make sure that not only does the clinic remain open, but that we continue to make Daniel proud."

Reyna looked around at the assembled staff. "I will need to meet with each of you individually over the next few days." She addressed Mary, "Can you arrange that for me?" Priya's heart had been sinking further towards her shoes as she listened and now she felt it hit the ground.

∞

Reyna left the meeting without another word and Priya avoided Aidan's eyes and retreated to her office. Tara wandered in ten minutes later, a grin on her face.

"So, I'd love to be a fly on the wall when you go in for your meeting." Tara was rubbing her hands together looking a lot like the fly in question.

Priya put her elbows on her desk, rested her head in her hands and groaned in response.

"My life has got to get better soon." She was determined to wallow at least for a minute in self-pity.

"You'll be fine, love, at least this time, with *this* boss, you might actually live up to the rumors. She'll certainly be more your type, all that repressed passion in *such* an attractive package." Tara was on a roll.

Priya looked up to see Reyna standing behind Tara in the doorway to the office and the expression on her face changed so fast that Tara winced and made a silent 'she's behind me, isn't she?' gesture then turned herself around to face the door.

"Ms. McFadden, isn't it?" Reyna voice was the gentle slice of scissors through silk. Priya was relieved that she wasn't at the receiving end this time.

Tara smiled. "Please call me Tara," she said. "As you can see, I suffer from 'foot in mouth disease'. Now, unless it was me you came to see, please excuse me as I am just going to the Ladies to wash my mouth out with soap." She brushed past Reyna and her footsteps beat a retreat down the hall leaving Priya alone with Reyna.

Reyna stepped into the office and closed the door behind her. She placed one of the spare chairs beside Priya's desk and sat down. Priya was getting fed up with the burning in her cheeks every time this woman looked at her with that critical gaze. But as the gaze continued, her cheeks grew even hotter. Reyna still hadn't said a word to her.

"I assume you will want my resignation."

"Dr. Joseph, I wouldn't make any assumptions if I were you. I have many things to sort out, you worked closely with Daniel and I need you to fill me in on the ongoing projects. I would like that to happen as soon as possible before I meet up again with our research partners."

Priya said nothing.

"There's no need to look so confused, Dr. Joseph, I intend to find out everything there is to know and it seems to me that you know quite a bit more than you let on."

"Ms. Fairer, I can fill you in on the Program Controller which is the project I was working on with Daniel before he... died. And our past projects and some of the ideas Daniel had been thinking about. But apart from that, I don't know in what way you think I can help you. I really haven't been that involved in any more than routine checks on patients for the last while."

Reyna's voice was sharp. "You were in his apartment that morning. My mother did not mention a little Indian woman being there when she found Daniel. She had a very strong feeling that there had been a woman in his bed. I assumed when he didn't call on Saturday that both of you were spending the day together."

Priya said, "Why didn't you tell your mother you brought me there. Why let her keep thinking that there was someone with him in bed?"

Reyna leaned forward, a harsh expression on her face. "Women like you think you can get away with a sweet smile, all innocence. But you are not innocent. I blame myself for taking you there but you were the one who slept with him, and then left him there. Did you even think of calling for help? What were you trying to save, your reputation?" Priya flinched at Reyna's tone; in it, there was no reputation worth saving.

"I was *never* Daniel's girlfriend. I woke up in a strange apartment; I didn't know how I had ended up there. I had a vague memory of meeting you. I didn't really want to stick around anyway, and then I found him. He was dead already. I just reacted. I know it was a mistake. I'm not proud of it. I don't know why I ran away. Why on earth did you take me there anyway?"

"You were drunk. I had the keys and I didn't know anywhere else in Galway." Reyna looked slightly discomfited for the first time. "Besides, Daniel said that he had a thing with a researcher and he mentioned your name a few times."

"Your mother said you were supposed to meet him at Massimo?"

"He sent me a text to say he wouldn't make it, that he wasn't feeling too well and was going to bed."

"Why did you stay on?"

"You had come over. You were very friendly. I knew you didn't know who I was."

"And you were curious to see why Daniel's girlfriend would be chatting up a total stranger? And a woman at that.

If you thought I was his girlfriend why didn't you just say who you were? Or were you trying to see how far I'd go, see if you could report me to Daniel?"

"No, it wasn't like that." Reyna stopped.

"Why did you not just send me back to my workmates? They must still have been there, Aidan saw us getting into a car."

"No…, they weren't there. They'd left before that. You didn't notice them going." *Was that a blush?*

Priya said, thinking out loud, "Why would they leave me behind? Not even say goodnight? Tara recognized you from the pub, surely she would have come over before she left…" She paused at the growing redness on Reyna's face. "…Okay, so she *did* come over and… what…? You might as well tell me, I'm just going to ask Tara anyway."

"You were kissing me, I looked up afterwards and saw her walking back into the crowd and then I think your group left."

Priya sat in stunned silence.

Reyna stood up and her chair screeched on the floor. She walked back to the door opening it with a quick pull. Tara had her hand raised to knock, and Reyna ignored her and walked out and away down the hall.

"Girl! Ye weren't at it again, were ye?" Tara glanced down the hall to make sure Reyna had disappeared before she spoke.

Priya didn't react; she just sat there in a silent huddle.

"Priya? Are you okay?" Tara walked over, took Priya's hand, and rubbed it between hers. "Was she giving you a hard time? You know, you don't have to put up with it. You could get her for harassment; from what I saw that night she was really into you too."

"She wasn't into me. I seem to have just thrown myself at her. And she thought I was with Daniel." *And then I find her brother and I leave him dead and she thinks I was having sex with him when he died. Or that I killed him?*

"Well, you weren't with Daniel. And as I said, and I'll say it again, no matter what Miss Ice Queen says she certainly looked like she was enjoying herself that night."

∞

The rest of the day blurred by her. Priya gathered what she could on the projects she had worked on with Daniel. She placed the material into neat piles on her desk. She worked through lunch and ignored Tara's frequent glances as well as her invitation to lunch.

When she had finished collating the information she had, it was after 5 p.m. She didn't want to go home. She could hear others still working in the building but she didn't want their company. A visit to Michael, he often worked from home, maybe dinner at their favorite Italian restaurant. The city centre would be busy but distracting with the Arts Festival in its second week. She made up her mind and grabbed all the notes she had made and stuffed them into her briefcase.

There were still cars in the car park as she walked out of the clinic. No dark car waiting for her this time. Probably all in her mind anyway. She wasn't sure she would have noticed it this evening, her mind was still replaying the conversation with Reyna, and struggling to remember the night they had spent a part of together.

"Dr. Joseph." Reyna's voice was real; it cut through Priya's imaginings and she dropped her briefcase. A few sheets of paper spilled out and the wind caught them and blew them towards Reyna's feet. This time as she reddened, Priya cursed out loud. She chased after one sheet that was wrapped around the base of one of the young saplings planted along the walkway. When she had retrieved the paper, she turned to see Reyna examining the other sheets.

Reyna asked, "Taking work home?"

"Just some notes." Priya held her hand out and Reyna gave her the crumpled sheets.

"My mother asked me to invite you to dinner tonight. She seems to have been quite taken with you." Reyna's tone seemed to suggest surprise.

"I'm not really organized for anything, it's quite short notice." Priya was annoyed at the arrogance of it. After the things this woman had said to her.

"I'm sorry I didn't mention it earlier, that's why I actually went to your office. If you want to leave your car at home, I could follow you and give you a ride to my mother's place. It's very hard to find. I'm staying with her. Maybe pick up some things at your place; I could give you a ride back in tomorrow." Reyna was already starting to turn away.

"Maybe I had plans already." Priya felt as childish as she sounded. Almost like she had just stamped her feet and sulked. There was that annoying smile again on Reyna's lips.

"I was merely passing on an invitation from my mother. You are free to refuse. I'm sure I'll manage to eat what my mother has prepared. She is an amazing cook. I was only trying to help by offering a ride; you are of course free to bring your own car as well if you want." Reyna said it so graciously, the words so subtly flavored with a smile that Priya now felt like a teenager and a gawky one at that. And she knew she couldn't avoid the talk with Catherine.

"You are very kind." She tried not to choke on the words, tried to sound like a 35-year-old adult. "I live in Barna, it's on the way out to Connemara. If you want to follow me, I'll pick up some things for the night. Which one's your car?"

Reyna pointed to a silvery blue Mercedes coupe parked beside James' quiet Lexus.

"Okay, I'm in the blue Volks over there; it'll be easy to keep in sight." Priya set off for her car without waiting for Reyna's response.

∞

She was tempted on the drive home to lose Reyna but she kept a steady pace and pulled in to her driveway with the Mercedes still behind her. Reyna had the top down and her hair had come loose from its ponytail. She took off her sunglasses and looked at the house with curiosity.

"Would you like to come in while I get my things?" Priya was hoping the woman would stay put but Reyna nodded and got out of the car. Her sleekness reminded Priya of her first impressions of Catherine. They didn't look alike, Catherine's face was softer, her eyes a pale shade of blue. But they shared a grace in their movements.

Priya opened the front door of her house. She was trying to remember whether she had left the house in a fit state for visitors. She was aware of every movement that Reyna made and conscious of the slight air of neglect that permeated the house.

"Come through to the back, you could wait out on the deck. Would you like a glass of wine while you wait?" Priya rushed Reyna through the front room and into the kitchen suddenly anxious to show off the nicer side of the house. She was pleased to hear the intake of breath as Reyna caught sight of the view from the kitchen window.

"No wine for me, thanks. The drive is difficult enough as it is. Remembering to stay on the right side of the road, or the left side. At least I was able to rent an automatic, I don't drive stick shift. Perhaps a glass of water?"

Priya fetched Reyna the water and left her on the deck admiring the view. She ran upstairs and grabbed her toothbrush and a change of clothes that she threw into her little overnight bag. She leant out to close the window and saw that Reyna had stretched out on one of the deck chairs right below her. Reyna's face was tilted to catch the shy rays of the Galway sun, the dark glasses sparkling. Priya stared at the bow of Reyna's lips, a memory flicked; of touching those lips with hers. Her gaze moved down; that body had lain beside hers, her body remembered the slight weight, the warmth against her back.

"Did no-one tell you it was rude to stare?" Priya jerked her head back into her bedroom. She heard Reyna laugh. It was a quiet sound and she was irritated to realize that she liked the tone of it even through her intense embarrassment.

∞

Priya went down the stairs ten minutes later to find Reyna in the living room looking through the stack of her paintings. Reyna had lined them up facing out from the wall and their colors brightened and warmed the gloom of the small room. There were a mixture of portraits and landscapes. Reyna was staring at the large canvas she held in her hands and didn't seem to notice Priya entering the room. It was a seascape in oil, stunning in its vitality, the sound of the waves almost crashing into the room, evoking the taste of salt spray on lips.

"Those are private!" Priya felt the hurt and anger flash back into her. She walked over and took the canvas out of Reyna's hands. "I don't mean to be rude. Can we please go now?" Priya was collecting the paintings as she spoke, placing them back in the stack, turning them around to face the wall.

Reyna didn't say anything, just looked at Priya with a faint tinge of pity in her eyes. Priya stalked to the front door and held it open and Reyna, still silent, strolled past her to the rental car.

11 CHAPTER ELEVEN

They had not spoken since they'd left Priya's house. Priya was conscious of Reyna's energy; it flowed through the car and filled every corner. Reyna's body appeared relaxed but it hummed with the lazy current of a sheathed cable. Her hands on the steering wheel, clean cut nails, long fingers, slender wrists. A little crescent scar nestled within the junction of the index and middle finger of her right hand, white against the cream tan. Priya imagined herself reaching out and touching that scar. A little jolt of electricity seared the tip of her finger. She shook her head and turned to look away, to watch the landscape flow past in barren waves. Her finger tingled.

"Look, how about a truce for the moment? For Catherine's sake. I'm sorry I looked at your paintings, I was curious and they were just lying there."

Priya remained silent for a few minutes. Then she sighed and turned her attention back to interior of the car.

"I don't get many visitors, in fact, apart from my best friend, Michael, I don't get any visitors. So I just forgot about them being there," she said.

"They're wonderful. I'm surprised you haven't become a professional artist. Or, are you? In secret, painting at night and selling your work in galleries around the world, under a pseudonym, I saw that you didn't sign your work."

"One does not become a painter, one does Medicine or Engineering, or Science." Priya had put on a slight Indian accent.

Reyna laughed. "You're kidding me! And that sounds nothing like your father. He has an American accent."

Priya had a sudden thought that laughing came natural to this woman though her face had seemed to settle in unsmiling lines.

"My mother. How do you know about my dad's accent? Did you meet him after he retired from the clinic? I got the impression you weren't at your grandfather's clinic till way after my dad left."

"I only started working for my grandfather in 2009; I think your dad had already been gone from there for about 10 years. I used to call him up and ask him stuff about the early records and patents from his work with my grandfather. I liked him, still do. I'm so sorry about your mum; I never got to meet her, though I occasionally heard her in the background telling him where to find the stuff I asked for."

"Thank you." Priya sighed again, then spoke in a very quiet voice. "They were such a weirdly mismatched couple you know, but they were together for 45 years. Went everywhere together, fought like cats and dogs. He's a tall man but he seems tiny now without her."

∞

As they drove over the rough sweeping asphalt roads deeper into Connemara, the weather changed. Gusts of wind blew slow drizzle like grey insects across the windscreen. The sun was still shining but was too weak to dry out the air. In the car, the heater battled against the condensation and Reyna fiddled with the controls trying to clear the glass.

"How do you deal with this weather?" Reyna muttered as she finally found the right setting and the windows cleared within seconds. The sun broke through the cloud as if in protest.

Priya said, "I've had time. My experience of the phrase 'it was a beautiful day' came from Enid Blyton books I'd read in India in which the Famous Five took picnics with ginger beer any chance they could. When I was a kid, I wondered at that phrase. What was a 'not' beautiful day? Why this fascination with the sun and its level of shine? What was so wrong with rain? I have to say when we moved here my world expanded to include new concepts of need, Please God let the sun shine, Please God let it not rain today, Please God let them be able to identify me when they find me dead from the cold but still attached to this radiator."

Reyna laughed and Priya pointed to the crisp jut of mountain against sky in the distance. "When the sun shines like this there is no place on earth more beautiful than Ireland. I remind myself of that when the grey dampness gets too much. Every time I landed back in Shannon after visiting my parents I used to come out of the airport and just breathe in and feel that particular mix of cleanliness and moisture wash out my lungs. I know there are other places with clean air but I don't know what it is about the Irish air. I guess it feels like home."

She stared out again at the brown and gold of the sparse landscape with its latticework of stone.

"Is that why you didn't go with your parents when they went to New York?" Reyna asked.

"I was just starting college and I'd been on my own so much at that stage that it didn't seem to make much difference. They were such a unit, you know. When I graduated I went on to do my postgrad and then when I realized I was gay I couldn't tell them."

"Did you ever tell them?"

Priya turned to her. "Yes, that was a surreal experience. I'll never forget sitting them down at the kitchen table, two Indian people in their seventies. I'd never spoken to them about anything even vaguely relating to sex or sexuality before. And now I was telling them that their only daughter was a lesbian. I think my mom thought I was changing nationality again."

She smiled as Reyna laughed again.

"For all their worldly travels, they really were quite innocent. My mother never really got it. She still suggested guys from good families every time I saw her. You know, if she'd been able to talk when I saw her in India the last time she'd probably have told me about a great guy she had found for me." Priya found her eyes were filling and she whispered as she turned away again, "And I probably would have agreed."

Reyna laid her hand on Priya's for a second and then jerked it back to the steering wheel. She said, "Seems so strange to me. Leo and Catherine were so easygoing about everything. It barely even seemed to register with them that I was gay."

They had reached the turn-off from the already narrow road onto a road that was barely one, with tufts of grass popping up in between two worn stone tracks. It was the bog-cutting season and stacks of turf were piled at the sides of the deep cuts in the dark ground on either side of the road.

"I used to spend some summers here. Leo had the house and the three of us used to visit." Reyna had to slow down as the car skewed sideways a few inches on the loose stones. "It's okay, the road will get better soon. It'll be worth it, Catherine really is an amazing cook."

"How come he had a house in Connemara? I thought foreigners couldn't buy or build here."

"Leo was Irish. It's his family home. He left Ireland when he was very young."

They turned onto a slightly wider road.

"Was Daniel not with ye? You said the three of you came here for the summers."

"Daniel stayed with his grandfather in New York when Catherine left to go to California with Leo. She was pregnant with me."

"I never heard Daniel mention his father at all."

"I don't think Daniel ever forgave Leo for causing his mother to go. Daniel grew up thinking of his grandfather as more of a father. And his grandfather didn't have a son of his own so it was the same for him."

"Yes I heard him talk about his grandfather. He was in awe of him, I think. But then I only really spent any time with Daniel after he opened the clinic. How old was Daniel when Catherine left?"

"He was nine. She wanted to take him with her. He chose to stay. Daniel didn't really know Leo, our father, at all. Leo had set up the place in California and wanted to move there and Daniel wouldn't leave his grandfather. I don't think he ever forgave Leo; he never attempted to meet him. But when Leo died 6 years ago, Daniel agreed to meet Catherine, and me."

"Wow, so you've only been in contact for the last few years. That must have been weird, knowing you had a brother, or did you?"

"I knew. I guess I had a very unusual upbringing. I grew up in what you'd probably call a cult. Leo was a very charismatic healer and Catherine developed her skills over the years. We lived on this farm-like place in Southern California. A commune of people, who shared everything, and worked and lived off the land. Very hippyish."

"That's funny; I can't see *you* as a hippy."

"I wasn't. I got out of there as soon as I could and I went to college to do Business. Did the usual, worked all kinds of jobs, and took student loans, got through it. I was somehow never taken that seriously in business though when I told anyone my name was Rain. I didn't get around to changing my name till a few years ago." Reyna smiled. "But the Irish used to have a lot of fun with my name when I visited."

"So were you working in a business before you went to work for your granddad?"

"No. I was in a totally different field."

Reyna didn't say anymore and the sudden quiet was uncomfortable after what Priya had found an easy journey so far. She was surprised by that ease between them after the accusations Reyna had leveled at her.

Priya said, "By the way, I was doing the practical research component of my PhD at the Fairer Research Company when I met Daniel. He asked me to do the interview for the job at the clinic. I didn't get the job there through my dad."

Reyna had that smile on her lips again; the one that annoyed Priya while at the same time sent her pulse rate higher.

"I apologize if I got that one wrong. I thought your dad had helped."

"He was the one who suggested I do a PhD in the field because he knew there would be opportunities and he gave me the idea for the thesis and pointed me towards the research company but he didn't get me the job at the clinic. I guess he was far-sighted and made sure I was in the right place at the right time. But according to Daniel, he'd never have taken me on just because of dad; he said the role was way too important to him for any friend or family influence to play a part."

"As I said, I'm sorry. I was wrong obviously."

"You were also wrong about Daniel being my boyfriend."

"You're determined to set me right about a few things, aren't you?"

"I don't understand why Daniel would tell you we were together. What exactly did he say?"

"Well, I don't remember the exact words but he hinted that he was having a thing with a researcher and I got the impression he was really 'involved' you know, which was so unusual for him, he had always been such a lady's man."

"He had a certain way about him. It wasn't just his looks or the money. He had a charisma. He could sell ice to the Inuit. I could see that for a straight woman he would definitely be interesting."

Reyna laughed. "I think that's snow to the Eskimos."

"Daniel could have patented the stuff and sold it back to them in truckloads."

"Did you like him?"

Priya said, thinking about her words, "I admired him as a researcher, and as a man who could make things happen. And yes, he could be very charming."

"That hasn't really answered my question."

Priya wanted to just give an answer, any answer. Reyna was glancing at her, waiting. But she found she couldn't say anything and just turned to look out of the window.

∞

They had travelled about an hour away from Priya's house and were deep in Connemara. As the Mercedes glided over the road, now asphalt and winding, rising as it hugged the side of a mountain, they were silent, and the silence was now filled with tension. The scenery was overpowering, the fjord stretching out as far as the horizon, its blue water a hundred necklaces of diamonds in the late sun. Clumps of trees covered the shores and the occasional house perched on the surrounding hills.

"I live so close to this beauty and I never come out here." Priya broke the silence.

"You've never been out here?"

"Oh I have. Over the last twenty odd years, any visitors were taken on the tour of Connemara. But it's been a while, and I never just get in the car and come out here."

"You've never been tempted to paint here?"

Priya thought for a moment. "I painted from my memories. I guess I lived in my head and painted what I saw."

"Wow. You must have a photographic memory! Those paintings were extremely detailed."

"It's hard to explain. I think in pictures, even numbers and code, they're expressed in my mind like images. And when I see something, it is stored as an exact image almost. Means I can usually see when something has been moved. It annoys Michael no end."

Priya felt uneasy as she remembered her bookshelf. And the research figures. She added, "It's not anything special, a lot of people see things in a more visual way. It's not really like I can look at everything on a page and reproduce it or anything."

"So why did you stop hanging up your paintings? And why did you stop painting? You have, haven't you?"

"I stopped liking my memories."

Priya turned to the window again. She sensed Reyna's frustration at her withdrawal but Reyna said nothing.

∞

The turn onto another dirt track came up a few minutes later. The track went down as it outlined the side of the fjord. Reyna pointed to the clump of trees stuck on the side of the hill in front of them. "This is the front entrance, see that gap, the house is in the clearing there."

A little trail of smoke crept into the air above the clearing tugged and dispersed by the breeze.

"Catherine always lights a fire, even in the summer. I think she's just addicted to the smell of burning turf."

The track wandered into the forest and the relative darkness under the trees made Priya shiver.

She whispered, "Does Catherine not mind living here on her own? Especially in the winter?"

"When you see the house you'll understand. There's a wonderful view and there's such a sense of peace. She has that ability to create spaces like that wherever she goes, but the last few years she's been the happiest I've seen her, until now obviously."

12 CHAPTER TWELVE

The sunlight streaked through the canopy of trees as they approached the house. It sat in a clearing, the denseness of forest behind it and surrounding it on three sides. Priya glanced over her shoulder and saw the fjord spread out in a vista of blues, the mountains on the other side solid and green.

"I see what you mean. That view is spectacular!" Priya said as she turned back to look at the house.

It was an old two-storey cottage, its painted facade was old stone, its windows had obviously been updated but the newer looking double-glazed units with red frames looked a perfect fit. The flowers in the yellow window boxes were shades of purple and red and blue. The roof had also been re-done but the work had been carried out with skill and the cottage settled comfortably in its setting. There was a stone barn to the side of the house and the shell of another building further back. A board with a white sheet pinned on it leant against the jagged stone shell.

"She really has done a lovely job of the house." Priya said.

"Yes, she did it with the help of some very skilled local tradesmen, over the last 5 years. It certainly wasn't like this when we used to stay here."

The cream-colored stones crunched under the wheels as Reyna drove the car up to the red front door.

The door opened and Catherine came out to greet them. She looked relaxed in faded blue jeans and a pale purple top, her silver hair falling loose to her shoulders.

"Welcome to our little corner of Connemara, Priya." Catherine's smile was as warm, her eyes clear and blue and the sunlight shaded the deep creases in her face. She seemed more grounded than she had appeared on the day of the funeral.

"Thank you for inviting me. You have a gorgeous place here." Priya took the overnight bag out and stood beside the car.

"Come in, come in. Dinner will be ten minutes. Reyna, will you show Priya to the guest room and I'll just set the table on the patio." Catherine ushered them in through the door.

The house felt draughty, the flag stone floor of the small foyer leading to a large hallway. There was a smell of turf as they stepped into the hallway. There were doors off each side of the hallway and a thick oak staircase rising into the darkness of the first floor. Catherine gestured down the hall and then hurried off through one of the doors.

Reyna led Priya down the hallway. The heat leaked out and hovered around the open door through which Catherine had disappeared. Reyna opened the second door down the hallway and they entered a room with a double bed covered in a knobbly white bedspread. A chair and a large dark wood wardrobe were the only other pieces of furniture in the room that was warm, heated by a wall-hung radiator that was one of the few signs of the modernization of the house.

"Sorry about the lack of luxury, Catherine hasn't gotten to all the rooms yet."

"It's lovely and toasty." Priya dropped her bag on the bed.

"Yes, Catherine made sure every room had good heating. That was one of the first things she saw to. I'll leave you to freshen up. There's the bathroom." Reyna pointed down the hall as she left. "Come through to the living room when you're ready."

Priya took her few bits out of the bag and placed them on the chair. The room felt like something out of the early part of the last century. It reminded her of the set that was on display at Maam's Cross, a little cottage with life-sized mannequins of John Wayne and Maureen O'Hara in 'The Quiet Man'. She took a towel and her toiletries down to the bathroom and washed her face. Even through the thick stone wall she could hear voices in conversation, two voices similar in tone. She heard Reyna's laugh, and again the sound vibrated through her.

∞

Tendrils of smoke floated in the light streaming through the window of the living room. There was turf burning in the open fireplace and stacked around the chimneybreast. The flagstone floor was covered in rugs and two couches were set around the fire, with throws draped over them. Through the open door, Priya could see another room with a dining table and an archway leading to what sounded like the kitchen. A large custom-built bookshelf full of books completely hid one wall of the living room.

"I think Catherine has read more books than anyone I know, she reads everything she can get her hands on, she'll even read instructions manuals if you let her," Reyna said from the door. "Can I get you a drink, a glass of wine perhaps?"

Priya shook her head. "Maybe with dinner. Something smells really good." She realized how hungry she was, she'd skipped lunch to work on the figures and her stomach was making rumbling noises.

"Come on in, dinner is served," Catherine yelled from the kitchen.

They ate out on the patio that had been built on to the back and side of the house in such a way that it was sheltered in parts, but on a good day it could be used for eating in the company of the stunning view. The large earthenware plates were full with rice and vegetables, and a variety of salads were placed out in bowls. Priya devoured what was on her plate and was surprised at how tasty the meal was.

"I hope you don't mind that it is vegetarian," Catherine said. "I don't think you are?"

"I'm not but I don't mind at all, it is delicious!" Priya said, "I keep meaning to go vegetarian and every now and then I try cutting down but I guess I'd have to go cold turkey." She realized what she'd said when Catherine and Reyna burst out laughing. She laughed as well. "Sorry, didn't mean that literally. I'd say I could happily be a vegetarian if I got this kind of food served to me every day."

∞

They cleared their plates and sat back.

"I'll wash up, you guys can chat." Reyna started collecting the dishes.

"Are you sure you don't want a hand?" Priya didn't want the conversation that was coming despite having been aware throughout the evening that Catherine had issued the invitation for a reason.

Reyna waved away her offer of help and carried the plates into the kitchen.

"Perhaps a glass of wine?" Catherine asked.

"No, I think I'm going to need a clear head for this."

Catherine smiled. "I actually did invite you out because I wanted to see you again and I knew you'd enjoy this place. But I also want to finish the conversation we started. Have you had a chance to think about what I said?"

Priya bowed her head. She said, "Reyna obviously hasn't filled you in on what happened that night has she?"

"She hasn't said anything but I know something must have happened between you two."

Priya jerked her head up. Catherine smiled. "I know you were both at the pub at the same time. My dear, there is enough electricity between you two to take care of my ESB bills for a year."

Reyna chose that moment to walk back out to the patio wiping her hands with a dishcloth. She halted as she heard Catherine's words and Priya felt the heat in her face reflected in Reyna's face.

"So, which one of you is going to tell me about it?" Catherine asked.

"It would probably be better if Reyna filled you in on the first part as she remembers what happened in Massimo." Priya felt herself blushing harder as Catherine raised an eyebrow. Reyna was leaving her to explain to Catherine that she was the woman who had been in the apartment with Daniel. Some kind of twisted punishment. Seemed rather sadistic towards her own mother though, not to relieve her mind. Unless she still thought that Priya had something to do with Daniel's death.

Priya took in a deep breath.

"I was in the apartment that morning. Reyna dropped me off there."

Catherine looked stunned. Reyna sat down and the patio chair creaked under the sudden weight. She had changed into a pair of stonewashed jeans and a white top with a pale blue sweater. Priya could not meet her eyes; she focused on the blue of the sweater.

Priya rushed on.

"I was in the guest room. I didn't sleep with him." She lowered her head. "I found him though."

Priya gave Catherine and Reyna as much detail as she could about the morning, about finding Daniel, and about her feeling that something was off, about the faint smell. Their eyes widened when she told them about the voices she heard when she was in the stairwell.

Catherine was shaking her head slowly. "I got a strong sense that someone had been in bed with him."

Priya was hesitant to tell them about her suspicions that someone had searched her house or that she had been followed. She didn't think they'd get how particular she was about her books or how her mind mapped patterns. And the car could have been a coincidence, the noises outside could have been the imaginings of her heated mind.

She felt like an open book when Catherine said, "There's more, isn't there?"

Priya told them about her suspicions.

"Who were all the people with you that night?" Reyna asked.

"Tara, of course, she's the other tech, that is, she carries out the regular checks on the pacemakers using the controller." She saw the look of confusion in Catherine's eyes. "When a pacemaker is installed at the clinic, the patient has to come in for regular checks for a while after that. Once a month for the first two months post-op and then every three months for the rest of the year after that and then it goes to six monthly, then annual visits. Tara and I use something we call a Controller to read data off the pacemaker and to communicate with it if necessary."

Catherine nodded and Priya continued, "Let me see, Aidan was there, and Sheila, Lorna, Maeve, and Laura, they're the nurses at the clinic. Lorna's husband and Maeve's boyfriend were there too. James doesn't go out to these things; he lets Daniel do the socializing bit. And of course, Clodagh, she organizes all of these things, when it's someone's birthday or when we're celebrating anything; she's the one who lets everyone know and picks the place. I think Sean was there too, he's the other doctor. So really, all of the clinic staff except James, and Sean really just showed his face and then left early. I remember meeting the others there, I was a little late and I drank a bit too much and a bit too fast. The rest of the night is a blur, actually to be honest; I don't remember anything after the first hour." *Except the memory of Reyna's lips and her body beside mine.* Priya pushed that sudden and unwelcome thought out of her mind but she had glanced at Reyna's lips involuntarily and was mortified that Reyna caught the look.

Priya turned to Catherine trying to keep Reyna out of her line of vision. "Did Daniel say anything to you, anything at all, about tiredness, or chest pain or shortness of breath or any other physical symptoms?" she asked.

Catherine said, "No, in fact, he said at the last Sunday lunch I had with him, two weeks before he died..." She paused and cleared her throat. "He said he was feeling great physically."

"Physically? Was there something else? And why ask me about the people who were there that night?"

Catherine looked at Reyna and said, "I think we should tell Priya."

Priya felt a flash of annoyance when Reyna hesitated.

Priya said, "I know what you think of me, leaving Daniel like that. But I've been thinking since that he died of a heart attack and in a strange way, that fact had given me a little relief. It made me sure I didn't have anything to do with his death. Since Catherine spoke to me in New York, I've been scared again. I had this underlying fear that I might have been involved in some way. But, you know what? I wasn't in his bed and I didn't do anything to him!"

Reyna leaned forward. "You sound like you're trying to convince yourself. Because you really can't be sure, can you?" The harshness had come back into her voice and face.

"No, I racked my brain. And my gut. Reyna, there are good reasons why I wouldn't even have gone to Daniel's in the first place, and I certainly wouldn't have been in his bed, even with all that drink in me."

Catherine said, "I believe you Priya. I wouldn't have talked to you about it in New York if I felt you had anything to do with Daniel's death. Do you want to tell us what happened last year with Daniel?" She reached across the table and took Priya's hand. "You don't have to if you don't want to. I got the feeling from Daniel there was something he wasn't proud of and it concerned you. But that's all I know."

"It's complicated. And I don't think it had anything to do with Daniel's death. It happened last year on my birthday in October and the police got involved but that never went anywhere and then my mom died and nothing mattered anymore. Daniel and I eventually found a way to live with it. He was very good to me when my mom died; he seemed to understand more than the others."

"Are you saying Daniel raped you?" Reyna's voice was strained and unbelieving.

"No. I said it was complicated. Some things happened the night of my birthday." Priya took her hand away from Catherine's and rested her face in her hands. "I haven't told anyone this. I was too ashamed. I came on to Daniel that night to stop something happening with someone else. It worked; he ignored her and gave me a lift home. I was drunk but there was no way I would sleep with him. But, as I said, I was drunk, and I really don't drink much, never have, I can't handle it. It's just since… since things went wrong…and I felt like I had led him on…"

Catherine came around the table and sat in the chair next to Priya. Reyna was staring across the table with a stony expression on her face and Priya's voice got weaker.

"I have this stupid sense of responsibility so when he parked outside the house and kissed me, I didn't stop him. But I came to my senses almost immediately and stopped him and he seemed fine at first and then he figured out what I'd done and he started talking and this anger just started to build in him. I could feel it like it was some kind of physical wave rising in him. It wasn't directed at me though, but I guess I was the one there."

Priya continued, her voice tight and small, "I panicked when he slammed the steering wheel and I tried to get out of the car. I think he just reacted too; he reached out and grabbed my hand as I was getting out and something snapped in my arm. It felt like that anyway."

Reyna's mouth had dropped open. Catherine put her arm around Priya's shoulder as Priya continued.

"I screamed, and Daniel released my hand. He came around and told me to get into the car while he examined my arm. He said we had to get to A&E immediately. He drove us there. We didn't speak at all. When we got there, he came in with me to the waiting room but then I think it dawned on him how it would look. I think he panicked. He left. When I was eventually seen, I told them I had twisted my arm but the doctor could see the bruise on my wrist and with that type of spiral fracture, of course he asked who had done it. The admissions people had seen Daniel with me. They thought we were in some sort of abusive relationship and that I was protecting him. They reported to the Guards who spoke to Daniel. He said I had come on to him, and that it had just been an accident. There was enough of the truth in there and I wasn't saying anything so they had to drop it but I got the impression that they thought there was a lot more to it. It took weeks, during all of that time my mum was sick in India, and I didn't go to see her. I hated them all for that after she died. I asked them to drop it, they'd never have done anything to him anyway, he was too important. And at that point, I didn't care. It seemed so minor in comparison."

They were silent for a few minutes. All Priya could hear was the soothing of Catherine's hand on her shoulder.

Catherine said, "It's not my place to apologize for Daniel's actions; I think he did try to make up for it in his own way. I know he was feeling bad about something but he wouldn't talk about it, not to me anyway."

Reyna butted in, "I am sorry. He mentioned you quite a few times to me. I got the impression you were on his mind a lot and you were someone important to him. And then when he said he was seeing one of the researchers I assumed you were together. I can't believe I took you to his apartment. And left you there!" Reyna got up from the table and stalked into the house.

Catherine said, as she watched Reyna go, "She's got a temper like Daniel's I'm afraid. But it comes out very rarely. Her anger is usually directed at herself. She doesn't get mad at other people even when she should. She's not able to see things clearly at the moment." She turned to Priya. "I'm grateful you were able to tell us about it. And I'm always here for you if you want to talk more."

Priya felt a bit lighter than she had since that night, a small portion of the weight carried away on the stream of words that she had let flow.

Catherine said, "I know there's something else that's happened. You're not ready to share that yet. You've been through a terrible time losing your mother, what happened with Daniel, but there's something more. Something that happened before last year."

She nodded as Priya looked at her in surprise.

"My dear, something must have got you to a place where you as a comfortably gay woman would come on to a man to stop him going after a woman." Priya cringed and Catherine said, "Don't get me wrong, I am not judging you. I get the sense that you've been through hell in the last while but you're not facing up to it. You're running and you've found yourself in a very bad place." She sighed. "Like Rain."

Catherine examined Priya's face. "The two of you as individuals have got all this negative energy surrounding you at the moment. And you're both too proud to admit that. So you both go bouncing around the place hitting off things. I just hope this chemistry between you is not a result of all that. Because there is a potential for so much good. Rain doesn't trust her own judgment anymore. So she doesn't trust anyone now. Always thinks the worst of people, especially women."

∞

Reyna walked back onto the patio. She was carrying a large brown package and a glass of water that she placed on the table in front of Priya.

"I don't know if you'd still want to help us but Catherine received this in the post. It's from Daniel. It was here when she got back from the funeral."

Catherine patted Priya on the shoulder and got up.

She said, "Thank you for telling us what happened. I know it was difficult."

She sat back down in her chair across from Priya and picked up the package. It was thick and papers were sticking out of the open end.

"As Rain, sorry, Reyna said, you may not want to help us and I'll understand if you don't. I don't understand what the papers are about. There seems to be a lot of information on pacemakers and frequencies, a lot of figures and graphs. I called Reyna when I got them. She's looked through them too and she doesn't understand them either."

Priya sipped at the water. She sensed that Reyna was just being polite phrasing it as a request for help rather than a command. But she was curious. She reached for the envelope and Catherine handed it to her.

Reyna said, "Daniel had been worried about something in the last month. He came to New York a few weeks ago and he went through a lot of papers and filing cabinets. He spent a bit of time with our grandfather. He told me there was something wrong but he didn't tell me what it was all about."

"When did he tell you this?" Priya took the papers out of the package and laid them on the table.

"He came to New York in the first week in July, a week before he died. He actually got me worried, that's why I came to Galway to see him. I arrived on the Thursday and stayed with Catherine. He was supposed to meet me on the Friday evening. He said he always went to the birthdays of staff members so I agreed to meet him in Massimo. I waited there and I saw you with a group. I presumed it was the group from the clinic because Daniel had spoken about you and there were no other Asian looking women there."

Reyna stopped and looked at Catherine.

Priya said, conscious too of Catherine sitting there, "Much as it embarrasses me because I don't remember, I need to know what happened that evening."

"You were with the group for the first while. It was a noisy bunch. You and Tara were coming back with drinks and you saw me. You stayed with the group but you kept looking at me and smiling."

Priya felt the familiar heat creep up her face as she cringed inside.

"You came over after about half an hour and asked if I minded you joining me. Daniel had just texted to say he wasn't feeling well. That was around 8 p.m. I think. He also added that he had been worrying about nothing and that he'd see me later over the weekend. And then when you told me your name, I knew I should have just left. I was going to but you were very … interesting. We spent the next few hours talking."

"And then I kissed you and Tara and the others left without me. So you took me to Daniel's place."

"Yes. It was around 1 a.m. when we left the pub. I was surprised when you flirted with me. I thought it was because you were drunk so when the others left you there I thought taking you back to Daniel's place was the right thing to do. I didn't want to disturb Daniel so I put you in the guest room."

Reyna seemed to be spitting the last few words out and Priya saw what Catherine meant. The anger was self-directed.

Priya asked, "Why did you leave?"

"I didn't want to be there in the morning. That would have been too weird. I assumed you and Daniel would spend the day together and I came back here."

"Was there anything different about the apartment?" Catherine asked and her quiet voice startled the two of them.

"It was dark. I was trying to get Priya settled. I didn't notice much."

Priya gathered her thoughts. "Okay, so we have a text from Daniel at around 8 o'clock on the Friday. I woke up just after 5 a.m. and found him. When I was leaving I heard a voice or voices from the lift..., elevator. Then I think someone looked through my stuff when I was away on the Thursday or Friday after and someone followed me yesterday."

Catherine said, "Daniel was worried for the last month about something to do with work. He went to New York at the beginning of July and worried Reyna enough that she flies here to see him. He doesn't make it to the pub and he's dead the next morning. The postmark on the envelope is 5 July and it was sent from New York; the day before he was to come back to Ireland. Why didn't he keep a hold of the papers till he got here?" She paused. "I'm more confused now. But the papers are obviously important. Will you look through them and see if there's anything there that might explain any of this?"

For the first time that evening, Catherine looked like a tired woman in her sixties. Her eyes were faded and the lines in her face stood deeper. She took a deep breath and stood up.

"I'm sorry your first visit out here happened at this horrible time. And thank you for agreeing to look through the papers. I'm going to go to bed. You'll both have to leave early to get to the clinic tomorrow so I'll say goodbye for now. But we'll meet up as soon as you've read them, if that's ok?"

Priya got up and hugged Catherine. "Of course it is. I'll look through it tonight but there's a lot of stuff there so maybe at the end of the week."

Catherine held the hug tight for a long moment and then wandered into the house.

13 CHAPTER THIRTEEN

Priya's chair was turned to face the view but she had not looked at anything but the papers in front of her. After Catherine left, Reyna had finished clearing, brought them out coffees and then sat in a hammock chair that swung from an upright beam fixed to the patio. An hour had passed in silence.

Priya's head was starting to pound. She hadn't slept well for the last few nights and had been up early as well. The graphs were beginning to blur. She'd done a quick scan and separated the papers containing notes on the design of the original Mark 1 Pacemaker from the results of trials on it. The notes and the testing of the Mark I Controller were also in two separate piles and she made a fifth pile with anything that didn't fit into the other ones. The papers she could see were all densely packed with typing and graphs, figures and code. They looked like photocopies.

She started with the Mark I Pacemaker. She had never been shown these details before. Her specific area of interest during her year with Fairer Research had been the security protocols used in the wireless communication between pacemakers and their program controllers. The Controller

Home was being discussed and she had been given data to work with but in a very restricted range.

She found some of the sheets on the Mark I Pacemaker that were darker and were actually old carbon copies. Or copies of carbon copies.

"It's been a long time since I've seen carbon copies. Do you remember when they were being used, those purple sheets of stuff?" Priya said, and Reyna swung the hammock around with her feet.

"That would have been the 80s, I think."

"These seem to be the notes your granddad made then for the first pacemaker he designed. He patented the use of a new and alternative way of powering the pacemaker." Priya pointed to the second pile of papers. "They seem to be some of the results from the clinical trials on that pacemaker."

"What was the technology he patented?" Reyna asked. She got out of the hammock chair and sat down across the table from Priya.

Priya laid out the copies of the older papers. She said, "I'll try and explain. I know some of this from my studies in the field obviously; I just never had this kind of detail on it before now. Do you have the internet here? I could show you some pictures that would make it clearer."

Reyna shook her head. "I'm afraid not. Catherine didn't get the place hooked up, we're lucky to even have a phone line, there's no cell phone signal out here."

"I don't know how anyone could live without an internet connection! Okay, do you know what a pacemaker does, where it goes and stuff?"

"Well, I helped my grandfather on the business and finance side not the medical bits. I manage the foundation he set up. I know that pacemakers are used when there are problems with the heart and I know the different product ranges. I need us to get to a point where we can figure out why Daniel gathered all this stuff. And why he didn't give it to you."

Priya felt the anger rise. "So you still think I had something to do with this?"

Reyna tapped one of the piles on the table. "I guess we'll see how capable you are."

Priya glared at her. "You want me to explain all of this but you don't trust me. How can you trust anything I say then?"

"I know you're good at your job. And that you used to be some kind of genius when it came to coding. If you don't have anything to do with whatever was worrying Daniel then you don't have anything to hide, do you? You'll be as eager as I am to figure all this out."

Reyna looked at her and the challenge in her eyes infuriated Priya. But Priya thrived on a challenge, at least she had. And, like Reyna, she couldn't understand why Daniel hadn't spoken to her about his worries, or sent these papers to her, why he'd sent them to Catherine when he'd given Priya the readings and code on the Controller II with no apparent reluctance. What was so important that he had gone to New York, called Reyna in, and sent the papers to his mother?

Priya closed her eyes and stopped the questions crowding her mind. She tried to simplify and arrange the concepts instead. She was aware of Reyna's eyes on her face.

She opened her eyes and said, "Okay. I'll start with the basics. Pacemakers can be used when there are problems with the heart's normal rhythm. The heart has its own built-in electrical system that creates the signals that tell your heart when to beat. It has a group of cells called the SA node that creates the electricity. This SA node is called the natural pacemaker. It 'self-fires' at regular intervals to cause the heart to beat with a rhythm of about 60 to 70 beats per minute. There's obviously a lot more to this but problems can occur with the natural pacemaker or the rest of your heart's electrical system, which could lead to a slower rhythm or a faster rhythm, and you get symptoms like fainting or shortness of breath or palpitations. When people say pacemakers, it's actually a pacing system. It includes the bit that generates the pulse, the leads, and the programmer, what we call the controller. The pulse generator part is implanted in the upper chest; around here," Priya pointed to the area just under her collarbone and then felt conscious of her heart beating as Reyna looked, "under the skin and fat but above the muscle. The leads are fed through the vein and into the correct area in the heart and then the other ends of the leads are hooked up to the pulse generator. All clear so far?"

"Yes, keep going."

"Modern pulse generators are programmable with information and settings and we can also get information by transmitting data from the pulse generator to a controller which is called telemetry. The telemetry and programming communication uses a wireless technology. We usually do this at the clinic but some of the newer ones can even download their data to the internet or can be checked over the telephone."

"So you're talking to a device that is inside somebody and it's telling you stuff about itself?"

"Yes. It can tell us how efficiently it's working, how much energy it is using, whether any arrhythmias occurred. Now, normally we would be checking battery life with a view to replacing it if necessary but that's where the technology your granddad patented comes in."

"Right, you said it was a new way of powering the pacemaker."

"Yes, in the 50s Medtronic's founder developed the first pacemaker that was wearable and it was powered by mercury batteries. In the 60s implantable pacemakers were produced. They've used nickel cadmium rechargeable batteries and zinc-mercury batteries. Each had problems. There has been work on biological batteries - biogalvanic cells, fuel cells utilizing oxygen from blood and hydrogen from body proteins, kinetic body energy. Even nuclear batteries. In the 60s there was a pacemaker that used Plutonium. The life of this type of pacemaker is around 14,000 years so these pacemakers would generally survive longer than the patient."

Priya laughed at Reyna's expression. "I love dropping that fact in. Some use the ceramic plutonium oxide to reduce the possibility of spillage in the case of the accidental impact of a rifle bullet. Plutonium could be used for other dangerous stuff so they stopped making this type of pacemaker, the U.S. government closely monitors the few that still have them in, and they come to collect the material from the pacemakers when the patient died. Anyway, in the 70s they started using lithium batteries. These batteries would last from 5 years to 10 years depending on their usage. Your grandfather was very interested in alternative self-sustaining sources of energy for the pacemaker and he figured out a way to use the voltage changes from around the natural pacemaker, the SA Node, and feed that back through the leads in the heart to the pulse generator. Quite ingenious really."

"But the patient who has a pacemaker has a bad SA node, yes?"

"That area of the heart has a lot of self-firing electrical activity. And the SA Node itself is not necessarily damaged; the arrhythmia might be due to a problem with the conduction system. The leads that are placed in the heart sense the electrical activity there, he just found a way to harness that energy and use it to run the pulse generator. The pulse generator senses when there is an abnormal rhythm and there are different types, some only discharge when they detect a problem, others give out a regular beat and others change their rate with the body's activity."

"So the person's natural pacemaker could still be working away."

"Yes." Priya was impressed with Reyna's grasp of the information. She was beginning to wish she hadn't spent the last two years suppressing any intelligent thought.

She continued, "There is a small lithium battery in the pulse generator just as a backup. We check its remaining battery power at the regular checks but it is really just routine."

Priya said thoughtfully, "I just checked the battery on a patient with an implanted pacemaker and her lithium battery seems to have been used."

"But you said it was only a back-up."

"Yes, that's why I found it strange. I need to go back over the battery readings for her and for the other patients. I should have caught it last week but what with everything that's been going on."

"So, what do the papers show?"

"I have really just separated them out. I need to look at them properly. They developed the Controller Mark I to communicate with the Pacemaker Mark I. They used to use the Controller I in the clinic to check on the implanted pulse generators. The Controller II replaced it then, it works using wireless technology as well but it incorporates the ability to communicate on the MICS channel as well as the older 175Hz frequency."

Reyna looked confused.

Priya explained, "The older pacemakers communicate on the 175Hz band. The Pacemaker Mark I does too, despite the fact that the FCC in the U.S. brought in the new range in 1999. All implantable medical devices are now to communicate on the 402-405 Hz band. This will help for longer-range communication, for devices that can be controlled at a greater distance. Like the new Controller Home that the Research Company is just finishing. They are also going to launch the Pacemaker II which operates on the longer-range frequency."

"The Controller III or the Controller Home is almost ready, that will be used by patients or their carers in their own homes and the information can be sent over phone lines if necessary. The papers here relate to the Mark I pacemakers and controllers. Nothing that I can see on the Mark II controller." She hesitated.

"What?" Reyna asked.

"I have the notes on the Mark II controller, that's what I had in my briefcase when you invited me out here." Priya made up her mind. "I took the research papers home a few weeks ago. Daniel gave them to me and I had a feeling something was out and I know the security issues and the rules but I really wanted to continue working on them. I told James about it yesterday. I had to; whoever broke into my house probably saw the papers. I presume James will be talking to you about it at some point."

Reyna rubbed her forehead. She rested her chin on her palm and stared at Priya. A little line had appeared between her eyebrows and Priya had an urge to reach out and smooth it away.

Priya said, "You're thinking how come someone who appears to be bright enough can do so many stupid things, right?"

Reyna gave a smile that seemed to come out against her will. "Well…"

"I seem to have made it my mission in the last few years. I was probably right this time though. I mean Daniel wouldn't have collected this stuff and he wouldn't have sent it here if he hadn't also felt something was wrong."

"Okay, we'll have to deal with that particular mistake later. I'll have to hear it from James and I should consult with him and see what he thinks should be the consequences of your taking the papers home and possibly exposing them to the wrong eyes. I think Gerry and Valerie will have to make that call, it is their research material really that you've potentially exposed. So I think the faster we can work out what's going on, the better."

"I'd better get back to the papers then." Priya picked up the second pile.

Reyna sighed and got up from the table. She went back to the hammock chair and stared out at the view.

∞

"Did we, you know...?" Priya's voice ran out. She hadn't been able to concentrate on the papers in front of her for the ten minutes since Reyna had left the table. She was too conscious of Reyna, of the gentle movement of the hammock.

Reyna said in a softer voice than Priya had heard from her "You're a very beautiful woman, Priya, and you were *very* charming... If it hadn't been for the fact that I thought you were Daniel's..." She paused. "No, we didn't do anything, well... I lay beside you for a few hours because you said you didn't want to be alone."

"And you undressed me? Or did I manage that myself?" Priya was finding her voice and it had a bitter tone.

"I helped. And I lay on top of the covers."

∞

They were silent again and Priya tried to focus but she gave up after a half hour of alternating looks between the papers on the table and the weave of the back of the hammock chair as it swung slowly. She had glanced through the clinical trials on the Mark I pacemaker and nothing had jumped out at her. The summer light was leaving the fjord and the air was darkening in minute degrees.

"I'm going to take a walk. I need to clear my head." Priya said as she got up from the table.

"You don't know the area, would you like me to come with you?" Reyna asked.

Priya looked at the forest lining the road leading from the front of the house down to the lake. The road was a dark pause before the brightness in the distance. She hesitated, not sure if she could relax with Reyna beside her but the thought of walking through the gloom alone didn't appeal. She accepted the offer.

Reyna had gotten out of the chair and was standing waiting for her. They walked on the light stone driveway, the crunching of their feet magnified in the quiet that enveloped them as they entered the avenue of trees. In the distance ahead of them, the lake glowed vivid through the shadow frame. They emerged from the forest and stepped off the road onto a small path that wound around the lake. Priya stopped and stared at the interwoven layers of blues and whites and greens.

"Don't you find beauty sometimes to be so painful? I look at this amazing view and it almost hurts," Priya said.

"Yes, sometimes beauty can affect us in unexpected ways." Reyna was looking at the mountains on the far shore but her eyes focused closer as she spoke and Priya felt her breath catch as she met Reyna's gaze. They were standing a few feet apart and Reyna moved nearer. Priya stood, fixed to the spot, unable to look away. Reyna rested her fingers under Priya's chin and ran her thumb gently over Priya's lower lip. Priya could see the faint black and blonde striations in the dark gold of Reyna's eyes. She saw helplessness struggling with desire. From the little she knew of Reyna, weakness wasn't characteristic but Priya was struggling too.

"I haven't been able to look at you without remembering that kiss. And you didn't even know what you were doing at the time." Reyna's voice was husky.

Priya could hear the rustle of leaves and the gentle splash of the water beside her but the sounds were dulled by the thud of her blood pulsing loud in her ears. She stared at Reyna's lips and heard a gasp as Reyna lowered her head and replaced her thumb with her lips. She could hear moaning but she didn't know which one of them it was coming from. She hadn't let a woman kiss her since Valerie. When she had slept with a woman in the last few months she'd been the one in control, never losing control, never feeling this overwhelming weakness, her legs trembling so she rested against Reyna, not just resting, pushing, straining to melt into Reyna's warmth. She had her hands in Reyna's hair, the thick strands worked loose from their restraint wrapping themselves around her fingers in bonds of brown silk.

They were falling, lying on a bank of grass, the water licking at the shore by their feet, Reyna beneath her, around her, on top of her. And then a cold breath of air on her skin as Reyna rolled away. Priya opened her eyes in a daze. Reyna was sitting on the ground, knees drawn up to her body, arms tight around her knees, visibly struggling for control.

Reyna spoke; her voice muffled through her arms, "I'm sorry. I shouldn't have done that."

Priya got up. Her movements felt heavy, slow, feeling the weight of a shame that swept through her. *She'd done it again.* Lost control. What she'd sworn never to let happen to her again. Her eyes filled and she swiped the tears away before they fell. She walked by Reyna and then half jogged half ran back through the trees. The light had almost completely faded and it was difficult to see the track but she was glad for the shadows as she headed for the house.

She took a shower in the small bathroom; drowning in scalding water pushed through at high pressure by a pump she could hear working from the cupboard. She tried to wash away, rub away, burn away the feeling of shame but it tingled in every pore, the fine hairs on her body standing up straight, muscles aching from the pounding heat of the water outside and the restless quivering inside. She held her head back and let the water run over her face, over her lips, trying to erase but remembering instead, the softness, the pressure, the fit. Between their lips, the perfect match, the unexplored that felt familiar, and so right.

A while later, as Priya lay huddled in the bed, she heard Reyna's footsteps in the hallway and pulled the cover tighter around her. The footsteps stopped at her door and she heard a gentle tap. She didn't respond and a long pause later Reyna walked away down the hall and she heard the opening and closing of a door.

14 CHAPTER FOURTEEN

Wednesday, July 20, 2011

The instructions had arrived as usual in the diplomatic pouch. But this time, there was a problem. The diplomat's meeting with the politician was still to go ahead as planned. Actually, that was out of anyone's control. No matter what problems the man in his dark suit encountered, the meeting would go ahead. As it had every year since they had been allowed to set up in this country. Meet, shake hands, smile, go in to a private office and talk about their two nations, come out, smile and shake hands for the camera. But this year, their meeting fell on the day before the hand he shook would sign in a small change to the economic structure of this country. The ripples would spread in a slow outward movement that would eventually trickle onto his shores. But the effects would be those of a tsunami.

They had 11 days left to stop it.

The problem was, there was a problem with the device. And they had no contingency plan.

15 CHAPTER FIFTEEN

Wednesday, July 20, 2011

The drive back to Barna was tense. They had not spoken, both getting up early and meeting in the living room. Priya had struggled to sleep and she was feeling the drain of the travel and the nights of broken sleep. Priya could not decipher if Reyna was feeling anything, the only visible effects were tightness around her lips and eyes. Priya had brought her work clothes and she sat stiff in the car hiding in the lines of her formal attire. She had stuffed the jeans and crumpled top she had worn the previous evening into her bag, shoving out of sight what Reyna had touched.

Reyna pulled into the driveway of Priya's house and opened her mouth to speak but Priya thanked her for the lift and hurried into the house. She attempted to do it with a modicum of dignity and was gratified to hear the wheels screech as Reyna pulled out onto the road and drove away.

Priya added the envelope of papers she had taken from Catherine's house to her briefcase with her notes and made it to the clinic on time despite the heavy traffic. The clinic car park was full; everybody seemed to be at work today. In the building, the air felt heavy and subdued with an undercurrent of electricity. Reyna was somewhere in the clinic and Priya didn't want to see her so she hurried to her office.

Tara was already sitting at her desk. She said, "This is getting to be a habit. You don't look good."

"And Good Morning to you too." Priya dropped the briefcase onto her desk. The papers were crammed in, stretching the leather. Priya saw her glance at the briefcase.

"Is everything ok?" Tara asked. She was looking fresh and there was a hint of pink in her cheeks.

Priya sat down at her desk and leaned back in the chair. *No, everything was not okay.*

"Yes, I'm just a bit jet-lagged still," Priya said. She looked closely at Tara, the new top, a glint in her light green eyes. "You, on the other hand, are looking interesting. What have you been up to?"

Tara laughed. "You'll never guess?"

"Hmm… let me see, Aidan…?"

"You are good! How did you know?"

"I've had my eye on you two for the last while. By the way, he was looking for you when you were off on Monday; I forgot to tell you yesterday. So, how, when? I want details."

"Well, he's been giving me the eye for the last month, and then the night of my birthday, we got together. But with what happened after that, we didn't do anything until yesterday evening."

"I'm happy for ye. But I have to warn you, you might be the target for an assassination attempt." Priya laughed at Tara's puzzled look. "Jacintha will be out to get you."

Tara frowned. "I don't think it's Jacintha I've to worry about. I think he's been seeing someone on the sly for the last few years and he says now there's nothing going on with anyone but I'm not so sure. I never thought I'd end up with someone's toy boy."

"Toy boy?"

"Just my impression. You know how he wasn't doing too well in London and then next thing he gets this job through Gerry and, I don't know about you, but I couldn't afford the

BMW and the clothes, and that watch on my salary and he only started here in February."

"Maybe it's all on credit."

"Yeah, like anyone would give that kind of credit anymore. With this recession and the credit crunch. Even with his job." Tara shook her head. "Anyway, as long as it's over." She looked at Priya and said in a lower voice, "So, what's happening with…?" She pointed towards the open door.

"Nothing. Why would there be anything? I'd better get to this stuff, I've loads to do." Priya started taking papers out of her briefcase.

∞

Before she left for New York, Priya had cleared her appointment book for the rest of the week. She now had a lot more information to get through. She laid out the papers into the same piles as the evening before with the additional pile for her notes on the Mark II controller. Laid out in front of her was the summarized history of the work carried out by the two Daniel Fairers. From patent to development, trials and results. She wondered whether despite Reyna's focus on the studies, that Reyna felt Daniel's death was not an accident, that it had something to do with what lay in front of her. And suddenly Priya was scared. Because if that was true, and if she had been followed, then she was in danger.

She tried to control the curl of acid panic in her stomach. Reyna must be wrong. This was Galway, a quiet city in a quiet country. Besides, Daniel had had a heart attack. She shivered. She had managed to spook herself to the point of imagining crazy things. She just needed to go through all the material and convince Reyna, and Catherine, that nothing was out of the ordinary. Perhaps Daniel had meant to do some writing and needed reference material. But then, why had he been so worried and distracted over the past month or so? Priya's mind was going around in possibilities. She decided the best thing to do was to calm down and study the information. This approach had always worked for her before.

She started with the top sheet from papers covering the trials of the Pacemaker Mark I. She made notes as she went along. Tara went in and out, covering appointments, glancing over at Priya, attempting conversation. Priya nodded and mumbled an occasional answer until Tara gave up after the first hour and they worked in silence for the rest of the day.

It was late afternoon and Priya was in the middle of the stack of papers on the pacemaker trials when she found a pink Post-It note stuck between two of the typed sheets of paper. The note had what she recognized as Daniel's writing on it. His handwriting had actually been very neat, an almost formal penmanship but the note seemed scrawled.

It read, "Check Priya re Liam (? Tara)."

Liam? Liam Whelan? Jacintha's son and Tara's patient. What did Daniel need to check with her about Tara's patient? Daniel had talked to Tara after Liam's heart attack in the clinic because the incident had happened there. But James had carried out the permanent pacemaker implantation to replace the temporary pacemaker used for the immediate period after the attack.

"Tara? You talked to Daniel about Liam's heart attack, didn't you? What did he say about it?"

Tara looked up in surprise. "He went through what happened at the time and got me to type out my account of what happened. And then a while back, I think in March, yes, in March, I had done Liam's check and then just after Paddy's Day when I was barely able to think he asked me to write out a more detailed description of what happened. I assume it was just for the record. I wrote it out by hand at home, didn't get a chance to type it up, he said it would be fine. Said nothing much about it after that. Why?"

"Just wondering." Priya got up and fetched Jacintha's file. "Could I look through Liam's file if you don't mind?"

Tara rooted around in her filing cabinet and handed a slim folder to Priya.

Priya looked through the folder. It was a typical medical record for a patient at the clinic but it didn't have details on the usual investigations that would have been carried out on a patient presenting to the clinic in the normal way. The attack had happened at the clinic; Liam was kept alive with CPR and hooked up to diagnostic equipment within minutes, and fitted very soon after with a temporary pacemaker. Priya couldn't find any handwritten description in Liam's folder. She continued her perusal of Liam's paperwork. She noted that they had not implanted a Fairer Pacemaker but had used one of the other models instead. Which meant Tara would have had to use the specific controller for that pacemaker.

Tara left a few minutes later and Priya realized it was late. And then she remembered that she hadn't checked Jacintha's battery power readings in detail. She looked for the printouts at the back of Jacintha's folder. The printout for each check had a line entry for the different parameters. Priya highlighted the entries for the Remaining Battery Power.

Post-Implant Check June 10 2010
Remaining Battery Power 100 (N)

July 12 2010
Remaining Battery Power   100 (N)

August 9 2010
Remaining Battery Power   100 (N)

September 13 2010
Remaining Battery Power   100 (N)

Dec 13 2010
Rem Batt   100 (N)

March 14 2011
Remaining Battery Power 95.83 (N)

July 11 2011
Remaining Battery Power 90.28 (LOW)

Priya couldn't believe she had forgotten to check Jacintha's file for the battery readings. She knew it had only been a little more than a week, and the week had been eventful, but this was un-professional. And the figures were surprising. The lithium battery in the Pacemaker I was not meant to be utilized. It was there as a back-up.

She looked back at the readings. December's entry stood out as different from the rest. The printout was a shade darker and the date and entry shorter. Tara had taken that reading when Priya was away.

∞

The clinic was emptying; Priya could hear the goodbyes and the footsteps, the occasional laugh, as the rest of the staff left. She had not seen Reyna and she wondered which poor staff member had been on the list for Reyna's interrogation that day. Priya looked at the pages of notes she had taken. She had made it through most of the papers on the results of the trials. There was a large chunk of information covering the transmissions between the Mark I pacemaker and controller, figures showing graphs of frequencies, code. Her head was full of Kilohertz, Packets, and C++ code. And capital letters; acronyms seemed to take the place of every third word. If there was something there, she hadn't seen it. Or it was staring her in the face and she didn't know its significance.

She closed her eyes and tried to form a picture from the information scattered in her mind. She needed to explain in non-technical language to Reyna and Catherine what she had gathered from reading the very technical papers. She was in the middle of an image that encompassed an implanted pacemaker chatting to a controller, both of which seem to have morphed into herself and Reyna, when a quiet voice startled her.

"Sleeping on the job?"

Priya kept her eyes closed. Just once, she would like to be at an advantage. Just once in this battle with this infuriating woman. But no, after a day spent looking at figures until her eyes hurt, she just had to have them closed when Reyna came in.

"Are the papers that interesting?" Reyna wasn't going away.

Priya opened her eyes. She raised her head up to the highest she could manage without straining every muscle in her neck. "I was imaging the data," she said.

"Is that what the Irish are calling 'sleeping' these days?" There was a laugh straining to get out in Reyna's voice.

"No, it's what this Irish Indian does to solve problems. Problems raised by visiting Americans, I might add."

"So, have you come up with the solution?" Reyna's tone turned serious.

"It would help if I knew exactly what the problem was. Daniel was worried. He texted you to say he needn't have been worried. Then he died of a heart attack brought on by the unnecessary worry. It could be as simple as that. Have you considered that?" She was tired and getting crankier by the minute.

Reyna slumped down into the chair beside Priya's desk. She looked tired.

"I have been looking through the financial side, studying the funding, investment, royalties. I wasn't involved so I need to see how it was set up." She tapped the desk with her fingers. "I have always believed in that saying 'follow the money'. It all comes down to money in the end, doesn't it?"

"That's a very mercenary way of thinking."

"But I've found it to be so true. Anyway, I've collected whatever information I can from the computer and I need to go through that as well as all the paper financial records. However, if there is something untoward it's not going to be obvious."

Priya got up from her chair and started gathering her papers.

She said, "I'm going to take these home and continue working on them there. One has to take advantage of any sunny day in Ireland."

Reyna asked, and there was a shy note in her voice, "Have you eaten anything today?"

"No. But, I'm not hungry." Priya had finished packing her briefcase and she looked at the door.

Reyna shrugged and got up. She walked out of the office and Priya heard her go into one of the other offices and close the door with a short sharp click.

Priya felt bad as she drove home, she wasn't usually so rude. *But the woman deserved* it. By the time Priya had changed into a pair of old shorts and T-shirt and was stretched out on the deck surrounded by papers she had managed to convince herself.

∞

The doorbell rang and it was a sound Priya was so unused to that she jerked, spilling water from her glass onto some of the research material. She was cursing and wiping the papers with a dishcloth when the bell rang again. She gathered everything into a pile, weighted it down with her glass and rushed to the front door.

Priya was shocked to see Reyna balancing two large pizza boxes and a satchel that was overflowing with papers on one arm while raising the other to ring the doorbell again. Reyna dropped her arm and looked sheepish when Priya opened the door.

"It's really not healthy to work on an empty stomach. You haven't eaten all day. I thought you might like a pizza." Reyna held out the pizza boxes.

"Two pizzas?"

"Well, I didn't think you'd want to eat on your own."

"For a visitor to this town, you seem to know your way around."

"I had the misfortune to have to wait in the ER of your hospital once and I popped across to that Supermacs place. So, can I come in?"

"I see you've brought your work along too. A bit presumptuous of you, isn't it?"

"Priya, I get the feeling you're not normally mean to people, so it's just me. I know I deserve it after last night. Just give me a chance to explain, please."

Priya glared at her. "This should be good," she muttered, as she turned sideways to let Reyna in to the house.

∞

They ate the pizzas out on the deck. The sun warmed the Atlantic Ocean and it responded with white-capped smiles and waves. The seagulls were holding a loud conversation as they swooped and waddled on the beach, their screeches punctuating the silence between the two women. Priya was conscious of her attire, the T-shirt she was wearing, its original cerise now faded to a dull pink. And the cut-off denim shorts were a relic of the 70s that she had bought in a clothing store run by a local animal charity more with the aim of supporting the charity than for the fashion.

Reyna looked as cool as usual. She still had her suit trousers on but she had taken off the jacket and her pale blue top set off the gold in her eyes. The woman had an effortless style even when she dressed down and Priya had that feeling of inadequacy she always got around beautiful women, especially when she felt such a strong attraction. She had to concentrate to keep from spilling pizza sauce down her front, *now that would really complete the image*!

Reyna had brought her a vegetarian pizza with so much on it that Priya groaned after the second slice. "I *was* hungry after all. I see you got me everything that could possibly fit on a pizza."

"Had to cover all bases." Reyna curled that smile at her and Priya looked away.

Reyna put down her plate. "Priya, I am really sorry about yesterday. I was completely in the wrong. I started something and I shouldn't have. I know you're going through a difficult time. And, right now, things are pretty weird for me. So, I shouldn't have dragged you into anything."

"Am I going to get anything more than 'pretty weird' or is that the standard excuse you use for all the women you make the mistake of kissing?"

"I guess you deserve a better explanation. And no, it is not an excuse, standard or otherwise. I have not looked at a woman in that way, not to talk of kissing any, for the last 3 years." Reyna was staring at the grain in the wood of the deck and her voice was angry. She looked up at Priya and her tone softened. "The last few weeks have been strange and confusing. I thought you were with Daniel, I thought you were straight. But I was so attracted to you and mad at myself."

Reyna stopped and closed her eyes. Her voice was quiet and she said,

"Priya, I'm still married."

16 CHAPTER SIXTEEN

Priya sat back in the chair, her back smacking against the fabric. She stared down at the pizza, its gaudy dressings clashing with the red and yellow. She put down the slice in her hand and closed the box. *Still* married. She hadn't even known Reyna was married at all. And now Priya was what, the other woman? She was finding it hard to think. She'd vowed never to hurt anyone again like she'd hurt Kathy, she'd promised herself she'd never have been able to do what Valerie did, insert herself between two people, be the other woman. And now she had, without even being given the choice.

"Priya...?"

Priya looked at Reyna. She said, "You didn't think that mentioning you were married might be a good idea? At any stage? Perhaps when I was kissing you in the pub, or wait, maybe even before that. Or when we were in your car for an hour, talking. Or before you kissed me?"

"Priya, it's not as bad as it sounds. We've been separated for two years and honestly, we might as well have been separated for the year before that. It's just that the papers for the dissolution haven't been signed."

"So you are still married."

"I know how it sounds. But it is not as simple as that. In fact, it is pretty complicated."

"Catherine said you were in a bad place at the moment."

"That would be one way of putting it." Reyna took in a deep breath. "I have a lot of stuff to sort out. On a personal level. I wasn't really dealing with it as I should have and I ran to New York and buried myself in work and getting to know my grandfather, and Daniel I guess. And then when I was needed here by Daniel, when he died, and I knew something was wrong, I just haven't been thinking clearly…" Reyna stopped. Her shoulders were bowed and there was a look of defeat in her eyes. "I would really have liked to have seen where things could have gone with us. As I said I haven't even thought about the possibility for years."

"Well, don't worry about it. I wasn't looking for anything. I'm sorry I came on to you in the pub. It's no big deal." Priya picked up her pizza box and gestured towards the box lying on the deck beside Reyna. "Have you finished?" She didn't meet Reyna's eyes but she saw them widen. She took the boxes into the kitchen and placed them on the table. She told herself she was used to disappointment, that the feeling would pass, but she found it strange that the sense of loss was so crushing.

She got two glasses of wine and sauntered out onto the deck. She handed a glass to Reyna who was sitting in the same spot, staring out at the sea.

"The quicker we can go through the material and you see that there's nothing to be suspicious about, the quicker you can get back to your life." Priya retrieved her papers and pushed the satchel towards Reyna who looked like she was going to say something but instead just nodded and took the satchel and started examining the papers in it.

∞

An hour passed as they concentrated on their individual study and thoughts. Priya stretched and rubbed her eyes. She had now looked through all the papers on the trials of the pacemaker and the data on the communications between the pacemaker and the controller.

She said, "Do you want me to catch you up?"

Reyna nodded. She put down what she was working on.

"From what I've seen so far, the Mark I pacemaker passed the clinical trials over a two year period and was launched with no problems."

"Is that the usual scenario?"

"Sometimes it happens that defects occur and are discovered after the device has been in use for a while. Things can go wrong not only with the pulse generators but also with the pacing leads that can corrode or break. The companies actually say in their literature that nobody is perfect and because large teams of people design these devices, that sometimes things go wrong. The manufacturers say that failures have happened in the past with all types of devices and that they'll happen again because these devices are too complex and changes in the technology happens so fast that they can't guarantee against failure. They complain that if they had to go through the many more years of testing then patient care would suffer and maybe hundreds of thousands of patients would die by the time the devices were available."

"So, they don't test the devices properly? Devices that are put into people and keep their hearts beating?"

"No, they do. They test them as well as they can in the shorter period of time. And they track the implanted devices and send out advisories if a serious technical problem is discovered. But what I'm trying to say is that there are problems that might occur over a longer period of time than perhaps the two year testing period. Like, there was a device advisory issued because there was a possibility of a sudden device failure and another because there was a higher than normal risk of the leads fracturing. See, these are possible future problems or the potential for a danger to the patient. But to the patient sitting there with the device and the leads already in them and working, there has then got to be a discussion with them and their doctor to see what the risks are with replacing the devices and everything that goes with that."

"There's a lot of money involved in this business."

"Yes. The devices are life-saving. I mean, think about how you would feel if something went wrong with your heart. We don't even think about how our heart beats. It is just something that happens. But if you were to think about it, it is almost like you just hope that the next heart beat arrives. We can't control it. And then out of the blue you faint and the doctors can't find anything wrong with you. But it happens again. And you're never sure when it is going to happen next, you could be driving, or in the supermarket, or as one of my patients, you could be singing in the choir. Another one of my patients fainted in the bathroom and fell against the radiator. She damaged her eye so badly that they had to put in a glass eye. Sometimes the fear is more about the next time you're going to faint rather than the implantation surgery which is actually quite minor. So when they're living normal healthy lives after the surgery it is not about the big money industry. For them, it is about their lives which they have been given back. But yes, it is huge money. And professional prestige. Every money-making industry has its conflicts. There's a big study being released that recommends more vigorous testing and that study is already being attacked by a big business group before it has even been released."

"From what I am reading here, the amounts of money involved are staggering."

"We don't really see that side of it but I guess they would be."

"One of the biggest companies reported that its revenue in the last quarter was actually lower than the previous years because of a recall of one of their product ranges. And looking at the figures for 2011 the two biggest companies in the industry that have plants in Galway reported export sales of over 4 billion euro for the year. Now obviously that is not all for pacemakers and controllers but it is a huge market."

Reyna sorted through the papers and pulled out a presentation folder.

"There's stuff here on the proposal for the setting up of the research company and also on the clinic. Galway seems to have a number of the largest medical device manufacturers located here."

"UCG, that's University College Galway or at least that's what they called it in my time, anyway, they concentrated on biomedical research and really made it a priority. I remember the fuss about the biomedical research area that was being developed. I was finishing my M.Sc. at the time and there was a drive by the college to bring our Faculty and Medicine and Engineering to collaborate on research. By that time, I'd gotten interested in IT and I was actually looking towards working more in the IT field so I wasn't paying as much attention as my father thinks I should have. There was a lot of funding and because there were huge medical device manufacturers based in Galway, a lot of the research was in the cardiovascular area."

"So Daniel was encouraged to set up the clinic."

"He did his cardiology fellowship here and met Gerry Lynch in the program… and Valerie Helion. And Daniel and Gerry studied further in the U.S. after that. The three of them started the research company. Well, the other two contributed time and some money I think. Daniel brought the patent technology from your grandfather and most of the money I'd say. That's why it is called the Fairer Research Company."

"Valerie Helion..? Valerie, Lynch? Gerry's wife, right?"

"Yes. I don't know why I keep referring to her as Valerie Helion. They got married at least five or six years ago but most people seem to refer to her by her maiden name. Gerry is a lovely guy. I worked with him for the second year of my PhD. He's extremely intelligent but very humble about it. He's Aidan's brother, you know."

"Did you work with Valerie?" Reyna's tone was casual.

Priya gave Reyna a look then sighed. "Is there a reason you're asking me about her?"

"I guess… I get the feeling there's something you're leaving out. And, she came with Gerry to see my grandfather in New York at the end of June. She was…very friendly."

Priya felt a sharp sting of jealousy. "Friendly… to you?"

"Yes."

"Well, she's a 'friendly' sort of woman." Priya was shuffling the papers.

"So, what happened?"

"It was a long time ago. And it has nothing to do with what's going on now. Would you like me to continue with the pacemaker explanation?"

"It is not just out of curiosity that I'm asking. I'm going to hazard a guess after what you told us yesterday about the night of your birthday and after meeting Valerie, I would say that the woman you were trying to stop Daniel going with that night was Valerie."

Priya's closed her eyes, squeezed them shut.

Reyna said in a gentle voice, "I think you had an affair with Valerie at some point. She struck me as a woman who has a lot of power and knows how to use it. I think she plays games. Perhaps you were caught up in one of her games?"

"What has this got to do with anything now?"

"I know you would rather not be reminded of all this. But think about it for a minute. We have been avoiding the main question. I may not think Daniel's death was an accident. But the doctor signed the death certificate stating heart failure as the cause of death. No one but the family knows that there was an autopsy arranged in New York. And the results showed no abnormality anywhere else and also concluded Daniel died of a heart attack. A diagnosis of sudden cardiac death."

Priya was puzzled. "So why are you still searching?"

"I want to know what happened to him before that, what was worrying him. I think it has something to do with the work of the research company. So I want to find out what I can about Valerie and Gerry. Especially before they come and meet me tomorrow. We'll be going over the research work that has been done in the partnership between the clinic and them. So, I think a heads-up might be in order?"

"Why would stuff that happened over two years ago be relevant?"

"And last year if I'm right about the night of your birthday. And possibly was still going on when Daniel died. We're studying the pacemaker stuff because that's what Daniel was looking at but as I said, follow the money, and I'd add to that, follow the emotion. People do things for money mostly but sometimes when there are all these hidden connections, you might find a reason by uncovering them."

"Do you still think *I* had something to do with this?"

"I think that there was something strange about the relationship between Valerie and Daniel. I think when he said he was with a researcher and I assumed it was you that he actually meant Valerie."

Priya tried to absorb this thought. She said, "As far as I know, Daniel met them in the late 90s. They set up the research company in 2000 but he was mostly in New York at the clinic there. Valerie and Gerry got married in... 2005, I think, because when I worked with them in 2008 they had been married about three years. From the way Valerie talked about Daniel, I think she was with him before she got together with Gerry. It was weird. She married Gerry but I would have put Valerie and Daniel together, they were more suited than Valerie and Gerry. Gerry was too nice for her."

"So, what happened between you and Valerie?"

Priya was silent for a few minutes. Then she sighed and said, "I met her in 2008 when I went to do my second year research project. I was in a relationship at the time. Seven years. I was such a black and white person, you know, no grays existed in my innocent little world. In a committed relationship, never cheated, never thought of cheating. I was such an arrogant little shit. I was so sure of myself, of my relationship, and my honesty. Well, I guess Kathy and I were both so secure, took it for granted. And then Valerie happened. And I'd never met someone like that in my life. She had a way of looking at you, like you were the most important thing in the world, of listening to you, saying just the right things, stroking your ego. I fell for it hook, line, and sinker. I fell for her and slept with her. A few times. But I felt so guilty that I told Kathy almost immediately. It was the worst conversation of my life. And she reacted badly, of course. Went a bit crazy for a while after that. She would have taken me back but I knew it was over and, I just couldn't continue, not with the way I felt about Valerie and with what I'd done. We split up. Valerie of course, had just been playing around and didn't want to know me after I'd come clean with Kathy. She never told Gerry. I felt really bad about that too; he had never been anything but nice to me."

"Seems like you're taking on everyone else's guilt as well."

"I'm good at that. Besides, I *was* guilty."

"You made a mistake. You lost your relationship because of that. Seems like you're still carrying that guilt for what, the last 2, 3 years…?"

"Kathy killed herself a few months later."

Reyna sat back in surprise, her mouth open to say something but she didn't.

"I know, it seems a bit of an extreme reaction, but Kathy seemed to go off the rails after we split up. She'd call me at weird hours and tell me she was going to kill herself. And I'd go running. And she'd have this elaborate situation all set up, usually razors. And I'd talk her out of it and it seemed pretty easy to do that so I thought she was just trying to get back together but she never actually asked. Michael would be so mad at me. He kept saying she was unbalanced and that I should not respond to it by running when she called, that I should get her professional help. I tried to get her help but she wouldn't take it, she just kept calling me. And the last time, when she did, I didn't go. I thought…"

She shook her head. "I don't know why I am telling you this. You wanted to know about Valerie."

"Have you talked to anybody about it?"

"Well, a bit to Michael, but I couldn't really. Just went a bit crazy myself."

Priya realized that she had said more about her personal life to Reyna in the last two days than she had to anyone in the last two years. No more. She gulped down the glass of wine that had remained untouched beside her.

Priya asked, "What did Valerie want in New York?"

"You need to talk about it Priya." Reyna's eyes were kind.

Priya shook away the effects of those eyes. She said, "You didn't answer my question."

Reyna seemed to give a little sigh. She said, "Valerie and Gerry came to see my grandfather about something. He didn't tell me what. She asked me out for dinner, used some excuse about not knowing anywhere in New York."

"Did you go?"

"Yes."

Reyna looked at her watch.

"It's getting late. I'd better get back to Catherine." She started gathering up her papers and stuffing them into the satchel.

Priya said, "Why is it that when you ask me, I tell you stuff I haven't been able to talk about to anyone for years? And the moment I ask you a personal question, you clam up?"

Reyna finished her packing without answering. She was gone a few minutes later, and the house seemed lonely for the first time in years.

17 CHAPTER SEVENTEEN

Thursday, July 21, 2011

Priya felt like she was carrying her ankle weights in the bags under her eyes. The morning had come quicker than expected but slower than she wanted. She had slept badly, her mind filled with memories, bad ones. Tara frowned when she arrived and saw Priya's face.

Priya managed as genuine a smile as she could.

Tara said, "I thought you were down when I came in. You really have a lovely smile. But with those dark shadows under your eyes I think maybe someone got lucky last night...?"

Priya shook her head. "We're not all cougars like you."

"Cougars!? Girl, cougars are older women, like, over 40, who like young men. Aidan is 36!"

"Oh, my mistake. I thought he was so much younger than you. I thought he *did* look my age. You know, young..." Priya couldn't stop herself as she burst out laughing. Teasing Tara had been her tonic, she felt herself slip into the comfort.

"I am only 30 as you well know!" Tara stomped over to her desk and then laughed too. "Why do I let you wind me up? And you can get away with it cos you look twenty no matter what age you really are." Tara sat down at her desk and looked over. "Maybe not today though. I like that top, by the way. The white really highlights that lovely skin tone. Girl, I am soooo jealous. This stuff is a nightmare to deal with. Can get all orange and caked up if you're not careful." Tara held out hands and examined between the fingers.

Priya said, "You don't need that fake tan stuff, Tara."

"Easy for you to say. Although from what I see with you, it isn't easy to meet anyone if you're gay in Galway. But I never thought it would get so hard to meet someone if you were straight! Have you seen the perfect specimens of women out there on a night out? They're all done up to the nines. Even on a Wednesday night! I hate all that, the high high heels and the skimpy skirts. And even when it's freezing out. And then they're falling over at the end of the night, pissed out of their minds, climbing into cabs with God knows who." She sighed. "Those were the good old days. I feel old."

"Well, you don't look it, much as I like teasing you. Aidan's a lucky guy. By the way, how is our Aidan?" Priya said as she set up her desk.

"Our Aidan is actually very nice. More than that. He's the first guy I've really liked in ages. This could be the one. I'm hoping the actual cougar is not lying in wait for him. Or for me."

Priya looked up at the note of concern in Tara's voice.

There was a knock at the door and Mary popped her head into the room.

"Priya, Ms. Fairer would like to see you in her office if you're free."

Priya forced a smile but Mary didn't wait for an answer and Priya felt a spark of irritation as the door closed.

Tara said, "Aha, I knew you'd get it together with her. You too make a beautiful couple, you know, such a contrast, and yet so, so matched somehow."

Priya stopped smiling. She got up and walked to the door saying as she did so, "Tara, I am not 'with' Reyna. Apart from too many reasons to go into, she's married." She didn't wait to hear Tara's reaction.

Reyna was sitting at Daniel's desk and Priya realized how alike Daniel and Reyna had looked. Both exuded strength but Reyna's was a quieter line of steel that seemed to hold her upright. James was sitting across from Reyna. He was wearing green scrubs, his dark hair neat before a day under the scrub cap he was holding. It was Thursday which meant surgeries all day.

James got up as Priya knocked on the open door.

He said, "Sorry about this, Reyna, but I'll see you later, as soon as it's over." He nodded to Priya and walked past her out of the office.

Reyna looked tired. She said, "We've had to postpone the meeting. Valerie and Gerry will be in before lunch, could you come in as well. I'll get Mary to call you when we're ready?"

Priya hesitated. The thought of sitting down in the same room as Valerie made her feel sick. Reyna was looking at her, pushing for an answer. Priya nodded and turned to go.

∞

Tara had been in and out of the office all morning. Every time she came back in, she talked about Aidan but Priya could not concentrate on what she was saying and resorted to nods at what seemed to be appropriate times. It was obvious Tara wanted to ask about Reyna but she sensed Priya's reluctance. It was almost midday now. Priya needed some air and walked down the corridor towards reception. She heard Valerie's voice and stopped. She could see Gerry's back and heard Clodagh's reply. Priya backed up a few steps and turned back into her office and closed the door. She didn't want to see them, to deal with her emotions and Valerie's games.

From behind her desk she watched their silhouettes pass the clouded glass sidings as they walked to Daniel's office.

Priya wondered if her conduct was an item on the agenda for this meeting.

She tried to focus on the figures in front of her but they refused to settle into a pattern. She had not been able to concentrate since she'd seen Daniel's body and nothing that happened since had helped.

She tried to put together a list of questions for Gerry and Valerie. She assumed the future of the research company was being discussed and after that Reyna would want to know about the specifics of the pacemaker product from the people who had worked on it with Daniel for so long.

Priya was beginning to think she couldn't help. For too long, she had just been going through the motions, working in a job, not a career. Using equipment to communicate with devices, just seeing data, code, frequencies. Not heartbeats, messages, lives. She had chosen to see the world as black and white, as a problem to be solved, but patients were different shades of grey and she'd fled to the crispness and logic of code. Which was deserting her now.

What was bothering her about the figures? In the papers that she had risked her job to bring home. She closed her eyes and focused. The Controller II had not needed the same level of approval as the other devices as it was a second version of an already approved device. So it qualified for the 501(K) process. It used wireless technology to communicate with the implanted pulse generator.

She looked at the design of the Controller II. The schematics made no sense to her, she wasn't an industrial engineer. She used a test version of the actual device, to communicate with an explanted pulse generator, to test the data flow between the pacemaker and the controller. She kept this version in her clinical room along with a version of the Controller I and the actual Controller II she used for the routine checks on her patients.

Priya looked through the files. The clinical trials on the pacemaker itself had started in 2001. It had been implanted in thousands of patients after the two years of trials. The first version of the programmer, the Controller I, had been in use in many clinics around the world until it was replaced in 2006. TechMed Devices had weighed in heavily behind the pacemaker product vaunting the alternative form of powering the device that promised less surgery because of its self-sustaining nature. The marketing was effective, speaking directly to the natural fears of people, reassuring them.

She now had the voltage readings for the Controller I since its launch in 2003. Her initial mental translation of the numbers for the Controller II had highlighted dips in the voltages in a few cases. The readings for the Controller I showed similar dips. She was going to have to trawl through thousands of readings and find the dips and try and find a reason for this.

She checked her phone. It was almost lunchtime. Tara must have been doing checks; she hadn't come back into their office for a while. Priya now missed her presence, missed the chance to tease her; it would take her mind off the impending meeting, if it ever happened.

The knock on the door startled her. Reyna pushed open the door and Priya could see Valerie and Gerry pause to shake hands with James and then continue down the corridor towards the front desk. James was still wearing his scrubs and he hurried off in the direction of his office.

"Sorry Priya, we were so late starting and we got tied up, we didn't really get through anything important. Perhaps you could come to lunch with us now instead? I'm off to Dublin this afternoon with the funding agency and I have another meeting with Valerie and Gerry tomorrow at their office." Reyna's tone was light but again Priya had the feeling she couldn't refuse.

Reyna continued when Priya nodded, "I'll be leaving for Dublin from there, so you'd probably better take your car as well. We're going to that hotel up the road from here, the…"

"Westwood?"

"Yes, that's it. See you there in a few minutes?" Reyna was already moving down the corridor as she spoke.

∞

The lunchtime traffic was heavy and Priya saw that Reyna's rental car was parked in the hotel car park when she drove in. Valerie's red Jaguar Coupe was crouching in the space beside Reyna's car. The car park was jammed. The Arts Festival was coming to a climax this weekend to be followed next week by the Galway Races. July in Galway seemed to be a month long festival. Priya had to drive around the side of the hotel and park near the service entrance to the restaurant. She walked slowly back around to the front, memories of other meals at other pubs were crowding in to her mind. She steadied her nerves, if the others could carry it off, this pretence that nothing had happened, she could do it too. She had become an expert at suppressing her thoughts. She had a mental picture of the fairground game where you hit gophers on the head as they popped up and she smiled as she exaggerated the image into one of her with a big-headed hammer hitting little blond thought gophers that had Valerie's face stuck onto them.

The lobby was busy, business suits moving by in a hurry to grab a lunch. Priya turned into the bar and caught sight of Reyna and Valerie standing by the stairs leading to the upper level. There was no sign of Gerry; Priya assumed he must have gone upstairs to get them a table. Valerie was around the same height as Reyna but she had her face tilted up, her eyes focused on Reyna's face as if nothing else existed in the bar. Valerie's blonde hair shone against Reyna's dark jacket and Priya stopped dead, her breath catching in her throat. *She couldn't do it.* The memories were too strong. She turned and walked out of the bar and the hotel and into her car fighting the traffic to get back to her desk.

18 CHAPTER EIGHTEEN

Priya had refused Tara's invitation again and had walked down to the petrol station at the corner to buy a sandwich. She ate her lunch at her desk. The routine act of eating and the sounds of people entering and leaving the clinic dulled the memories but the pangs of jealousy remained sharp.

Annoyed with herself, she threw the half-eaten sandwich into the bin and emptied her briefcase onto her desk. She picked up Liam's file which fell out. Where was Tara's second detailed description of Liam's heart attack? She remembered that she'd seen some handwritten sheets in amongst the typed sheets of the papers Daniel had sent Catherine. She had separated them into the pile that didn't fit into any category and hadn't got to them yet.

She found the sheets and was about to read them when Reyna walked in without knocking. Her eyes were cold and Priya saw them go colder when Reyna noticed the half-eaten sandwich in the bin.

Priya spoke before Reyna could say anything. "I'm sorry, I got caught up in this stuff." She waved the sheets of paper, the feebleness of the gesture not creating enough of a draught to cool down the heat of her face as she lied. "Did you have a nice lunch?" She looked at the clock on her phone, "I thought you had to go directly from there?" The light tone felt forced but she kept her expression casual.

Reyna stared at her, as if trying to get into her head, and then she said, matching Priya's nonchalance, "Yes, lunch was delicious. I just popped back in to get my... bag."

"Find out anything useful?"

"I'm meeting them again tomorrow morning at their offices. I plan to get all the financials from them, for the Research Company."

Priya waited for an invitation to join them but Reyna nodded a curt goodbye and turned to leave the office then paused and turned back.

"I won't be back here till Monday, can I take the material Daniel sent Catherine. I think it might be better if I held on to that stuff for the moment."

"Wow, must have been an interesting lunch." Priya couldn't keep the bitterness out of her voice.

"It would be safer, that's all." Reyna looked at her watch and grimaced. "Sorry, I really have to go."

Priya's muscles felt stiff as she gathered up the relevant papers, grateful that they were still in separate bundles, and handed them to Reyna who took them and left without another word.

∞

Priya examined the doodles she had drawn on her notepad. The afternoon had slipped away. Tara was handling all the new patients for the moment and had finished at 4 p.m. She was in a good mood leaving, looking forward to her day off the next day. Priya could hear the chatter of the nurses. She had held on to Liam's file and she looked through it again. Daniel had asked for more information from Tara in March. He'd made her write it out in detail. Priya thought back, Daniel had been moody and withdrawn for the last few months. He'd gone to New York in early July, searching for something, worried about something. Was it something about Liam's case that had triggered the worry?

She wished she'd had a chance to read Tara's second report. She couldn't even ask her now till Monday.

So she'd have to work it out herself.

Liam was a healthy 39 year old when he had suffered a massive heart attack at the clinic. There had been no signs of electrical activity in his heart and he was extremely lucky that the attack had taken place where it did. It wasn't unknown for young healthy men to have heart attacks but it was unusual which is why the doctors had investigated. She presumed they had found nothing.

She logged onto her PC and went to Google. She typed in 'Cardiac arrests in young men' and the usual surge of information was displayed on the screen. The first link was to a study that highlighted the sizeable rise in the death rate in the 1990s from sudden cardiac death in young adults aged 15 to 34. Right, so it wasn't as uncommon as she'd thought. The multitude of links after that just confirmed it.

Liam's file had a diagnosis of sudden cardiac arrest of unexplained origin. Priya spent the afternoon clicking on links, wandering deeper into the navigational forest. As the afternoon turned to evening she decided to try another tack. She made an assumption. That Daniel had not considered Liam's heart attack as a random incident. Daniel had been troubled by something about the way it happened.

She searched through the files she had received from Daniel, the ones he had given her a few weeks before his death. She had seen a sheet of paper with a list of links printed on it, the blues and green and black on the computer screen reminded her of it the printout. She found the sheet and examined the links. They had been copied from a Google search and put into a Word document.

She typed in the first link including all the question marks and numbers and was taken directly to an article on the online version of a local newspaper in Boston. The article was from 2004 and it described the life and death of a 29 year old woman who had been born and brought up in Boston but had been working as an electrophysiology technician in a clinic in Singapore. The picture showed a woman in her twenties, her plump face widened by a smile, the graduation cap dropping its tassel into her curls. The article described her death as a cutting short of the promising life of a much-loved daughter, wife, and mother. The cause of death had been a heart attack and the journalist highlighted the irony of a death from a sudden cardiac arrest occurring in a state-of-the-art cardiac facility.

She looked at the list lying on the desk. There were 3 links in total. Her fingers were slow as she typed in the second link. This time the article on the newspaper site was from 2006. It was a local paper from France. Priya had limited French but it was enough to work out that the death of the 35 year old woman had occurred at her place of work at a cardiac clinic in the south-western city of Limoges.

The other link was to a clinic in Seattle. No death mentioned. But it was a cardiac clinic.

Priya sat back in shock.

Priya took down the number for the clinic. It was now after 5 p.m. Irish time on a Thursday evening. She did a quick search online for time zones around the world. There would be no problem with Seattle as it was 9.23 a.m. there. She could call Seattle from the phone on her desk but she was reluctant. The clinic around her was bustling with activity as the nurses were discharging the post-op patients. Most of the staff would be around until 6 p.m.

Priya decided to make the call from her house. She was working out the time as she collected all the paperwork she had left and filled her briefcase. She folded the sheet with the links together with the one with the number for the clinic and slipped them into her pocket feeling the crackle of paper loud against her thigh.

∞

The clinic in Seattle put her through to her counterpart immediately they heard that she was an electrophysiology technician working at the Fairer Clinic in Galway. It was just coming up to lunchtime in Seattle.

"John Landon here. I had the pleasure of speaking to Daniel Fairer himself a few months ago." He still sounded pleased.

Priya said, "I'm sorry to trouble you, Mr. Landon. I don't know if you know that Mr. Fairer passed away two weeks ago." His shocked exclamation told her he hadn't heard the news and she continued, "I worked closely with Mr. Fairer and I'm trying to sort out some of the things we were working on in the last few months. I was just wondering if you could fill me in on your conversation with Daniel."

"Of course, of course. I can't believe he's dead. He was so kind to call, I think it was in May, I don't know how he found out or why he would put himself out to call me after the attack but he did."

"The attack?"

"Yes, I suffered a massive cardiac arrest in April 2006. I would have died if I hadn't been at work when it happened."

Priya sat down. She had been standing at her living room window watching the evening traffic file past.

She said, "What were you doing when you had the attack?"

"I was carrying out a routine check on a patient with one of your pacemakers. I don't actually remember much before, just remember coming around after in the ICU. Though I do have vague memories of the ambulance. I explained this to Daniel and he asked for my medical records and I was happy to send him copies. And a description of what I was doing during the check. They should be there by now although I honestly don't know how long the post would take from here to Ireland. They used a temporary pacemaker and now I have a permanent implanted one." He laughed. "Talk about empathy with your patients."

Priya wondered where the medical records were, the post shouldn't have taken that long.

"Could you email me through the description of what you were doing at the time of your heart attack? The one you posted to Daniel."

"Sure. I did give all the details to the TechMed rep a few months after the attack. I didn't hear back from them until they gave us the Controller II upgrade that year. And then there was the software patch a couple of years later. Why all the interest now?"

"I think Daniel was just following a research interest of his." Priya did not know what to say. She gave him her personal email address.

Priya's heart was thumping. She got John to confirm the equipment that he used, chatted for a few more minutes about Daniel's contribution to their field, and then got off the phone. She wondered if John had been as exuberant a person before his brush with death.

She didn't have to wait long. The email arrived within the hour and she printed it out and studied it.

John had been using the Controller I to carry out a check on the pacemaker of a 67-year-old woman. He went through the various routine checks he had carried out. Then he had carried out a Controller programming test and the patient had complained of a slight discomfort. John had leant over her and the next thing he remembered was waking up in the recovery room at the clinic.

Priya wished she had asked him for the details of the patient who had undergone the test. She emailed John back thanking him and requesting any details he could provide on the patient and on all the checks that had been carried out on her. The reply came back in minutes and John promised to collect what he could and scan it and email it to her.

∞

Priya had another bad night's sleep. Her mind was churning. She hadn't been able to get through on the mobile phone number Reyna had given her. She realized she had never gotten Catherine's landline number. She decided just before she finally fell asleep that, invited or not, she would go to the meeting at the Research Company in the morning.

19 CHAPTER NINETEEN

Thursday, July 21, 2011

The lack of sleep was getting to him. The diplomat knew there were things going on in the background that he didn't need to know about. He knew all he needed to know was how to work the device, with no awkward movements, with nothing to show in his demeanor. He wasn't looking forward to the meeting with the man the next day. Probably their last one. And then facing another long weekend, sitting and staring and thinking. He couldn't even contact the kids, didn't want to betray his tension. He hoped that later, after he had killed the woman, he would still be able to look them in the eyes, to pick up his grandkids without his guilt rubbing off on them, staining their souls. He rubbed his eyes. He was getting fanciful but the waiting was getting to him.

He had 11 days.

20 CHAPTER TWENTY

Friday, July 22, 2011

The rain had washed the tarmac clean and it winked in the alternating sun and cloud that hung over Galway. Though the research company's office was in the same complex, it was separated from the clinic by the lines and trees and the irregular shape of the car park. Priya had been able to ignore it, out of sight, out of her consciousness. Priya walked into the foyer of the clear glass and grey steel building feeling the weight of memories. She had first gone through those whisper smooth doors oblivious to the threat, innocent of the guilt she had carried now for what seemed like a very long time but it had only been three years.

The foyer was small but bright. There was no receptionist. Just a set of buttons on a panel by the lift. She remembered the code from her days working here and guessed Gerry wouldn't have changed it. The sequence of numbers worked and the panel for the lift buttons slid open. Her finger shook as she pressed the button for the first floor. The doors opened and she started at the sight of herself in the mirror. She got another fright as the voice announced that the lift doors were opening. On the way up, she examined her reflection. She looked more confident than she felt. She looked like nothing could reach her, as if she had drawn a dead shade of black over her eyes. She had worn her smartest pair of grey trousers and they hung off her hips. She looked professional; her black hair untied but neat nestled on the shoulders of her loose cream shirt.

The lift opened onto a corridor lined on one side by glass through which she could see the river. There were rowers bending and straightening in their pushes, their boat leaving a wake of ripples that swam to the shore. The doors on the other side of the corridor were closed but she headed for the one at the end of the corridor. As she walked away, the voice from the lift followed her and suddenly she realized what she had heard that morning when she was running from Daniel's apartment. She hesitated for a moment, gripping the handle, and then took in a deep breath and opened the door to Valerie's office.

The office had glass walls on two sides and the sunlight washed pale the burgundy of the other two walls. The other three were already seated at a conference table set into a corner of the room. Expensive looking office furniture took up another corner and paintings of the college grounds were positioned on the walls. The light wood floors shone with a dull glaze.

Gerry got up immediately Priya entered the room. He came around the table with a wide smile and took her hand. He wore a conservative dark blue suit; his tie today had a Simpson's motif with yellow-headed Homers juggling donuts on a red background.

"Priya, good to see you again." Gerry seemed to assume that Reyna had invited her. He led her to the table and pulled out a chair for her. He looked like he had aged by a decade, the grey in his hair marching further inwards.

Priya looked at the two women sitting across from her. Valerie never tied her hair back and it fell in blonde layers. Her eyes searched into Priya's even as she smiled and nodded a greeting. It was a habit that Valerie did not even seem to notice anymore, her eyes on remote control seeking a weakness, a hold. Reyna's eyes were shuttered, the taut lines of her jaw highlighted by the pull of her hair tied back in her usual business-like manner. She acknowledged Priya's presence with a nod and continued her conversation with Valerie. Priya's mind was still trying to deal with the possibility that there had been no one around on the morning Daniel died and that, without meaning to, she had misled Catherine and Reyna.

"So, the funding that we received from the government was used to build…" Reyna gestured around her.

Valerie flicked back her hair and said, "It was used for the setting up of the research company in 2000. As you can imagine, it took a lot of money. We re-invested to build this facility 2 years ago. We are on the cutting-edge here. Ask Priya. She did her PhD research component here with us. We have given a lot of students a chance to work with the latest research." Valerie turned to Priya and smiled, and Priya noticed a slight narrowing of Reyna's eyes.

Gerry said, "Yes, we shook up the industry when we launched the Mark I pacemaker. Your grandfather's patent provided us with a groundbreaking technology. The Fairer Mark I pacemaker uses an alternative source of energy powered by the electrically charged cells in the heart muscle which sends current through leads to the pacemaker itself so it is a self-generating system. Daniel II had developed the idea for the alternative energy source in the 90s. He worked all his professional life in the field. He invented and patented different technologies. Amazing man. Well known and well respected in the field. I couldn't believe it when I found out his grandson was doing the fellowship with us. When we set up the research company in 2000 with Three." Gerry paused as he noticed Reyna's raised eyebrows. "Sorry, erm… your brother, Daniel, we used the technology, which was patented by Daniel II, your grandfather."

Reyna asked, "So, is that the only research work carried out by the company?"

Valerie said, "Mostly. We worked solely on the Mark I pacemaker and Mark I and Mark II controllers which were very successful. We have just developed version III of the Controller which allows the patient to be monitored at home. The Mark I pacemaker was developed by us and manufactured and marketed through TechMed Devices and captured 43% of the market for that particular class of devices. Millions of dollars involved. Our company's continued future is dependent on this range of products and technology. The Mark II controller was offered at a deep discount to those returning the Mark I controller so it obviously did not have as good a return. The Controller II was really just a change to the available frequency and getting ready for the Mark II pacemaker. The Mark II pacemaker will be launched soon and that will help TechMed Devices regain its share."

Priya spoke up. "Were there ever any problems with the Mark I pacemaker or controller? I know we didn't get any product advisories, did Daniel ever mention any worries he had about those products?"

Valerie focused on Priya. "There were no product advisories necessary. The pacemaker worked beautifully. Daniel set up the clinic here on the basis of the success with the product. He was encouraged to do so. We only had to issue one software patch in 2008 for the Controller II."

Gerry said, "When I decided to go into research rather than work as a clinician I never realized I'd get the chance to work with technologies that can make as much of a difference in the lives of patients as I could have working as a doctor."

Reyna said, "Did you have much contact with my grandfather? Was he very involved in the work you do here?"

Valerie turned her attention back to Reyna. "We went to see him as you know. He liked to keep in touch with everything. For a man in his eighties, he was very energizing to be around, he still has a fire in his belly." Priya felt Gerry tense beside her but then relax as Valerie turned to him and smiled. "Like Gerry here, all their lives spent knee-deep in saving other people's hearts."

Priya asked Gerry, "The clinical trials for the pacemaker lasted two years, didn't they? And were very successful." He nodded and she continued as Valerie and Reyna turned to look at her, "Did anyone follow through on the reports of the 2 deaths and the heart attack suffered by technicians over the last 7 years since the launch?"

Priya felt the shock in the air. Reyna had a look of surprise on her face as she turned to Valerie.

Valerie said, "I don't know anything about this."

Priya rushed on. "Well, all 3 were carrying out routine checks on the Mark I pacemaker using the Mark I Controller. They were all in specialized clinics when they had their heart attacks so one managed to have a temporary pacemaker installed and then he went on to have a pacemaker implanted. The other 2 weren't so lucky."

There was a sharp edge to Valerie's voice as she asked, "And you think this has something to do with the product? Where did you get that information anyway?"

Priya glanced at Reyna and answered, "I was reading up and doing some searches on the Internet for a project I'm working on and I came across the information on the woman who died. I did some more digging and found out about the heart attack and the other death." She sensed Reyna wouldn't want them to know about the papers Daniel had given to Priya or the ones he had sent to Catherine, and she agreed. The incidents had been spread out over the 7 years but Daniel had found them and connected them.

Gerry got up from the table. His face had reddened with the usual darker patches over the tips of his ears and the back of his neck.

He said, "This is incredible!" He turned to Valerie. "How could we not have known about this?"

153

Valerie shrugged and held out her hands with the palms up. "This is the first I'm hearing of this, Gerry. For all we know, it might be a coincidence. Do you know how many pacemaker checks are carried out each day all over the world?" She got up from the table and said to Reyna, "Let me do some investigating. We're just back in the office today after the shock of the last few weeks. How about we meet up tomorrow evening and I'll fill you in with what I've found out. I would like to return the hospitality," Priya felt her stomach tighten as Valerie purred out the word, "so perhaps we could take you to dinner? We have some extremely fine restaurants in Galway; of course the seafood here is excellent."

Reyna got up. She said, "You don't need to but that would be nice, thank you." She turned to Priya. "Are you free tomorrow evening?" Priya could see Valerie's face tighten and she wished that she was free but she'd promised Michael she'd go with him to a concert.

She said, "Sorry, but I have to go to a concert at St. Nicholas's church. I promised my friend and I haven't been to anything with him at the Arts Festival."

Valerie said, "Not Michael? Are ye two still an item?"

Priya reddened with anger. Valerie knew Michael had been her close friend since their college days. Valerie had cut Michael off the few times all of them had met socially, dismissing him as though he didn't exist. Valerie also knew Kathy and Priya had been in a long-term relationship and she'd oozed her charm on the two women, leaving Gerry and Michael to talk. Priya was struggling to contain her anger. This woman had wreaked havoc on her life, what right had she to continue to play games?

And how had she managed to diminish Priya's findings so adeptly.

Gerry said hurriedly, "Valerie, you know Priya's gay, why do you continue to tease her?" He smiled at Priya. "Michael's a nice guy, is he still living in that apartment he managed to buy before the boom?" Priya nodded. He continued, "Nice guy, and lucky guy then. Everything went up so high, of course, we bought at the height, and then it all crashed. Valerie was saying it would happen but I wasn't really listening, real estate really isn't my thing, but she was saying all right, the boom was built on nothing, housing industry feeding off itself."

The tension in the room had defused and Valerie said to Reyna, "Reyna, how about I show you around? And we can get Gerry to put all the financials in your car. Priya, Gerry will show you out, or you know your way, you've been here often enough." Valerie had her hand on Reyna's elbow as she guided her out of the office. Gerry smiled and was moving towards the door to see her out but Priya waved him back with a forced smile.

"I don't need an escort, Gerry, but thanks." She reached for his outstretched hand to shake it and then impulsively gave him a hug. He squeezed her tight and then released her and examined her face.

"Thank you, Priya, I needed that." She noticed close up the lines on his face, the dark circles under his eyes, and worst of all, a new pain in his eyes. She wondered again, as she had many times before, did he know the type of woman he had married. Or was his head so filled with his research? He had not had a clue of the undercurrents when they'd all sat in the bar on the nights out. Of the looks Valerie had given her. Of the orchestrated seating. Of the hand touching hers under the table. Or the crazed fumbling in the bathroom. Valerie had hunted and Priya was trapped as surely as a rabbit. And left flopping weakly, dust settling around her in the wake.

"Take care, Gerry." She left the office, the guilty click of her shoes echoing down the glass-lined hall.

21 CHAPTER TWENTY-ONE

She was not due back at the clinic today. She didn't feel like being around people anyway. The sight of Valerie had brought up too many bad memories, the sound of her speaking reminding Priya of a now silent voice. Priya wandered down the path that ran alongside the river, from the college past the shiny buildings that housed the commerce, and now the new engineering, faculties as well as research facilities. The student village was visible in the distance, colored blocks spaced around green areas; it was used for student accommodation during the college term and as a holiday village in the summer. The new university term was not until September and the buildings were mostly empty, the path deserted.

Priya left the narrow tarmac of the path and picked her way over the loose stones that lay on the rough ground leading to the edge of the water. She sat on a large boulder, molded into a smooth seat by generations of river gazers. She couldn't remember if she'd sat here before. Maybe with Michael. Never with Kathy. When they had met, Kathy had been living in the heart of what was now Galway's trendy pub scene. Then it had been a slightly dingy collection of back streets with an air of menace. Kathy had moved in with her into the house in Barna after they'd known each for six months, they'd often joked with their friends about the 'second date U-Haul'. But they'd been together for years, seven surprisingly happy ones. Until Valerie. Priya couldn't even blame the seven-year-itch; she hadn't felt anything but contentment. They'd even been discussing having kids. Which was why Priya had been so shocked at her own treachery.

"Priya?" Reyna's voice broke through her thoughts. Priya looked back at the path; she could see the glass walls of Valerie's office over Reyna's shoulder. Reyna slid down the little track and joined Priya beside the river. She sat down beside Priya, the boulder large enough for more than two people. It was a quiet cocoon. The hum of traffic crossing the river on the bridge drifted down to them. The intense blue of the water was shadowed under the span and she could see the cars through the railings.

Priya broke the heavy silence that had seemed to surround them since Reyna had met Valerie again.

"They still call that bridge the New Bridge despite the fact that it's been there since at least the mid-80s, about 25 years or so. I guess its real name is too much of a mouthful, Quincentennial. Celebrating 500 years of Galway. Me, I don't believe in history."

Reyna laughed. "You can't not believe in history! It isn't something that can really be disputed, it happened."

"Yes, but we can never be sure exactly what happened, can we? Depends on who tells you about it. It just seems that all history is bad, everyone always fighting. Show me a place with no history of fighting and I'll bet it's probably full of animals rather than humans." She rubbed a little pebble loose from the boulder and threw it into the river. "I try not to study the history of any place where I've lived, India, America, Ireland. I try to see them with blank eyes, a blank canvas, undiluted by the centuries of hatred. Michael gets so frustrated with me, he loves history, but then he can see the good that's happened. Me, I can't see it. And I don't want to get involved in it, all that hate."

"I have to keep believing that it's not all hate. Leo and Catherine were good teachers in that sense, they believed in compassion, in sending out love. They said it was the only thing that could work. My grandfather, on the other hand, is always warning me about people. Daniel said once that he was not always like that, that he had changed, became withdrawn after what happened in New York."

Priya wanted to say something, to warn Reyna about Valerie but the words stuck in her throat and they were silent as they watched a branch struggling in the moving water. Reyna seemed as reluctant as she was to talk about the research, about the deaths, Daniel, Valerie, the reasons they had met.

Reyna asked, "Have you moved a lot?"

"Yes, this is the longest I've stayed in one place. Even after my parents moved to Galway, there was a lot of travelling. Before that, my grandparents in India brought me up. So, citizen of everywhere, but nowhere to call home."

"But you're an Irish citizen, aren't you. And you've lived here a long time. Surely you consider this home."

"The closest thing, I guess. And I find myself relating to the Irish more than any other race. But, I'll never be Irish to them. Not at first, when they see me first. Do you know, I studied and paid a fair whack in college fees, and then worked and paid taxes but when the boom came in the last ten years and the refugees and asylum seekers arrived, I was assumed to be one. Made my blood boil and I had this speech all worked out about my contributions to this country but I realized no-one was interested." Priya laughed. "That speech was so good too, but I condensed it into this perfect glare which I threw out at anyone who mistook me for a refugee which unfortunately now meant that they felt smugly confirmed in their belief that I was an unwelcome, and now also unfriendly, leech that didn't speak English."

Reyna looked horrified and Priya rushed in, "Don't get me wrong. There have been so many changes here over the last while I think the Irish are just besieged and bewildered. And I love this country, deeply. It has given me so much. I wish it could be happy."

They sat in silence for a few minutes. The sharp blare of an annoyed driver sounded loud. Priya glanced over her shoulder at the building that housed the research company. She was conscious that if Valerie looked out through the glass she would see them. There was no movement in the office.

Priya asked, her tone level, "Did you enjoy the tour?" She saw Reyna glance at her.

"Well, I saw a lot of equipment. Which wasn't much use to me. But I did manage to get a hold of the financials from the Research Company. Thank you for coming in. I know it was hard. When did you find out about the deaths and heart attack?"

Priya told her about the typed links and gave an account of the searches she had done and the phone call.

"I would never have found out about them if Daniel hadn't typed out the links. I couldn't get through to you. Sorry about that," Priya gestured with her head towards the building, "I certainly set the cat in with the vultures then, didn't I?"

Reyna grinned. "You certainly did set the cat amongst the pigeons there. Valerie was flustered and I get the feeling she's not a woman that is easily thrown."

"Do you think she knew? About the deaths of those women, the heart attack. Before I said anything?"

"I don't know. It wouldn't be something they would be aware of necessarily. Maybe TechMed. As she said, it could be a coincidence when you think of the number of checks that are done every day and this happened over, what, seven years. I'll try to find out more tomorrow at dinner."

Priya got up off the boulder and swept the sand off her trousers. Her movements were rough.

Reyna touched her arm. "It would have been nice if you could have come too."

"I couldn't have sat down to dinner with that... woman. Though I might have, just to annoy her. Can't let Michael down though."

Reyna got up too, and they walked back down the path to the car park. They stopped at Reyna's car.

Priya said, as she turned to leave Reyna, "I promised your mother I'd speak to her at the end of the week. Maybe Sunday? I've got that concert tomorrow and you have dinner. I still have a lot of stuff to go through but I'll definitely have a better picture by then. I'll work on it for the rest of the day and tomorrow."

Reyna nodded. She seemed to want to say something but she got into her car without another word.

Priya wanted to ask Reyna to come back with her, to sit out, talk, to spend as much time as possible with her before she left. But, Reyna was married. And in Valerie's sights.

∞

Priya stood in the car park looking after the car as Reyna drove away. She heard the slick of tires behind her and the ruby red Jaguar slid up alongside her.

"Can I give you a lift somewhere?" She couldn't believe Valerie was actually being civil. To her. After what Valerie had done to her life.

Priya shook her head. She pointed to her own car. Valerie did not take her eyes off Priya's face.

"Get in Priya, we're going to have a little chat." Valerie's voice was quiet but determined.

Priya stayed where she was. She had kept the anger she felt at this woman at bay by refusing to think about her, by restricting contact with her to the absolute bare minimum. She turned to leave.

Valerie leaned her head out slightly and said, "Do you think about Kathy these days? Or is it all Reyna now?"

Priya stopped. She felt the pierce of adrenaline and her fists clenched. She took a deep breath and turned to walk away.

Valerie's voice was louder now. "Do you still think Kathy was the innocent martyr?"

Priya stopped and turned back around to face Valerie. The words spurted out. "She was a lot more innocent than we were."

"If you're so sure of that, then you'll have no problem hearing what I have to say, will you?" Valerie reached across the front seat and opened the passenger door.

Priya hesitated but the urge to know, to learn more about what had happened proved too strong. She'd never been able to talk about it to anyone, certainly not Valerie. She made up her mind. She'd hear her out. Even death-row prisoners were given a chance to confess.

Priya walked around the car and sat into the passenger seat as Valerie revved the engine. The car jerked forward and Valerie raced it out of the car park. Neither woman spoke as they moved through the traffic. Priya realized they were heading towards her house in Barna. She couldn't be in the house with this woman! Not after what they had done there.

"Not the house." Priya said. She crossed her arms.

"Wasn't going there." Valerie smiled. Another driver tried to cut her off as they exited the roundabout but she powered forward and glided the powerful machine through the narrow gap before the other car.

They turned off before Priya's house, at the road leading to Silver Strand beach. How appropriate, Priya thought. She'd confessed to Kathy here, as they'd sat in their car facing the sea. The wind had been howling, battering the car, shaking it on its wheels. And inside, in the darkness, Kathy had screamed at her, pounding the dashboard, her fists leaving indentations in the hard plastic.

Valerie pulled the car into one of the many empty spaces in the parking area. It was deserted and there was only one figure walking the beach bent against the wind, a raincoat pulled closed despite the watery sun, the King Charles spaniel leaping around in circles, hairy waves of fur lifting and falling.

The engine ticked as they sat there. Valerie now seemed reluctant to speak which was so unlike her that Priya felt a twinge of trepidation.

After a few minutes that stretched between them like the pulling back of a stringed bow, Valerie spoke.

"Gerry doesn't know anything about what happened between us. I want it to stay that way."

Priya turned to her. "Did you bring me out here to warn me off spoiling your happy little marriage?"

Valerie smiled. "I don't think anything is going to spoil my 'happy little marriage'. Unlike yours." She ignored the look of shock on Priya's face and continued, "What did you tell Reyna? Did you tell her about your 'little indiscretion'?"

"Little indiscretion! Is that what it was? Valerie, what we did, was, … I don't know how you can be so flippant about it. You pursued me, right under their noses, and we were all friends and those two people did not have a clue what we were doing. In the bathroom of a pub while they're chatting at the bar, in our bed! Don't you feel *any* guilt?"

"Guilt is such a waste of time and emotion." Valerie turned in her seat to face her. "My little Priya, I have to say you were fun. You were so reserved, proper… so honest. How long did that last, what, two weeks?"

Their words were echoing off the inside of the car and Priya could feel every jab.

Priya said, "At least I felt something for you. I didn't do it as some kind of screwed up game."

"You mean you convinced yourself it was okay because you felt something apart from just wanting to have sex with me. At least I'm honest about it. The sex was good, wasn't it Priya?"

Valerie was facing her, her eyes the usual weapons. She put her palm against Priya's cheek and turned Priya's face towards her, the soft caress controlled. Priya stared into

Valerie's eyes. The pupils were black voids in the sea of brown, the gold glittered. She had felt the lure of those eyes and her life had fallen into a black hole. She had loved this woman.

Priya's voice was a whisper between them. "I didn't just convince myself that I felt something for you. I did. At the time. I would never have cheated on Kathy otherwise. And I told her and ended things with her."

Priya shoved Valerie's hand away and turned to the sea outside. *Why was she excusing herself to this woman?*

Valerie cleared her throat. She said, "Yes, Kathy was very upset about your infidelity. Funny that…"

"Funny?!" Priya consciously unclenched her fists. She understood now that Valerie played games. Said things to get a reaction, to push her opponent off balance. She calmed her voice and said, "If you think that's funny, you have a sick sense of humor."

"Strange, then. Or what would you describe it if you knew that I had her too."

The words landed but Priya couldn't figure them out through the gathering cotton-wool daze in her mind. The walker on the beach had turned and was walking back; she could see the earnest face of the spaniel, its heavy ears drawing a straight line pointing back the way it came.

Her voice came out. "Had who? Kathy?"

"She was actually not as difficult to get as you were. With you, well, you were always struggling with guilt. With her, she enjoyed it. She felt guilty too but that was later."

The wind died down suddenly. The sun beat down through the quiet and Priya could hear the thrum of the waves. The walker had one of those tennis balls on a throwing stick and she had loosened the raincoat and flung the ball off its spring and down the beach. The spaniel raced after it.

"I don't believe you."

Valerie laughed. "You're actually like Gerry in a lot of ways. You just can't believe anyone could do anything wicked." She whispered the last word.

"Kathy wouldn't."

"Do you remember that time we went to the Skeff? I think Michael was there as well as the four of us."

Priya remembered. She had gotten into a discussion with Michael and Gerry about the economy. Priya and Michael had tried to convince Gerry of the approaching crash in the property market, of the abuse of power by the political leaders. It had been a playful atmosphere even though the argument at times was heated. Then the heat had been turned up even more as the discussion turned to the War on Terror. She tried to remember where Valerie and Kathy had sat. She couldn't picture them there.

Valerie said, "You guys were having this boring discussion. Kathy and I were not."

Priya closed her eyes. Her mind escaped into the details of that afternoon. They had sat upstairs. She could see the pattern on the sofa chairs, the red cream stripes behind Michael's shoulders as he leant forward to emphasize a point. Gerry leaning back and chuckling at something, his sleeves rolled up, the pattern on his loosened tie matching the ornate carvings on the wall. She could see the gleaming wooden floor stretching out in front of her. She could feel the warmth of the fire blazing behind her, the brick-lined fireplace with the chunky mirror hung above it. She could hear the voices of the two men in front of her and the cheers of a crowd coming from the large-screen TV perched in the corner.

And she could see Valerie coming back from the bar with their drinks, what had she drunk, a Baileys? Priya could feel the stare into her eyes as Valerie handed her the glass, the curls of cream liquor slipping off their cubed ice platforms as Priya sipped hastily trying to hide her reaction. And Kathy, coming back from the toilets, the flush on her face reflecting the heat of the fire.

No. No, no, no, no, no! There were no other words allowed. If she repeated the word over and over again, she would not have to let in the thoughts. But the knowledge crept into the space between her thoughts and set up home, a squatter she would never remove.

"She used to call me, after. After you two split up. She wanted more. She didn't seem to accept it was over. Unlike you. She used to call me and say she was going to top herself. Of course I never went." Valerie sounded surprised that Kathy would call her.

Priya thought of all the times she'd gone when Kathy had called, guilt and concern propelling her through the doors to pick up the pieces of the woman she thought she'd shattered. She opened the door and struggled out of the car. The walker and her dog had disappeared. She hadn't noticed them getting into a car and driving away. The beach was empty. She heard Valerie call her but she ignored her and walked down the ramp leading off the concrete promenade and onto the sand. She heard the engine roar as Valerie drove off a few minutes later.

∞

She sat on the rocks for hours and let the wind batter her. The sun and the clouds were still playing the same games. Walkers came and walkers went. Some with dogs, some in couples, all glancing curiously at her especially on their return leg, surprised to see her still sitting there, her light jacket soaked through, her hair sprawled on her skull.

The movie reel of her mind turned, projecting pictures onto the back of her eyes. The images were over two years old, and the same; her eyes were different. And she saw it. What she would have seen had she not been so blinded by Valerie. The gaps when Valerie and Kathy weren't with the rest of them, the screaming reaction to Priya's confession, Kathy's desperate phone calls after her first ones to Valerie had been ignored. The unspoken request to get back together had not been spoken because it had not been felt.

And the woman with who she had spent seven years had mirrored her betrayal, magnified it, and left her with the guilt.

She walked home as the light faded.

22 CHAPTER TWENTY-TWO

The doorbell was insistent. It scraped through her mind, jangling her nerves. She didn't know how long she had been sitting on the sofa in her living room, her clothes drying into wrinkles. The lights were not switched on and the growing darkness outside had slunk in further, cozying up to her as the hours passed. There was a full bottle of wine on the floor by the couch, uncorked but untouched; a glass lay beside it.

She'd opened the bottle earlier but had decided not to take any alcohol while she was upset. She didn't like alcohol, in college she'd argued against its over-use, but the last few years had changed many things. She'd tried but hadn't managed to drown anything in drink and the last few times she'd had too much, she'd made a fool of herself or worse, ended up with a dead man. She was going off alcohol rapidly.

She looked at her phone. There were five missed calls from an unknown number. She knew they were from Reyna but she hadn't wanted to talk to anyone. For two years, she had done a good job of suppressing. No one at the clinic had seen anything but the mask. The effort of holding it up was draining. She could feel it slipping despite her frantic efforts.

And cracks had been appearing since she'd found Daniel but Valerie had just taken a hammer and smashed holes through.

The ringing of the bell clamored at the corners of the room. Whoever was at the door wasn't going away. Then there was silence and Priya felt her body relax. The knock at the window sent her rigid again and she twisted to see a fist poised to rap again.

Priya got up and opened the door.

"What's happened?" Reyna's face showed her anxiety.

"I'm sorry. I switched my phone off."

Reyna stared at her but Priya summoned up a smile as she turned and walked into the living room switching on the light as she went. Reyna followed.

"We have more of a problem." Reyna's voice was tense, and there was a sense of defeat in it.

Priya reached down for the bottle of wine. She waggled it at Reyna who shook her head. Priya shrugged and poured herself a glass. She took a long swallow.

Reyna asked, "Are you going to tell me what's going on?"

She was looking at Priya's crinkled clothes, at her damp hair, at the look in her eyes. Priya took another gulp of wine then finished off the rest in the glass and placed the glass on the floor. She gestured at the armchair and sat back down on the sofa, pulling her legs up into her and hugging the rounded arm.

Keeping her voice steady, Priya asked, "We have a problem?"

Reyna remained standing but she'd moved around in front of the couch.

"I don't know how to say this, especially since you're obviously not okay." Reyna knelt beside the couch and took Priya's hand. Priya stared at their hands and then back up at Reyna. Even through her daze, she felt the power of Reyna's eyes. They were brown like Valerie's but a million shades away. The pupils were wide and Priya saw a universe inside the shadows.

Priya closed her eyes. "Just say it."

Reyna took in a deep breath then let it out in a rush. "Gerry phoned James and demanded your suspension from the clinic and an investigation into your breach of security."

"Gerry? Or Valerie?"

"Gerry."

"And what did James say?" Priya felt surprisingly calm.

"He was under pressure from TechMed Devices as well. He said we have no choice and has asked me not to go against the decision."

"So I've been suspended."

Reyna got off her knees and sat beside Priya without letting go of her hand.

"I'm sorry. As far as TechMed and James are concerned, the rules were broken. Only you and I, and Catherine, know that it turned out to be for a good reason. And Gerry and Valerie have a right to demand this as it was their material."

"And you're not going to go against them." Priya yanked her hand out of Reyna's grip.

Reyna said, "Priya, I would have fought it but I actually think right now it might be a good thing." She hurried on as Priya turned to glare at her, "Have you considered the danger you are in? It would be safer if you weren't near the clinic for the moment. Not till we find out what's going on."

"Danger from what? The only thing in common between the attacks is the equipment the technicians were using. So if, I'm in danger, so is Tara and so are God knows how many others who use the same equipment every day."

"But you're the only one who's been followed. You're the one Daniel trusted along with Catherine."

"So, now you trust me? But you're going to suspend me?" Priya sprang up and felt the wooze of wine rush to her head. Or was it light-headedness from a rush of blood to her legs, or a lack of food. She hadn't eaten since that half of a sandwich at lunchtime yesterday. Her hands trembled as she poured out another glass, splashing a few drops onto the floor, the red drops brightly dark against the black and white tiles. She drank the glass in one go and poured another.

"Don't you think you've had enough?" Reyna said.

"Don't you mean 'Priya, you obviously can't handle your drink as you've proven before'? What is it, Reyna, can't you 'handle' me when I'm drunk. You've done it before. Or is it when I'm sober that you don't want to know?" Priya spun around to face Reyna.

The fast motion made her head spin and the wine spilled out again and dripped down into the fold of skin between her thumb and finger. "Why do women like Valerie get whatever they want?" She watched the drops of red creep down towards her wrist.

Reyna got up, took the glass from Priya's hand, and placed it on the low table beside the window and stayed, staring out of the window. The night had snuffed out the lingering light of the Irish summer and Priya knew the occasional sweep of brightness from the passing traffic was not that interesting.

It struck her that Reyna was forcing herself to remain turned away. She felt a surge of power. For the first time. She wondered if this was what Valerie felt. Was it more satisfying when the woman who was struggling was strong?

Priya wanted to be in the game. To feel what it was like to participate, to control, to direct it. She walked over to the window, her steps deliberate. She felt Reyna's body flinch away as she took Reyna's face and turned it towards her. Keeping her eyes fixed on Reyna's, she placed her hands on Reyna's hips and pushed, slow but firm, until Reyna was leaning on the sill, her back pressed against the glass blackness. Priya looked down at the pulse that thrust against the line of Reyna's neck. She ran the tip of her finger over the movement and down to the edge of Reyna's top where it bunched at her collarbone, she could feel the grain of the cloth rough against the silk of Reyna's skin and she could feel Reyna's fast breath against her cheek, warm and cool, hot and cold. As she lowered her head to kiss Reyna, she saw the helplessness she had seen in Reyna's eyes before, but there was hurt attached now. The feel of Reyna's lips drowned out the protest that surfaced in Priya's heart. She wound her fingers through Reyna's hair, her knuckles tapped against the cold of the pane, her palms cupping the heat, pulling it closer, her body pushing Reyna's.

She was losing herself in their kiss, but the shade of hurt in Reyna's eyes wouldn't leave that part of Priya's mind that knew. She pulled her mouth away and laid her cheek against the base of Reyna's throat. She closed her eyes and inhaled the scent.

With as much strength as she could marshal she took herself out of Reyna's arms and sank down onto the couch.

She kept her voice calm and it came out low. "I don't play games, Reyna. I'm as competitive as the next person but not when it comes to feelings."

"I am not playing games." Reyna was still slumped where Priya had left her and her voice sounded like it was being forced through a rigid tube.

"Well, everybody seems to. And I honestly don't know anymore who's playing and who's not." Priya slid her body flat onto the couch and rested her head against the arm. "You've done what you came to do; I have been well and truly suspended. You know where the door is."

The click of the door closing a few minutes later stung deep in her chest.

23 CHAPTER TWENTY-THREE

Friday, July 22, 2011

The man sitting across from him was tense. The diplomat noticed that the man's blue suit had just one wrinkle, arcing its way down below the knee to the hem of the trousers. On the desk between them lay the device. The temporary one the diplomat was using. He was now expert at working the device. Hold it over the collarbone, wait for the beep, press the button. That was to communicate with his implanted pacemaker. For the meeting, he would be holding the device in his pocket, standing within three feet of his target. He couldn't get the device any closer without arousing suspicion. And when he pressed the button, everything would stop. And his pacemaker would start.

The diplomat said, "Why am I practicing with this? It is not the real thing. I will not need to hold it in the same way." His voice was harsh with fear.

The man frowned. "It is close enough to the real thing. Everything will be in the same place. It will work though."

"You are sure? We will never get another chance, you know that."

The man nodded. His eyes burned and the old acne scars stood dark against his tanned skin.

"I will make it happen. If it is the last thing I do."

The man got up and walked to the door. He used the same tone that he had when they had first met, the reassuring tone, the convincing tone. The diplomat found it disturbing, that flat confidence, the arrogance that still managed to creep through.

"I am going there today. I have a few things to clean up. The device will be ready before the 28th. That is the latest date for the device to be ready in time and get it to you for the meeting on August 1st."

As the man left the room, the diplomat tried not to think of the lack of options for him, and more importantly for his country, if the device was not ready in time.

They had 10 days.

24 CHAPTER TWENTY-FOUR

Saturday, July 23, 2011

Priya woke up on the couch, her spine fixed in pain. She groaned as she tried to crawl off without moving her back too much. Her neck was stiff too and she knelt on all fours beside the couch trying to work her muscles loose. The empty bottle was lying on the floor and it felt sticky as she picked it up as she got to her feet. Her head hurt; the light from outside made it worse.

She checked her phone, it was late morning already. She had slept for hours. The last few weeks had caught up with her. It was now two weeks to the day that she had woken up with a dead man. She wondered for how long more she would measure her days from that moment. Like she had done from the morning she'd found out about Kathy, and then the moment the machine was switched off. Anniversaries of death. After a lifetime with no close experience of death, they were now sudden and intimate friends; she had the mental photographs to prove their relationship.

She wouldn't look into the mirror as she cleaned her face. This time she remembered. Every detail. The strength and movement of Reyna's cheek against her palm, the softness of her earlobe as Priya's finger brushed against it, the scent of the hollow at the base of Reyna's throat. She remembered most of all the feeling of coming home as she laid her face against that scent.

She raised her eyes to look into the mirror. So, the long search for home ended with a woman who was married, emotionally unavailable, and in Valerie's clutches. And Priya would never play that game. At least she could look herself in the eyes on that count.

∞

Priya sat on her cliff at the end of the field behind her house, legs dangling, feet bumping off the eroded earth wall. She watched the seagulls argue on the beach as they chased the glint of the afternoon sun. The participants in the debate changed often, some joining in from the air, others leaving to go for a bob on the waves. She had observed them for years and she thought she could recognize some of the regulars.

She'd cleaned up and taken a taxi in to the clinic to collect her car. It had looked lost and blue in the empty car park.

She heard a voice calling her name and turned to see Catherine walking down the path that led by the house and down beside her field. There was a break in the low loose-stone wall and Catherine edged through it and picked her way through the boulders.

Priya's immediate feeling was that of a child about to be scolded but Catherine smiled at her with her usual warmth.

"May I join you?"

Priya nodded.

Catherine slipped off her shoes and settled down beside Priya. She refused Priya's offer of a drink and they sat for a few minutes absorbing.

Catherine took both of Priya's hands in hers.

Priya looked down at their hands and said, "I've noticed in the last while that people have held my hand when I wasn't feeling okay." She looked back up and smiled. "Do people see me as a child or something? Though I probably come across as one. Is it the height thing? Little Priya. My dad is tall, I got this from my mum, she was exactly 5 feet tall. My dad and I used to use her to measure the height of the badminton net when we played back there."

Catherine laughed. "You *are* little, my dear. But you certainly don't come across like a child." Her face turned serious. "In fact, you come across as a beautiful, confident, powerful, young woman. But you just see the child."

"Powerful?" Priya snorted. "You're kidding, right?"

"No, Priya. I'm not." Catherine turned to look at the sea and the blue reflections deepened the color of her eyes. "You know, we all have the same power, it is just that some people know it and use it and others don't and give it away. I used to be like you. My father was a powerful man; he wanted things for me, for his family. All for the right reasons, of course. When my mom died, I was 17 and he was only 39. He didn't realize what it would do to me, he was devastated and he withdrew but he couldn't see that losing a mother is as difficult as losing your wife. Maybe more. Because when she's gone, it feels like that one person in this whole lonely world that is there for you, isn't anymore. And I don't mean it was a perfect relationship or anything, we fought a lot, but I just knew, I just felt it, right here." Catherine took one of her hands and touched her chest.

Priya's eyes filled and she rubbed them with rough fingers.

Catherine's voice was gentle. "It is okay to cry. I wish I'd done that instead of lashing out. But then, I don't know. I wouldn't have had Daniel if I hadn't rebelled and hung around with Leo. I was only 17 when I met Leo and he was 30. I can't look back now and regret my mistakes because each one left me with something good too. I was young. I made mistakes. But, I'm still making them. Every day. Along with a few good decisions. You have so many bruises, Priya. And they are not all inflicted by other people. Stop beating yourself up."

Priya whispered, "There are things I've said and done that I can't forgive."

"So you've made mistakes. Did you mean to hurt anyone?"

"No. I can't stand hurting anyone."

"Except yourself. I guess that doesn't count." Catherine smiled as Priya shot her a look.

Priya said, "I seem to have gone through life with no direction, or letting other people and their needs be the signposts for me." She sighed. "But anything else means figuring out what I want and that always seemed selfish."

"It is not selfish, Priya, It is essential. I have been trying to tell Rain that." Priya stiffened and Catherine said in a softer voice, "You see yourself as this powerless person when it comes to women like Valerie and Rain. Yes, Rain told me about Valerie and about Kathy."

"Did she tell you Valerie 'had' Kathy too? No, she couldn't have, she didn't know. Like I didn't know." Priya's voice was rushed and angry. "How could someone do that? I've been paralyzed by guilt ever since I cheated on Kathy with Valerie. Then Kathy killed herself and I thought it was over me. Can you imagine what kind of guilt came with that? I tried not to feel anything for Valerie after that but somehow she got to me. That night, on my birthday, I tried so hard to ignore her. I didn't know about her and Kathy then, I was such a fool. Valerie played with me, she flirted with Daniel. I don't know why I reacted. She had that effect on me. I mean, how could I have flirted with Daniel, a *guy*, to stop her? She had that kind of power." Priya shook her head. "It wasn't a game. Her games affected too many people in such awful ways. I don't want to be powerful if that's what it causes."

They sat in silence for a minute.

Catherine said, "You know that saying, with power comes responsibility? Well, handing away power doesn't lessen responsibility. It is not a game but it is an interaction. And if you hand all the power to the other person, you're giving up your responsibility for yourself. The difference between a Valerie and you is that when someone hands you their power you don't abuse it, in fact, you seem to take on all the responsibility for them. Valerie just takes on all the power."

"And Reyna…?"

"Reyna is not like Valerie. Not one bit. But she has lost her power. For the moment." Catherine smiled, "She was such a cool kid, shy, but so naturally cool. She didn't have to try; people were just drawn to her. I guess that was Leo coming through in them, Daniel was like that too, but he knew it. Rain was the kind of kid that would hear you talk about something you liked and she'd remember and get that for you on your next birthday. She liked to find out what would make other people happy. There were a load of kids in the commune but I think she was the leader, not in a loud kind of way, it would just seem to default to her."

Priya said, "She still has that."

"Yes. But she doesn't trust it." Catherine's hand was tugging at the grass beside them. "She had her share of relationships; she was considered quite a catch I gather, but none of them really serious. And then she met Simone." The name hissed out.

"Her wife?"

"Yes. They got together about a year before Leo died. Simone was a sous-chef in a French restaurant in San Francisco. Rain had just finished college and was working at helping a start-up, a dot com thing. I think the relationship wasn't that serious at first, not for Simone anyway, and then Leo died, and he left money to Rain." She sighed. "Next thing, Simone wants to get married. And I think Rain was quite isolated from her friends by this stage. Simone had a way of doing that. And I had just moved to Ireland. Rain had withdrawn from me because I made the mistake of telling her what I thought of Simone. So they got married and I wasn't invited. And Rain set up a restaurant for Simone. I'm afraid I didn't handle it too well, Rain was such a responsible person with money and she did this without thinking. She said she wanted to make Simone's dreams come true."

Catherine's fist clutched a handful of grass, slender roots dripping dry earth into the open grave.

"But Rain didn't have any background in restaurants, did she?"

Catherine shook her head. "But she could usually do anything she put her mind to. And she did. She learnt everything she could, she used to work as a waitress there as well as manage it, while that, that… woman lorded it as the chef. The restaurant was actually quite good. But a month after they opened, Simone had an affair with a waiter there. A really young guy, only nineteen, twenty or something like that. Practically flaunted it in front of Rain's face. And when Rain confronted her Simone got violent."

"I can't see Rain, sorry, Reyna, putting up with that." Priya asked, "What happened, did she kick Simone out?"

"That's what I couldn't understand. How a strong woman like Reyna could let someone control her like that. No, she didn't kick Simone out. Simone created havoc in the restaurant. She would scream and shout and threaten Rain, sometimes in front of customers. And I think when there were no customers, she would hit Rain." Priya's mouth dropped open. "Yes, Priya, I thought that too, but it turns out it happens between women as well. I didn't know about this, one waitress saw something once but she didn't want to get involved. The bitch said to me later she didn't want to take sides. Sorry for my language, but if you see someone being physically threatening to another person who won't defend herself, at least *say* something."

"But you just said it. Why didn't Reyna defend herself?"

"She finally told me two years ago. When she moved to New York. She was embarrassed when it was happening. She didn't want to get physical; she couldn't believe it was happening. Everyone seemed to think it was just a tempestuous relationship and that they were both involved." Catherine sighed again, a deep breath out. "I understood then why she didn't walk away at the time."

Catherine stopped and was silent.

Priya leant forward. "Why?"

Catherine shook her head. "I've already told you more than Rain wants anyone to know. I know I shouldn't have, I'm not allowed to talk about her life, but I just couldn't bear to see you both tearing yourselves apart."

Catherine looked at the torn grass in her hand and laid it down beside the dug up soil. Her fingers ran over the dirt and she smoothed the rift as she talked. "I've just lost my son, this time it is final. But I am so grateful for the last few years when he let me back in to his life. And I think that time was cut short. I don't know why it was you that I asked but I had a strong feeling if anyone could work it out you could. And now you are in danger too it seems." She straightened up. "Whether he was killed or not, Daniel wanted us to know and to do something. Something he couldn't do for some reason. I am as angry as you are about your suspension but a part of me agrees with Reyna too. We have two days to figure it out. And then Reyna is going to go in and shut everything down at the Research Company. She is going to get a worldwide product advisory issued and all checks are going to be stopped until we can be certain the deaths and the heart attack have nothing to do with the equipment."

"Does she have the power to do that?"

"We don't know. But the better the case we have, the more chance she has with TechMed Devices." Catherine glanced back at the house and smiled. "She's in the car, looking through her papers. Any chance we can release her and all go in?"

"She's been sitting there all this time?" Priya asked. She grimaced and said, "I guess I wasn't too subtle when I kicked her out yesterday."

Catherine got to her feet and held out a hand. Priya took it and pulled herself up.

Catherine said, "I don't think Valerie is Reyna's type."

Priya turned and walked towards the house. "I didn't think she was mine. Or Kathy's," she said, over her shoulder.

25 CHAPTER TWENTY-FIVE

Reyna's face was tinged with red and a sheen of moisture was layered over the wary expression on it as she looked at Priya through the open window of the car.

Priya said, "You're not my boss for the moment so I can say, you look silly using a Merc as an office. You can come in; I'm not going to bite." She turned to hide her smile at Reyna's face and added, "Not yet, anyway."

She could hear Reyna start to gather up the papers draped over every available surface of the interior of the rental car. Priya turned back. "Do you need a hand?"

She took Reyna's snort as a 'No' and grinned as she went back into the house.

∞

Priya and Catherine were sitting at the kitchen table as Reyna carried in a cardboard box and dumped it down on the table.

Reyna said, "Most of the important financials and the stuff I took from your office."

Priya said, "I was just going to go through the basics of pacemakers and the industry that you and I went through already."

She went through it again in detail for Catherine and drew out pictures on an A4 notepad to illustrate.

Priya said with an apologetic tone in her voice, "My study in the field was very focused. And I didn't get to see the whole picture at any stage. I had some…distractions when I was finishing my PhD."

Reyna said, "You said before that you were in the second year of your PhD when you met Valerie. So all this happened with Valerie in that year, and you still finished the PhD, what, a year or two later?"

Priya nodded. "About a year and a half." She saw the confusion in Reyna's eyes and said, "Yes, my personal life had just been blown apart, but in our family that was not allowed to come before finishing what you started especially when it comes to education."

Reyna said, "But your seven year relationship had just come to an end, Kathy had committed suicide…"

Priya saw Catherine glance a warning at Reyna but Reyna was still looking at Priya in puzzlement.

Priya closed her eyes. She said, "Yes, I had to deal with a lot of stuff. And I did. I closed off for a month and then my dad came to see me and I had to get up and finish the PhD."

Priya opened her eyes. Catherine had a look of understanding in her eyes but Reyna looked angry.

Priya said, "Reyna, considering my background, I am a screw-up. My parents were highly educated, driven, professionals. And they were Indian. And I was their only child. The fact that I wasn't a doctor like them, or, since I'd half-heartedly followed the route and done Science, the fact that I hadn't won the Nobel Prize in Science by the time I was 30 was a huge disappointment. Especially, as they saw it, for someone with so much potential." She laughed. "When I switched to IT, my dad comforted himself by asking me to contact Bill Gates to see if I could get 'in' there on the whole Microsoft thing."

Reyna smiled reluctantly as Catherine laughed.

Priya continued, "I know it seems harsh but they were just trying to do the best for me, and trying to get me to do the best for myself. You see, I had one of the highest points you can get, in the Leaving Cert, and I could have walked on to any course. But I guess I had a mini-rebellion and stuck a finger onto the list of course options, of course, these only included everything to the rational side, and it landed on Science, so that's what I did. And I was let loose in college; my parents had left by then. I spent those years attempting to tear up every stereotype of a quiet Indian girl. I'm afraid to say I did a good job of that."

"But even then, you got so many degrees, didn't that make them happy?" Reyna asked.

"Yup, I guess. But then the job and marriage thing came up so they had something else for me to pursue. God, this is sounding bad, but it wasn't. I just wandered around after the IT postgrad, couldn't settle at anything. I was happy with Kathy, she was a graphic artist, and I got into painting and started doing an Art therapy course, which of course I didn't mention to my parents. And then the PhD came up. And Valerie… I told you she knows how to get to someone. Well, with me it was the 'you're just so intelligent' route. And because she's really smart and Gerry is too, I respected her opinion, She just knew exactly what to say and I fell for it. Jeez, it was like manna from Hell. So when I knew it was just an act on her part, I think I stopped feeling intelligent, in fact, I stopped feeling human. I guess a robot version of me finished the PhD and reported to work at the clinic when it opened."

Turning away, Priya said, "Daniel connected the deaths and the heart attack suffered by the technicians."

Catherine put a hand on Reyna's and Reyna closed her mouth.

Catherine said, "Is it possible that someone knew about the incidents before Daniel. That someone found out that the Controller I could possibly have caused the deaths of those women and the other heart attack and covered it up?"

Now Reyna was up and pacing.

Priya nodded. "Let's follow the logic. The people who could have connected the incidents in any meaningful way were Daniel and the researchers at the company, the staff at the clinic, and the unit in TechMed that dealt directly with the product. It could be anyone of them that covered up the connection."

Reyna stopped and turned to Priya with a shocked expression on her face. "You think *Daniel* could have been a part of it?"

"How can we rule it out?"

Catherine said, "I can't believe that of Daniel. He was too dedicated to his work, to healing people. All his life he wanted to make a difference and he worked really hard to get where he was."

Priya said gently, "He had the most to lose then, didn't he? If this came out, there would be product recalls, investigations, charges possibly."

Reyna cut in. "But Daniel was killed!"

Priya said, "We don't know that for sure. What if he found this stuff and covered it up but then died of a heart attack."

Reyna and Catherine were staring at her. Their faces reflected her confusion.

Priya said, "What do we have beyond a feeling that would point to Daniel's death being anything but a heart attack? The fact that he was worried and had discovered that technicians had died while using his equipment. That could still point to a heart attack brought on by worry. The feeling that Catherine had that there was a woman in his bed with him. Well, maybe that was because I was in the apartment that morning. The voice I heard when I ran from the apartment." Priya realized she had forgotten to tell them about her new hypothesis for that. "I actually meant to say the other day but it is possible what I heard was the recorded voice saying 'Lift opening'." She couldn't meet their eyes.

She hurried on. "And the autopsy showed no other cause of death."

Then Catherine said, "I know this is from his mother, but I am convinced Daniel would not have been a part of a cover-up."

Reyna nodded.

Priya remembered something. "Daniel must have received the medical records from John Landon, the guy who had the heart attack. He sent those weeks ago from Seattle. I can understand it taking a while but they should have arrived before Daniel died." She gestured at the mass of papers and files. "They are definitely not in there. This means either Daniel had them at the clinic, or he sent them to someone else, or he had them at home. I don't think he'd have kept them at the clinic."

Reyna said firmly, "There was a cover-up. And we know without a doubt that it wasn't Daniel that covered up the deaths and heart attack at the time they happened. He didn't know about the problem until this year. What we don't know is what convinced him that there wasn't a problem the night he died. Don't you think it is too much of a coincidence that he texts me to say that and then he dies. Just after finding out about the problem? And what happened to the medical records?"

Priya said, "So, someone else knew about the deaths, covered them up, and either convinced Daniel to send the text or sent it themselves from his phone to put you off...? And then killed Daniel. That leaves us though with the unlikely situation that Daniel was killed in such a way that it appeared beyond a shadow of a doubt to have been a heart attack."

Catherine was firm. "Then that is what happened. And we have to figure out how it could have happened."

Priya looked doubtful. "I need to try and get an overall picture of this. The note Daniel left..." She searched through the box, and held out the Post-It and then started searching through the rest of the stack. "I need to look through Tara's description of Liam's attack."

Reyna sat back at the table.

Priya found the handwritten sheets. Liam had had his heart attack in December while Priya had been away with her mother in India. Tara had described in detail what had happened that afternoon almost a year ago, December 13th. Priya tried not to let her mind wander to that date, only three days before the machine was silenced, but of course it ran there. Priya read the account out loud, her voice growing stronger after the first few sentences.

The appointment had started out as a routine six-month check on Jacintha's pacemaker at 2.15 on the afternoon of the 13th of December 2010. Liam was present as usual, sitting beside his mother. Tara described in detail the setting up of the Controller, of placing the wand over Jacintha's chest, of hearing the beep.

Priya continued reading. The trolley was placed as usual beside Jacintha. The controller had started the communication by sending the auto-identification sequence; the device implanted in Jacintha had in turn sent the response detailing its serial and model numbers. The controller had then sent an interrogation command that elicited Jacintha's name and diagnosis. So far, everything was routine.

Tara wrote how she finished the first part of the check and had started the programmer test, when there had been a knock on the door, and she had gone to answer it. She couldn't remember if she had left the wand on Jacintha's chest. Laura, one of the nurses, had needed the file for one of Tara's patients. Tara had left the room for a moment. She'd been standing outside the door to the room when she had heard Jacintha scream Liam's name. She had immediately entered the room to find Liam sliding down to the floor from what seemed like a slumped position over Jacintha's chest. He fell first against the trolley which rolled away from Jacintha and then onto the floor. Tara had raised the alarm and performed CPR. Liam's condition had necessitated a temporary pacemaker, as the ECG showed no spontaneous electrical activity. The printout of the results was stapled to the back of the handwritten sheet.

Priya said, "Strange that she described the way Liam fell."

Priya searched out the official typed sheet that Tara had submitted after the incident. "See, she doesn't go into those details in her official report. This is what I saw when I came back. Liam wasn't my patient but I checked to see what had happened. Liam seemed to have been leaning over Jacintha. And John Landon, the technician in Seattle, described leaning over the patient as well."

Priya stopped. She was looking at the printout of the results.

"What?" Catherine leant forward.

Priya said, "The printout for the check that Tara did is different. Older type, the Controller I or the Controller II before 2008. I don't use either of them for routine checks in the clinic. They are there for my research work with the company. I only use it to communicate with pulse generators, not the implanted ones, just to test the coding."

Reyna asked, "Does Tara know that?"

Priya tried to think. Tara knew the Controller I had been replaced. But the clinical room Priya used for her patient checks was also the room where she carried out the tests on the controller. They had not had time to sort out anything when Priya finally left to go to her mother. It was not a dangerous piece of equipment. The Controller I looked slightly different from the Controller II. The two versions of the Controller II looked very similar and were on identical trolleys.

Priya said, "It is possible that Tara used the Controller II without the software patch.. She had only joined the clinic a short while before that. She wouldn't have known much about the research work."

Reyna asked, "But why would that be dangerous? I thought the Controller II had passed the clinical trials and had been used successfully before it was replaced?"

Priya was up and pacing around the room. "It wouldn't have had to go through clinical trials. There still shouldn't have been any problems. It does the same thing. I need to see what the software patch does."

Catherine said, "So, Daniel asked Tara to write the description out. And then wanted to check something with you after he read it? Maybe the fact that the wrong Controller II was used by mistake?"

Priya said, "Could be. He got the description in March, why didn't he ask me anytime in the last few months. Unless he only wrote the note recently." She sat back down amidst the folders. "So what changed? He would have known that Tara used the wrong Controller II since March."

Reyna said, "According to what Daniel found out, the problems were when the Controller I was used. So Daniel did those searches because he found out that Liam's attack happened when the wrong Controller II was used."

Priya said, "But both Controllers would have been used so many times in so many clinics over the years. Why on those particular occasions did they cause fatal or near-fatal heart attacks? So far the similarities are that the people who had heart attacks were leaning over the patient and the Controller I or the Controller II without the software patch were being used."

Priya pulled at her sleeves in frustration. "I'm all over the place. Let's get the timing straight."

Reyna grabbed the notepad and pen.

Priya spoke slowly as Reyna scribbled down notes, "These attacks happened over the last 7 years since the launch. Liam's attack happened last December. Daniel got Tara's first report sometime shortly after that I'd say. We don't know when he did the searches on the internet and found out about the deaths. He would know a lot more about sudden cardiac arrest. He was probably investigating that, trying to find an answer. I can see him not letting it go as an unexplained cardiac arrest though that happens. In March, he asks Tara for a more detailed description of the incident with Liam so I'm inclined to think he had done at least one of the searches by then."

Catherine and Reyna both nodded and Priya continued, "Daniel called John Landon in Seattle in May. We don't know if he called other clinics around the same time. He gave me the figures on the Controller II in June before he went to New York and he seems to have searched through all the paperwork on the pacemaker and the Controller I which he what, sent to Ireland...?" She looked at Reyna who nodded. "So he makes a copy and sends it to Catherine. The postmark was 5 July so ..." she looked through the calendar on the wall, July's poster child was a rescued three-legged sheepdog searching for a home, "4th July would be a holiday, and he left what, the day after posting it, the 6th..?"

Reyna nodded as she finished writing and showed the page to them. Catherine and Priya examined the list.

Last 7 years – attacks
December last year – Liam
First report from Tara
Internet searches
March – Tara details, 1 search done?
May - John Landon Seattle phone call
June - Figures on Controller II to Priya
July 1st week New York – Pacemaker, Controller I
Makes copy, sends to Catherine 5th July?
Back in Ireland, July 7th

Priya filled in some more dates as she worked them out from the notes she had made.

Last 7 years – attacks – pacemaker/controller I launched 2003

attack 1 Singapore 2004 – death

attack 2 Limoges 2006 – death
attack 3 John Seattle 2006 – survived

Priya stared at the additions. "The attacks seem to have stopped after 2006…? We don't know for sure, do we?"

She drummed her fingers on the table as she thought.

"The Research Company started work on the development of the Controller II in 2004 after the launch of the Controller I. The Controller II replaced the Controller I in 2006. And what did Valerie say? They issued a software patch in 2008."

"Where were we?" Priya looked at the notepad. "Okay, Liam's attack in December 2010."

She added it to the list.

Last 7 years – attacks – pacemaker/controller I launched 2003
attack 1 Singapore 2004 – death - Controller I
attack 2 Limoges 2006 – death - Controller I
attack 3 John Seattle 2006 – survived - Controller I
Controller II launch 2006
Controller II software patch 2008
attack 4 Liam Galway 13th December 2010 – survived – Controller II (mistake – no patch)

She said, "If Daniel started looking because of Liam's attack, then he would have started after the 13th December 2010. I got back to work in the first week of January after my mum… Tara had done the typed report, I remember reading it, but I didn't really take it in. Daniel would have received it. He didn't discuss it with me, we were still very awkward with each other but he was really kind to me. He really seemed to feel it."

Catherine made a small sound and Priya saw the pain in her eyes and realized why Daniel had been so affected by the loss of her mum. He had lost Catherine too, until the last few years. She rubbed Catherine's hand, which had clenched on the table, and they both smiled.

Reyna was looking at the list. "I'd say Daniel didn't do anything till around March this year. Something must have triggered his request for the exact details of Liam's attack and I don't think he would have waited that long if he'd known about the deaths and heart attack before then. Let's say something triggered his interest in early March and he asks Tara for the details. Then he starts searching online. It takes him until May to call Seattle. He probably called Singapore and Limoges too."

Catherine said, "I'm getting the impression that he was finding out all these things but wasn't telling anybody. He didn't talk to me about it; he didn't say anything to either of you until a few weeks ago when he went to New York."

"But he was definitely moody and withdrawn at work before that," Priya said. "If he had found out something that he thought was dangerous, why didn't he tell somebody? Why didn't he work on getting a product advisory? Why didn't he make sure no one else could get hurt? I mean, he couldn't be sure all the Controllers were safe."

"Maybe he did." Reyna's voice was quiet. "Maybe he told the wrong person."

There was a note in Reyna's voice that made Priya look at her. Reyna's eyes were distant as if she was coming to some sort of realization.

"Reyna, Daniel didn't tell me any of this. He just gave me the figures and code on the Controller II and asked me to look through them."

"I didn't accuse you. But a lot of this seems to revolve around you." Reyna leaned back and ran her hand through her hair. She had a look of distress on her face.

Catherine said, "Rain, you're holding something back. You can't surely still think Priya has something to do with this?"

Reyna said in a low voice, "I don't. But I found something in Daniel's papers that I didn't show you."

She held her hands up at Catherine and Priya's exclamations.

"It was written across one of the pieces of paper. It said Priya was the key."

"So you've been thinking this whole time…!" Priya realized her behavior hadn't helped but she was furious.

She continued in a quieter voice, "Can I see the paper, please."

Reyna took a folded sheet out of the pocket of her jeans. She handed it to Priya who unfolded it and laid it out on the table. She looked back up at Reyna.

"It says 'Priya's key'. Not Priya is key."

Reyna nodded.

"Key is a term used in security protocols. I did my PhD on the subject. I wrote algorithms for God's sake! Did it occur to you that I might actually be innocent of all this, or do you just think all women are guilty?"

Reyna looked guilty herself.

Catherine said in a firm voice, "Enough. I said it before, you two with all that negative energy. Where do we go from here? Do you have the keys or whatever they are from your PhD?"

Priya said, "I never went back to the Research Company. They still have all my findings. Though…" She got up and headed to the door. "I'm a devil for hoarding stuff."

She came down ten minutes later carrying an armful of books and folders that she added to the pile on the table and sat back down. Catherine had put on the kettle and was making coffee. Priya patted away the dust on the first folder and opened it as the kettle screeched its readiness. The touch in her hair startled her, though it was as slight as a feather settling on a quilt. She looked up. Reyna had a strand of cobweb in her hand. There was a look in her eyes that made Priya's heart jump and then hurt. Catherine placed their coffees down and Priya broke the look and gazed back down at the folder waiting for her heart rate to return to normal and the pain to fade.

26 CHAPTER TWENTY-SIX

The folders contained mostly material on the new thesis. The literature search on the original thesis was there along with folders of printouts of Excel sheets. Priya hadn't realized how much material she had hoarded away and never touched since. She had stored the material out of sight in the space she had built in the eaves of the room where she painted.

Reyna asked, "I wonder why Daniel gave you the figures on the Controller II in June. I thought that product had been launched and was working fine."

Priya looked up. "I guess, apart from Gerry and perhaps Valerie, I would have been the one who knew the most about the wireless issues. When I started my PhD, I was concentrating on the communications between devices and their programmers. The coding, the frequencies. My original thesis was on the possible vulnerability of implanted devices to radio attacks."

"Original?" Reyna asked.

Priya sighed, "Yes. I picked the area because of my dad's work with Daniel's grandfather. My dad suggested it actually. He must have trumpeted my IT and Science background to your grandfather because he said that it would be very useful if I worked on the software coding for security issues. Your grandfather had patented the alternative source of energy for the pacemaker and Daniel developed that to power his pacemaker. Before that, the security issues were affected by the available battery power. There was always a trade-off between draining the limited resources by using the battery power to implement security. With a different source of power, and the wireless communications between the Controller and the pacemaker, the study of security issues was coming more to the forefront."

Reyna said, "You said, 'original thesis'. What happened, did you change it?"

"Yes. I spent the first year gathering the literature on the area and then I did my second year with Gerry, and Valerie. It was strange; I was only allowed access to a restricted range of data. I would do my calculations and submit them. I worked on bits of controllers and pacemakers. It was hard to work without a sense of the context into which the figures fit. I developed some algorithms based on very specific technical specifications."

Priya leaned back in her chair. She remembered the sense of achievement, of pride at having solved some coding problems that the researchers had obviously been struggling with for some time. She felt the memory of despair but she ignored its knocking.

She said, "Everything started to fall apart, after Valerie, and then it completely blew up when Kathy died. I just sat on the couch for a month. And stared. A real couch vegetable. Until my father arrived. I hadn't even told him how Kathy died. They had never considered it a real relationship because we were two women. They considered us just friends but he knew from my silence that something was seriously wrong. He got very upset on the phone because I was on my own here according to him. So he came to visit. I had to get off the couch to pick him up at Shannon. Anyway, we talked. He talked to the Faculty. He can be very impressive, especially when he's talking about me to other people. I went back to finish the PhD but on a very theoretical basis. I changed my thesis statement to something about the use of IT in developing pacemaker communications, I can't even remember, it bored me so much I was surprised I did enough to get the PhD but I can be very good on auto-pilot."

Catherine and Reyna both started to say something but Priya patted the notepad and spoke before they could.

"I have been trying since then to wipe away some images. I need to go back on auto-pilot if we are going to figure this out."

They paused for a few seconds and then Catherine nodded.

Priya said, "From what we've found, the problems were with the Controller I and the Controller II without the software patch. So the patch is the key. If I had access to the code for the software patch… I only have my notes; I had to leave the copy in the clinic." She paused and looked at the mass of folders. "If Daniel's right and it is my key then…I can look through the algorithms I developed and see what they could have been used for. Maybe the patch was based on my work, the timing would be right."

She saw Reyna check her watch.

Priya asked, "What time is your dinner?"

"They said to meet them around 8.30 at the restaurant. But I'm going to have to take Catherine back home and then come back in so we'll have to leave here at the latest… 6ish."

Priya checked her phone clock. It was just after 5 p.m. and the concert was at 8 p.m. She really didn't want to go; it was more Michael's scene. But he had bought the tickets, and given her the program months ago. And she hadn't seen him since the previous Saturday, hadn't been able to tell him everything that had been happening.

Priya realized that she hadn't told Reyna about Valerie and Kathy. She felt reluctant. Reyna was going to dinner with Gerry and Valerie that evening. If there was something going on between Reyna and Valerie, Priya was not getting involved.

Priya asked, "Have you found out anything from the financials of the Research Company?"

Reyna searched through the box and pulled out a folder. "When I was in Dublin, I got the tax returns of the Company. I also managed to get hold of the tax returns of the three directors."

Reyna held out a list of the board of directors of the Research Company. Dr. Daniel Fairer III was the Chairman, Dr. Gerald Lynch and Dr. Valerie Helion were directors. Valerie was the Company Secretary and Gerry was the Technical Director. There was no mention of Daniel Fairer II.

Reyna went through a set of sheets that showed the investors in the company. Here Daniel Fairer II featured prominently; the bulk of the investment was from him with significantly smaller amounts from the three directors. Priya had not been interested before in company structure or financing and she didn't know whether the amounts detailed were unusual for this type of investment but they were huge amounts to her.

Priya looked through a summary of the accounts that Reyna had written. The licensing of the technology to TechMed Devices was the main source of income for the Research Company. The first tranche appeared in the first quarter of 2003 when the device was launched. Followed by large tranches over the next 3 quarters. After that, there seemed to be annual royalties.

Reyna looked up from her notes. "Something is not adding up. I've written out the financial history of the clinic and the Research Company and something just isn't adding up. Their tax returns show that Gerry and Valerie declared a reasonable income for the first few years. They had a dip in 2006, which I guess is when the replacement of the Controller I with the Controller II happened."

Priya said, "Yes, didn't Valerie say they didn't have a good return because it was offered at a deep discount to make sure the Controller I was replaced? That seems a bit unusual to me."

Reyna nodded. "It would be. The Controller II didn't have to go through the full clinical trials because it was substantially equivalent to the Controller I. But it is still strange that it would be offered at a discount to clinics. So someone had to have made the decision and pushed it through despite the financial consequences. Who makes the decisions? Gerry is more the research man while Valerie deals with the financials. Daniel dealt with the medical side. But it would be the marketing people and the administrators in TechMed that would normally have the power to make that decision."

"So, who owns TechMed?"

Reyna shook her head. "I don't know. I was never involved in dealings with them. Anything related to them was kept under lock and key in my grandfather's study. From what I've studied about the industry, there are two huge players, both with facilities in Galway, and some smaller ones. TechMed Devices seems to have come out of nowhere and set up its manufacturing plant in the States despite the obvious benefits offered by Galway. It is still under private ownership, it never floated on the stock market so getting information on it is going to be difficult. It captured a large share of the global market for that particular class of pacemaker but because it only has that one pacemaker product and the associated controllers, it would not be anywhere near the same scale of the other players."

Priya said, "And it is very dependent on one product then."

Reyna nodded.

Priya continued, "So, if there was a problem with the Controller I and it had to be recalled, that would affect confidence in the pacemaker. As it is, we just know about the two deaths and one heart attack. We think it is the Controller. But it could be the pacemaker too. We are assuming that there have been no incidents after the

Controller II with the software patch was used. But even if the pacemaker turned out to be completely blameless, there would be a huge loss of confidence in it. And considering what the recall of one family of products did to the profits of the leading player despite its huge range of products, if TechMed knew of this problem with the Controller and the potential impact on their only pacemaker product..."

Catherine said, her voice brimming with anger, "That would be the end of TechMed and their millions of dollars. And enough of an incentive to murder my son."

27 CHAPTER TWENTY-SEVEN

Priya decided to go early to Michael's apartment. Reyna and Catherine had left taking the box of financials and they had arranged to come back to Priya's house the next day. Reyna was going to try to find out what she could at the dinner with Gerry and Valerie that night. Priya could not sit, could not study the figures. The thought of Reyna with Valerie kept intruding. Priya had gotten ready automatically and decided as she was leaving to stuff her PhD papers in with the other papers in her briefcase. The car would be locked and closer to her.

It was the last Saturday evening of the Arts Festival and the weekend before the Galway Races, one of the busiest nights of the year in Galway. She could not find a free parking space in town despite driving around the Spanish Arch area for twenty minutes. There were spaces available at the Jury's hotel, which hulked at the end of Quay Street, in its underground car park with its corners that a bicycle would have difficulty navigating. She hated the car park but she had no choice, she knew she was lucky to find a space at all. She left the car there and walked the hundred yards to Michael's apartment building her jacket slung over her shoulder. The main street through Galway, Shop Street, trailed off and became Quay Street, which had become the

Latin Quarter of Galway, a street lined with tourist shops and bars and cafes and restaurants with their maroon and blue and yellow awnings over the stone buildings, the creams and reds of the painted facades. The packed street was starting to empty into the pubs and restaurants.

She turned into the alleyway that ran along Michael's building. She tried the door expecting him to have left it unlatched for her. A little surprised to find it locked, she used her key. The staircase was ancient, its two ends twisted in opposite directions. She felt for the light switch in the relative gloom of the stairwell. The light bulb sprang to life shoving away the shadows and she relaxed. As she turned in the twist of the staircase she saw that Michael's door was closed as well. She was fumbling for the key as she climbed the last few steps. The key turned and she pushed the door open.

It was quiet. She found that strange and she felt reluctant to break the silence. The lights were not on in the apartment but the late evening sun sneaking in through the windows cast its fading light onto the dark wood floors and carried in the sound of laughter from the street below.

She was about to step into the apartment when she saw a shoe sticking out from behind the couch. Which was also strange as Michael was so tidy. But it looked like it had a foot in it. She moved slowly towards the couch and around it. Michael was lying on his back, his eyes open, his lips blue, his hair clumped brown around his face. Her eyes continued to take in impressions; the knife sticking out of his chest, the handle familiar, the stain on his concert shirt. She'd given him that too. Funny, she seemed to have gotten him many things that he wore, or used. Her heart had slowed and she felt every painful thud like a stone dropping into a well, heard her heart beat in the deep well. *So this is what my patients feel, bradycardia, a slow heart rate, am I going to faint?* Another part of her mind was wondering how she could be thinking of such things when Michael lay there. And the smallest part of her mind just screamed his name over and over and over.

And then over the roaring hiss of the screams in her head, her ears suddenly became aware of sounds from the bedroom. Her head turned and her eyes moved, still and sluggish, towards the bedroom. Her body was backing away, closer to the open door of the apartment. A man appeared at the door to Michael's bedroom. He was short and tanned and he was wearing luminous yellow rubber gloves. His expression went from searching to shocked when he saw her standing half-in, half-out of the apartment. But it was only a fleeting expression of surprise. The look in his eyes changed to those of a predator catching its first glimpse of its prey and the searing jolt of adrenaline jump-started her heart and she turned and ran.

Priya seemed to stumble over every narrow step; she registered more than one set of footsteps behind her as she almost fell down the staircase. She unlatched the door feeling the noisy wave of presence behind her and staggered out into the alleyway and ran towards Quay Street slipping into the heaving crowd.

She glanced over her shoulder and thought she saw the top of his head; he was pushing his way through the crowd less than a hundred yards behind. She was at the bottom of Shop Street now, at the clearing where it forked into Quay Street and Mainguard Street. A band of boys was playing Rod Stewart's 'Some Guys Have All The Luck', the drum kit perched on the edge of the pavement, the guitarists treading the cobbles, a thickening of the crowd surrounding them. Priya pushed through and found herself funneled up Shop Street, further away from her car and from the Mill Street Garda Station. As she ran, the strain of the boys' song was drowned out by the wail of a didgeridoo, the busker breathing heavily into the long windpipe.

On bad days, Shop Street was clotted and clogged up, sluggishly spilling its excess into narrower tributary streets. On good days, its flow is fluid, with occasional pools forming around pubs and cafes to enable fueling with coffee or alcohol, or a dip into the minds on sale in its bookshops.

This was not a good day.

Priya fought her way through the crowd, twisting to avoid the jabs of rucksacks wielded on the backs of unseeing tourists, top-heavy and dawdling. She fought the urge to cry, the even stronger urge to push them over. She couldn't ask for help, couldn't risk the slash of a knife in the press of the crowd. Slicing through her, or through anyone who she dragged into this nightmare. She drew in a deep breath, struggling for breath. Her mouth filled with the scent of perfumes, wafting from the people and from the shops mixed with the beer from the pubs, the grease smell of pizzas, fish and chips, and burgers as well as the delicate flavors coming from the finer restaurants.

She reached the top of Shop Street where it flowed out from Eyre Square, the heart of the city. There were still crowds of people but they were more dispersed. She felt the loss of the protection from the crowd and looked behind her again.

The man was disentangling himself from a buggy, its little boy screaming and red, his mother trying to quiet him. Priya started to run towards the tourist information kiosk nestled in the corner of the Square. A large 50-seater tour bus was just pulling out from on the street and she changed direction and jumped through its closing doors landing with a heavy thud on the steps leading up to the driver. He braked in surprise, and then jerked the bus forward again as the horns of the cars behind sounded.

"Are you that eager for the tour, love?" He was trying to keep an eye on the road and didn't seem too put out by her arrival.

She stayed seated on the step and tried to appear eager, tried not croak the words out.

"I'm so sorry, I didn't want to miss it, my last day in your beautiful city, you know."

"Ah sure, just find yourself a seat back there, you can pay me when we stop."

She kept her head down, peering through the glass panes of the door as the bus drove down towards the entrance to Shop Street where she'd last seen her pursuer. He was standing at the corner by the pedestrian posts that blocked Shop Street to traffic, looking up at Eyre Square and then to his left at the road where it continued onto Eglinton Street. She scrambled up realizing that if he looked he would see her crouching at his eye level as the bus passed him. But it was too late, his eyes widened as he caught sight of her just as the bus started its arc around the corner. She saw him read the signage on the bus that proclaimed its destination and many stops in large white lettering on its green shamrock covered exterior. And then he gestured to another man, and yelled something at him. The second man turned and they ran back down Shop Street.

She walked through the seats and found one at the back window. The bus was almost full just about ten seats vacant. There seemed to be a large number of American youths and they looked at her with curiosity as she passed.

The drone of the driver's voice came over the speakers, welcoming them onboard, his practiced spiel provoking the required laughs from the young passengers.

She slumped down in the seat. This was the second dead body in as many weeks. Shock had transformed into chaos in her mind. She would normally turn to Michael at times like these not that there had ever been times exactly like this. This time it was Michael, *her* Michael. She was struggling to see him as not there, as gone.

Priya couldn't understand why she didn't say anything to the driver, to the passengers. Why she didn't scream and cry. She had a sure sense that if she spoke somebody else would get hurt. The coldness of the stare, the sureness of the feet on the stairs behind her, the silent chaos of the chase through the crowded street all weighed in; into a chant in her head that kept her mute. She had never asked for help from anyone but Michael before. *And where had that gotten him?* The voice of guilt was cruel.

Priya sat up with a jerk. She didn't have her jacket. She tried to remember when she had it last. She had gotten out of her car, put her keys in her jacket pocket along with her phone, and then slung the jacket over her shoulder. She remembered getting her keys out of her jacket at the door to Michael's building and using another key at Michael's door. The jacket had been over her arm, the keys in her other hand. She had dropped her jacket beside Michael's body! Her phone was in it. She thought she might have dropped her keys on the stairs or at the door to the alleyway. So if the men went back, they would have her keys and her phone, and her ID. She checked her pockets. She had a twenty-euro note and some coins, a pitiful total of 26 euro and 30 cent.

The bus was heading in the direction of Connemara. She was hoping it would take the road past her house and when it turned in the direction of Barna she got up and walked down to the driver.

"Where's the first stop?" she asked him, waiting for a break in his patter and leaning over his shoulder.

"Just one stop for the moment, Spiddal. You do know this bus doesn't return tonight, right? This crowd are booked into the hotel further on. Do you want to change your mind?" He glanced over his shoulder at her. "Where are you from, love? You sound very Irish to me, though, no offence, you don't look it."

"I might just get off before Barna; I didn't realize it wasn't coming back tonight. How much do I owe you?"

"Listen, we won't fight over it, give me what you can, and we'll say no more."

They were coming up to her house and she was just about to ask him to stop when she saw the car parked on the road a hundred yards after the entrance to her house. It was the same car that had followed her the other evening. This time there were two men in it and as the bus passed the car, she saw them look at bus and then pull their car out behind it.

The bus was heading further into Connemara. *Catherine and Reyna were in Connemara!* Priya knew the general direction; she only recalled the initial part of the journey, somewhere after Spiddal and after the turn to the Aran Island ferries they had turned, she couldn't even remember if it was to the right or the left. She had to get off the bus without being seen by the men in the car behind. Connemara was vast and barren, she could hide in the bog, but only if she got there without their knowledge. If they saw her enter, she would be an easy target in the open landscape.

The bus was approaching Furbo and she made up her mind. She took out the three two euro coins and said to the driver, "Will 6 euro get me to the turn off to the Aran Islands ferry? I'll give you the rest when I can. I know it must be a lot more usually."

"I wouldn't want to drop off a young lady like yourself in a place like that. There's nothing out there. I tell you what. We're stopping at the pub in Spiddal for a meal and a few drinks, how about I drop you off there and you can get me another time."

Priya thanked him, aware that he wanted to ask her more and grateful that he didn't. She went back to her seat and peered through the headrests through the back windows. There was a line of cars behind the bus and in the dimming light of the summer's night, she could see that the dark car had let a few cars pass and was now five cars behind the bus. The car was far enough away that she couldn't see the occupants, but close enough for them to see the bus as its bulk heaved its way along the coastal ribbon road through the changing landscape, lined by gorse and trees, stone and sea to the entrance to windswept boggy depths of Connemara.

∞

Twenty minutes later, the bus stopped, whistling its air out and jiggling itself into a comfortable squat. They were in Spiddal, parked on the side of the road in front of a hotel. The chalkboard outside advertised daily specials of seafood and live music in the pub. She tried to see what was on either side of the hotel but she couldn't see through the kids gathering their belongings. She looked out through the back seat again and saw the car. It was parked on the other side of the road. She decided to follow the crowd into the pub and then figure out a way to get out without the men seeing her.

She hid in the bottleneck of people at the door to the bus. It squeezed and sprayed them out onto the street and into the hotel. The noise in the pub was deafening even from the lobby of the hotel. The band was playing traditional Irish music that battled for a place beside the loud conversations. The smell of sweat was a solid wall and she closed her eyes and allowed the crowd to carry her into the warmth of the bar, their American accents creating a memory of Reyna's voice.

Priya looked around the pub. She couldn't see the far wall through the crush of people. There was a sign for the beer garden over the heads of the crowd and it pointed to a way out. She looked back at the front door to the hotel. The two men had not followed her in. She wondered how long they would wait. She needed to get out through the back door before they realized there was one. She didn't know if they were locals, whether they would know about the beer garden, nothing at the front of the hotel gave a hint. She started pushing her way through the mill of bodies. She felt as vulnerable in the crowd, the thought of a knife thrust into her, her body kept upright by the others around her. The panic was tightening her throat, making it difficult to breath and she gasped in the warm air when she broke through on the other side of the room.

The cold air outside was even more welcome. The beer garden was deserted, its garden furniture tables with their attached benches lonely in the early evening breeze. Not completely deserted, she realized with a fright. There was one occupant. He sat by himself at the table closest to the exit from the beer garden to the side street. He was wearing a peaked cap and his navy t-shirt stretched tight over a large belly. His nose was bulbous and red but his eyes were clear and he looked up from his sandwich to peer at her with curiosity as she stumbled through the door.

She tried to get her bearings. She was at the back of the hotel she thought and a side alley led in the direction of the front of the hotel, back to the main street. There was no way out without placing herself in the sights of the men in the car. She walked towards the exit, a break in the waist-high wall that ran around the stone beer garden, meaning to check down the side street and see if there was a slim chance that she could sneak out undetected.

"Evening." His voice was deep, his accent so strong that she struggled even with the simple word.

She could see the small holes in his baggy trousers and the patch of grey hair on his belly that showed where the T-shirt had given up its effort to cover the expanse. He smiled and every line in his face stood to attention pushing back the folds of stubble-roughened skin. He took off his cap and wiped at the bald red patch that appeared covered lightly with wisps of grey.

"Hi. Good evening." *Wow, she was able to be polite, now.* Her eyes were searching the surroundings, a trapped animal seeking escape.

"Sit, sit…" He gestured to the bench attached to the other side of the table.

She sat in a daze.

Michael was dead, she was being chased by two…killers, and she was sitting with the stereotype of a Connemara man shooting the breeze. This could only happen to her.

The man was looking at her in the way that she was used to from most old Irish men, a mixture of appreciation and curiosity.

"You are not from around here. Where are you from?"

She was used to this too. She wanted to say Galway but decided on the shorter route.

"India, originally."

"Ah… I hear that's a nice place, that. You must find it very cold here."

"I've been here a long time. A very long time, you get used to it."

She looked at the cars parked in the small gravel area behind where they were sitting. There was a high wall surrounding the area, she tried to judge if she could clamber over the wall. She turned back to him.

She said, "Where are you from?" *Stupid question, Priya, it was obvious.*

"Down Connemara. I've a farm there. In the middle of cutting the bog." He pointed to a lime green van parked at the side of the gravel area. It had a trailer attached covered with a blue tarpaulin that was lumpy and she assumed packed with a load of cut turf. She looked back at him and saw that he wasn't as old as she'd originally thought maybe late sixties.

"A bit of sandwich?" He was holding it out to her.

She shook her head.

He took a swallow of his Guinness and held up the pint to her. "Do you want a drink? Do you drink Guinness?"

She shook her head again and smiled with difficulty.

He said, "I come and have one or two of these on an evening. Gets me away from the wife and kids, all six of them still at home. I keep Connemara ponies you know. Can't get the same price now, it's all the Swedish buying them now."

She couldn't do this. He was nice but this was crazy. She needed to find a way out. She got up and he held out his hand.

He said, "Powli. My name."

That didn't sound like any name she knew and she didn't even know if she'd heard it right, or anything he'd said that didn't involve gestures. She didn't want to tell him hers. She shook his hand and smiled at him, and heard him say as she walked off the stone of the beer garden, "Lovely girl."

The side street was rough and darker than the back of the hotel. She saw the cars passing on the main street. The street opened onto the road a few yards up from the entrance of the hotel. She risked a look out sliding just the side of her face out from behind the bulk of the building.

The car was there. But there was only one man in it. And he would see her if she left the side street.

Priya panicked. She looked back down the side of the hotel. How long before the other man discovered the beer garden? She looked at the van and trailer. She checked whether Powli could see from his perch and decided he couldn't. She didn't have time to find a better way out of here. She ran over to the trailer as quietly as she could, worked up one end of the tarpaulin and slipped into the dark crevice. She knew he would be driving back into Connemara, she just hoped he was at least going in the general direction of Catherine's house.

The tarpaulin weighed heavy on her, damp and hot in the cave of sharp edges. She could not see or hear now. But she would not think. Just strained to listen. Then she heard the rise and fall of music as the door to the garden opened and shut. And she heard and understood despite his thick accent.

"Sure, the little Indian girl. Are you her boyfriend then?"

The questioner must have nodded assent and Powli continued,

"Lovely girl, lovely. We had a nice little chat. Then she headed back into the bar, didn't you see her? Must be very busy in there. Good band, isn't it? One of my cousins is on the bodhran. What do you think of them?"

There was silence, the music, and silence again. Then Priya heard him again,

"If that's her boyfriend I'll eat my cap."

28 CHAPTER TWENTY-EIGHT

She estimated that she had been lying there for two hours. It felt longer because of the space for thoughts. On a few occasions, she heard people come out and she smelt the cigarette smoke. Powli started up conversations with all the smokers and a waiter brought him out another Guinness. So he had drunk two pints that she knew of, and was going to be driving her and a trailer-load of turf down the narrow bog roads in the coming dark. She didn't care. Her usual concern for the letter of the law seemed useless right now.

She took stock. The men were probably sitting out front in the car. She was finding it hard to figure out what a killer would do. Would they have given up when they didn't find her in the bar? She had no phone. If she could get to Catherine's house. She concentrated on that thought. *Would they have found Michael?* She pushed all thoughts of his body out of her mind, lying there, broken.

She felt the movement of the van as the door slammed. The engine was loud even filtered through the tarpaulin. The edges of the cut turf jabbed into her as the trailer went over the curb and bumped onto the main road. She needed to see whether the men were still there but she was lying with her head near the van. She didn't know whether it was dark enough outside her cocoon to risk moving. She stayed as still as possible, trying to move with the swaying of the trailer. She needed to work out the distance, the time it would take the van to reach the turn she remembered Reyna taking. If Powli kept driving straight, she would have to jump. *And then what? Walk to Catherine's?* She felt she could find the house, they hadn't made many turns, the road had just wound its way and though she had been lost in thought and talk for a part of the trip, her eyes had taken in the beauty, and the route.

She maneuvered her way around to face out the back of the trailer, inch by inch, holding in her breath as though the smallest dimension would make a difference. When she was positioned right, she nudged the edge of the tarpaulin and saw that the dusk that she needed was moving in. There were no car headlights in view.

They were reaching the area where Reyna had turned right onto a narrower road through the bog. Priya moved closer to the edge of the trailer praying that Powli would turn right as well. But he passed the turn and she hesitated for a second and then launched herself off the back of the low trailer aiming for the grass verge and ditch beside it. She landed with the upper half of her body on the grass and her legs scraping the tarmac. She felt the pain and heat through her trousers but stopped the cry that tried to escape. She rolled into the ditch and lay quiet, listening through her gasps. The sound of the van's engine lessened as it continued on its way, without a pause.

Her legs hurt but she needed to get off this road and onto the one through the bog, the road that led to Catherine's house. She staggered up the gravel track that led up a hill. At the top, she could see the stretch of the way ahead but the curve around the hill hid the road on which she had come. The track was edged by fields of bog, part dug up, part intact. She stumbled on the stones, the clicking of her shoes loud in the boggy silence.

She was halfway down the track when she heard the noise. She looked back but saw nothing. Then she saw two diffuse shafts of light winking between the hills. She ran.

She knew would be an easy target in the open and she searched the fields on either side for somewhere to hide. She made her decision and scrambled off the track and into the darkness of the bog.

The earth was torn like a dog's chewed up plaything. She was lying in the earth cut of bog, bricks of turf lying chunky and black beside her.

She quietened her breathing and listened. Her head lay against the base of the tunnel, the days' sun-baked heat still retained to seep out into her skin. The dense earthy smell crept into her nostrils. She felt the quiver of her pulse in her cheek and then the tremble of weight on the stone-chipped track. The clicking of wheels on gravel cut through the night air.

Priya felt tears trickle down from her eyes and drop to the black earth silent as pebbles in a raging current. The car had stopped, the thunk of its door shutting preceded the light footfall, shifting weight on an uneven stony ground.

As the footsteps grew closer Priya realized with horror that the moonlight was bouncing off her white shirt, glowing like a firefly in the deep blue night. She was possibly more visible to the occupants of the car than if it had been broad daylight. She tried to shrink further into the ground. Then the anger that had been building in her from the moment she saw Michael lying on the floor struck her hard. She felt around, her hands grasping and releasing crumbling turf, until her fingers gripped something that didn't disintegrate. She felt the edges of a solid object, it was shaped like an axe head, it was blunt but it was something, something solid.

The footsteps had stopped at her hole in the ground and she raised her head and then her torso. She gripped the axe head feeling the blunt edges dig into her palm.

The tall shadow figure was silhouetted by the lights of the car behind. Priya used her arms to launch herself off the ground and towards the legs. Her shoulder connected with a sharp knee and she heard the exclamation of pain, a surprisingly high-pitched sound that at first she thought might have come from her own crazed mouth. The axe head had fallen loose into the dark soil so she scrabbled for the throat of her pursuer and closed her hands around soft skin and a slim neck.

"Priya?" The accented voice was a woman's struggling to break free, to breathe. A voice Priya recognized. Her hands loosened and she felt strong hands grasp her own and hold them away. Priya rolled off from on top of Reyna and huddled against the sharp edged stacks of turf lining the pit.

Reyna sat up rubbing her throat. Her face was in shadow still cast into a sharp silhouette. The engine of the car whined and then sputtered out, the lights dimming in a faint flicker of movement. The breeze was quiet and couldn't conceal the sound of their breathing. Priya could see in a haze Reyna moving towards her like a zookeeper approaching a wounded lion. She felt the edges of shock nudging her towards nothingness and she battled to keep her mind present, adrenaline leaving its bitter taste in her blood as it ebbed.

She felt Reyna beside her, and then arms around her shoulders gentle but firm guiding her into a circle that cut off the cold of the evening air. Her trembling lengthened into a shaking, jerking, gasping string of words that made no sense to her.

When her words ran out, she felt the grip around her tighten and she sank further, emptied and silent. She didn't know how long they sat there; it felt like hours huddled against the rough edges of hardened earth.

∞

Priya felt Reyna whisper in her ear as the circle of warmth loosened. She felt the cold leak back into her arms and chest as Reyna got up. She acquiesced as Reyna stood her up, as fingers wiped away some of the tears, as she was led to the car that sat quiet its light cutting a weak path through the lightening night.

Reyna helped her into the front seat and Priya felt lost in the seconds it took for Reyna to walk around to the driver's side. The cold feeling of loss continued to numb her; she paid no attention to the route, staring silent out of the window unseeing. The occasional grinding of the automatic transmission punctuated the long drive, the road twisting and rising before settling into a level path darkened by trees bunched at its side.

One solitary light cut through the darkness, brighter than the lights of the car, bright in the darkness of forest that cleared to surround the house on three sides, the fourth side, at the back of the building was pale, no trees blocking the dawning sky. The car bumped up from a pothole and her head tapped off the side glass window. She sat up as Reyna brought the car to a stop at the back of the farmhouse, its white walls glowing pale the windowsills chipped dark where they appeared through the flowerboxes that rested in sleeping colors of red and blue and deep almost black violet.

Reyna got out and walked around the car to open Priya's door. Priya took the outstretched hand and the help to get out of the car. The back door of the house was unlocked and the warmth of the empty kitchen felt like a blanket on her face. The light went on, she was seated at a worn solid pine kitchen table and she heard Reyna opening a few cupboards. Reyna placed two tablets in her palm and helped Priya with the glass of water before finding a bottle of brandy from which she poured out a glass and the smell hit Priya with a memory of Michael and his neatly placed dishtowel. She rushed to the sink and retched but the old thick Belfast sink remained white and clean and mocking her efforts.

Priya leant against the solid ceramic, eyes shut tight against the tears. She felt Reyna hug her gently from behind and then lead her out of the kitchen and through a draughty hallway. They passed an open door that held the remnant smell and heat of a turf fire and then entered the small room with the bed covered in its knobbly white bedspread. Reyna pulled back the covers and Priya crawled into the space beneath closing her eyes and letting the cloth swaddle her as the covers were laid back over her.

Priya heard the scraping of a chair being pulled up and the creak as Reyna settled into it. She felt the light weight of a hand resting on the fabric covering her shoulder and then the blackness swept in and she felt nothing.

29 CHAPTER TWENTY-NINE

Sunday, July 24, 2011

Did it matter that it was a woman he would be killing? Did it matter whether she was attractive, charismatic, kind?

The diplomat swam laps of the pool, his arms pumping the questions into the water. There were a multitude of women like her in his country who would suffer as much as dying, as would the men, and the children.

He hoped the man was in control. He had 4 days before the device arrived. He couldn't practice with the real thing. That was one of the risks he would take. That it would all work out on the day.

They had 8 days.

30 CHAPTER THIRTY

Sunday, July 24, 2011

In her dream, she was sitting on the boulder by the river watching the water flow at her feet and the traffic overhead. She turned and Kathy was beside her, sitting on the rock. They watched the bodies float by, nameless, smooth movement then jagged as they bumped off the tree trunks resting on the riverbed. Kathy got up; she pushed Priya's hand away and walked into the river until she disappeared. Priya was in the bog pit, lying face up to the midnight blue sky. She was aware of lying on something, something warm. She felt under her with her hand but she knew even before she touched the arms and chests and legs. She was screaming as she woke, flailing at the covers, clawing at the edge of the pit, seeing even as she climbed out of the dream, the faces beneath her.

She was still struggling as Reyna pulled back the cover, freeing Priya's arms. Reyna was saying her name. She heard Catherine too. She opened her eyes and the daylight hurt. She closed them again, squeezed tight, kept them closed. She curled up into a fetal position. Her mouth felt thick and dry.

"Here, take some of this." Priya heard Catherine say. She felt Reyna take her hand. She felt the cold of glass pressed against her other hand. She opened her eyes. Reyna was sitting on the bed beside her. She looked ragged, the sharp lines of her face softened with fatigue. Catherine was standing beside the bed holding a glass of cherry colored liquid to Priya's hand.

"Go on, my dear, I put in a mixture of things that are good for shock." Catherine said.

Priya grasped the glass and took a swallow; it tasted of cherries with a startling aftertaste of bitter. She grimaced but drank all of it.

Catherine sank into the chair beside the bed. Priya closed her eyes again and the three women stayed in silence for a few minutes. Then, Catherine got up.

Priya said, "I'm sorry I came here. Now I've put you both at risk."

"You did the right thing. I tried ringing the Cop station last night after you'd gone to sleep but I couldn't even get through," Reyna said.

"Well, I for one am glad you didn't get through," Catherine said, "Not after what's been on the news."

Priya looked from one to the other. Reyna was silent. Catherine smoothed back a strand of hair that fell across Priya's forehead.

"Come in to the kitchen when you're ready." Catherine gestured at Reyna to follow her then turned and left the room.

Reyna squeezed and released Priya's hand. She got up and smiled at Priya before leaving the room.

∞

Priya washed her face, but was unable to look at it in the mirror. She rinsed her mouth out with the mouthwash but the bitter taste remained. Someone had left clothes neatly folded on a chair in the bathroom. They must have been Catherine's jeans, they fit her loosely and she didn't have to roll up the legs. The navy sweatshirt had California Berkeley emblazoned across the chest, the memory of another college sweatshirt swamped her, and she sank onto the floor clutching it to her. She muffled the sobs in the folds of fabric as she lay on the cold tiles. She heard a knock and a quiet voice asking if she was okay and Priya said she was fine as she dragged herself up the sink. She washed her face again and left the bathroom a few minutes later.

Catherine and Reyna were sitting at the table when Priya joined them in the kitchen. She gratefully accepted the cup as she sat down at the table, the aroma of coffee strong in the air, diluted by the waft of breeze through the open patio door. The radio was on and the voices squabbled over the evils of the European troika that had taken over the running of Ireland.

Catherine said in a gentle voice, "It was on the morning bulletin on Galway Bay FM. They found the body yesterday evening and named him as Michael Walsh." She paused as Priya flinched then continued, "Priya, they have released your name as a person of interest. They are saying that witnesses saw you running from the building."

"Did they say anything about the men?"

"No."

"How would anyone know who I was?"

And then she remembered,

"My jacket, I didn't have it when I ran. They must have found it."

She jerked her head up,

"Are they looking for me because they think I killed him?"

Reyna said, "They haven't come out and said it. The news report was vague but they said the police were searching for you for questioning. We first heard it on the 10 o'clock bulletin. Catherine has set up the TV but it is difficult to get any channels up here, and she hasn't got cable. Just the Irish language station coming through. You don't speak Irish by any chance, do you?"

Priya shook her head. "The few words I have wouldn't get me anywhere."

Reyna said, "We're going to watch it anyway and see if anything comes up on the lunchtime news. And we'll see if the noon bulletin on the radio has any more information." She looked at her watch and got up to turn up the volume on the radio. "It's almost noon."

Priya felt a wave of panic. The voices on the radio were now arguing about mortgage debt forgiveness. Her heart jumped when the familiar jingle played to announce the start of the news bulletin. And sank as the newsreader spat out the juicy details of a murder in Galway and the search for an Irish woman of Indian origin who had been a friend of the murdered man and had also worked with the recently deceased American doctor who had brought investment, jobs, and prestige to Galway through his cutting-edge involvement in the medical devices industry. The woman bemoaned the lack of detail in this breaking news story but hinted at more to come from unnamed sources. She ended the piece by mentioning that Dr. Priya Joseph had recently lost her mother and was known to the Gardai prior to this murder.

"They're making it sound like I'm some crazy woman who the Gardai have known about for a while!"

Catherine was looking worried. She nodded and sighed. "It's believable. If I hadn't met you, I would probably have thought... With all that has happened to you in the last few years. It's just going to get worse when they find out about the other things. And they're going to find out, they're going to dig and what they find is going to add to the picture of a woman unbalanced by grief."

"You two don't think I killed Michael, do you?" Priya's voice was rising with an edge of panic.

"Of course not. And we all know now this isn't a coincidence nor was Daniel's death an accident." Reyna's voice was firm. Catherine nodded.

Priya said, her voice barely audible, "Why did they not just kill me? Why Michael?"

Reyna said, "I don't know." She paused, her forehead crinkling. "But if the police are looking for you and you're on the run, then you're not trying to dig up any more on Daniel's death." She sat back and rubbed her forehead. "It would never pass as a coincidence if you died so soon after Daniel. But, if you were pushed over the edge and…" She broke off and paused for a moment.

Reyna continued, "No one would have been suspicious about Daniel's death because it seemed like a natural death. When I got his text, I would have just gone back to Catherine's and then contacted him the next day. If we hadn't ended up back at his place that night, I would have found him on the Saturday probably. I wouldn't have thought there was anything more to it than a heart attack. It was the fact that we went there that night, that I left you there and I thought you and he had been together, that made me suspicious. Even after that, when we got the package he sent. The things we found out since, it all comes back to him dying of a heart attack, which is throwing us off."

Catherine asked, "We're saying again that someone killed him and made it look like a heart attack? Is that even possible?"

Reyna smacked her palm on the table. "I know it sounds crazy."

The sound jolted Priya. She clenched her fists. "And meanwhile those bastards get away with it?"

Reyna asked Catherine, "Does anyone know that you live here?"

"No. I don't think so. Daniel never said it to anyone as far as I know, he probably just mentioned Connemara in general, I'd say."

Reyna turned to Priya. "Ok, I would say they don't know where you are at the moment. Neither the police nor the men who killed Michael. I don't know how long it will take them to work it out. But we can't sit around while they do that."

Priya said, "You are both going to be in trouble, and in danger. They are going to work it out. The bus driver would remember me; the guy at the pub will definitely remember me. They'll put it together, that Catherine, and you, live in Connemara."

Catherine shook her head. "They'll look for Catherine Fairer if they do go down that line. The house will still be under the name Leo Turner."

Reyna cut in. "We need to be fast. We have to work out why somebody would be willing to kill two people and destroy another. What in all the things we looked through? We need to finish going through the stuff. We're just not seeing something."

The female voice on the radio was now droning out the death notices for the Galway area. *Would they add Michael's name?* Reyna got up from the table and snapped off the radio.

Priya felt the guilt punch in her solar plexus. *What had she missed?* And then she remembered something else and slumped further down in the chair.

"I left the papers in my car. All the stuff Daniel sent and the notes I made. And the Excel sheets from my PhD."

"Where is your car?" Reyna's voice was patient.

"I left it in the Jury's car park. It's close to Michael's apartment. I went straight from work on... yesterday." She couldn't even remember what day of the week it was. Saturday. No, the concert was on Saturday. So Sunday.

Reyna got up.

Catherine said, "I'm coming with you."

Reyna shook her head. "We can't leave Priya here alone and we can't take her in with us."

"And you will take much longer to find the place. Besides, do you know how to get into a locked car?" She turned to Priya. "I presume you locked it, and the keys were in your jacket." Priya nodded but was too tired to correct her about the keys. They had fallen somewhere. Catherine continued to Reyna, "Also, your rental car is too obvious. We'll need to take my car, and it is stick shift."

"And you know how to get into a locked car?"

"Yes."

Catherine thought for a moment and then said, "We'll have to park in the little alley on the other side and I'll get to Priya's car and open it. I'll only have few minutes because the alarm will go off. Get the papers and get back to the car. Nobody is going to look twice at an old lady." Catherine smiled at their expressions. "I'll dress like one."

Reyna looked at Priya.

Priya said, "She's right."

She looked out at the patio. A brown speckled bird loitering at the far end hopped towards the door, stopped, and cocked its head. It flew straight up into the air bursting into a harsh birdsong as it rose.

Priya said, "Leave me the financials you were looking through. If that's ok?"

Reyna nodded. "Maybe you'll see something I couldn't." She looked out at the track leading through the forest at the back of the house. "You should stay upstairs. You'd be able to hear better." She looked back at Priya and hesitated. "Maybe, we could put you in the back seat and you could crouch down when we're in town?"

Priya shook her head. "Too risky. For all of us. I'll stay alert. You should too."

∞

The sound of birds singing and squawking occasionally broke through, sometimes from the forest, and sometimes from the patio. She sat in a chair by the window in the bedroom upstairs. The one with Reyna's things in it. Files covered the bed.

Priya tried to concentrate on the financial details Reyna had collected from the Research Company. Her eyes wandered every few minutes and she stared at the tops of the trees bending in the drizzle that moved in waves over them, at the potholes in the track twisting through, at the crows that perched on the bows of the telephone wire strung from post to post.

Reyna and Catherine had been gone for thirty minutes. They had driven off in Catherine's station wagon that grumbled out of the galvanized steel barn as if woken from a long nap. The worry was evident on both their faces despite Priya's repeated assurances that she would be fine. Priya had refused any thoughts though they tried to force their way in through the fog. She had locked all the doors and climbed the stairs, her steps heavy. She felt the dregs of whatever was in the tablets Reyna had given her but she was calm. She thought that was probably the effects of what Catherine had mixed in the glass for her.

Priya looked through the papers stacked in boxes beside Reyna's bed.

The sudden silence outside attracted her attention. The birds had found a reason to stop their noise. She opened the window and listened, willing her heart to slow and the blood to clear from her head, trying to tune in under the absence of natural sounds. She heard the vibration before the noise of the engine and before she saw the movement between the trees. It was about 500 yards away. The slightest of sounds and the slightest of motions but it was enough. The car was crawling. She rapidly calculated the distance the car would need to cover before it would emerge from the shaded entry to the clearing and reach the back of the house. Just enough time to get out the front and into the forest below the front of the house. She assumed it wasn't the Gardai; they wouldn't be creeping around if they had tracked her down. She was not going to sit and wait for the other possibility to break down the door.

She raced out of the bedroom and down the stairs trying not to let her momentum push her into a fall. Her shoes flapped off the flagstones in the hall echoing her rapid breaths. The large iron key was in the front door and her fingers tangled as she turned it in the lock but it opened smoothly on her second attempt. The rain was now heavier than a drizzle. She ran to the edge of the clearing where the cream stones stopped and the ground dipped down into the trees. The stones had shifted under her feet but they were steady compared to the wet grass and bushes on the slope. She grabbed on to the rough branches hanging from the bushes as she slid into the forest.

She could not see the sky above her, the trees crowded, fighting against the light shining through. The ground was a yellow green mush of leaves, her feet slipped and she fell as she stopped to listen. The forest was still and damp and dark, like the inside of a thermos flask of day old tea. Rain droplets clung to leaves then hurtled down onto her face.

All she could see around her were trees. Lines and lines of trees, their trunks bare and smooth, lifeless and slippery. She heard rustling, then silence. She heard a drumming and realized it was her heart thumping. She fought past the fear and scanned the surroundings for a hiding place.

Then she noticed a cave, formed by the roots of a large tree twisted into the air and then sweeping down to create a dark empty space. She looked around at the other trees. The larger ones she could see had the same arrangement of roots but there were no spaces beneath them. This cave was only visible because of the angle at which she had fallen.

She heard the crunch of shoes on the stones behind her and made up her mind. As quietly as she could she crept into the moss-lined darkness beneath the thick roots. The shoes had stopped at the slope into the forest and the wearer seemed to be standing still, listening as she was. She wondered if he could also hear the shadows cry from the rooted lairs. The water smelt of mould and mist as it ran back out of her nostrils.

In the distance she could hear nothing. Just forest, miles of it. The trees stood lonely in it, in the loneliness of the crowd. She tried to sink below the leaves. Into the soil. She tried to slow her heartbeat, to quiet her breathing. The darkness was suffocating but welcome.

Footsteps approached and she guessed there was a second person joining the first. The tread was heavier, firmer. She had only made it to the edge of the forest and was lying a few yards from the track. She prayed they would assume she'd go further into the forest. She had gambled on that.

She wanted to see their faces. For the first time in her life, she wished she had a weapon. Something she could use to smash those people, no, they were not people, those monsters into the ground. And she would stand over them screaming her rage into every blow. But it was Michael's voice in her ear, calming her, urging her preservation. He had never believed in revenge, he'd always felt the avenger lost more in the process. She wondered if he'd changed his mind.

"No-one in the house. What do you think?"

The accent was Irish but she couldn't pinpoint from where in Ireland. She knew she would recognize the extreme accents like the ones from Cork or Donegal and then she realized, it sounded like the people around her, from the West of Ireland, like her accent.

"We have about two hours. If she's here, they won't leave her for too long. We need to be gone by..." He paused. "2 p.m. at the latest. That's an hour and a bit."

This accent was American. She didn't know anything about American accents, even from which coast. It wasn't like Reyna or Catherine's accents. But it was the smoothness of his speech that terrified her, the confidence, even arrogance.

The American continued, "Search in there. Until 1.45. I'll be in the house."

The crunch of footsteps diminished as he walked away.

"Search in there. Meet me here. Yessir. Stay nice and dry, why don't ya?"

The grumbling was low but she heard the words and the giggle as the second man mimicked the American accent. He wasn't a good mimic and it came out flat. He was passing the tree under whose sprawling roots she lay and she pushed her soaked body further into the ground. She prayed again, that he wouldn't look under the roots of her tree and that there were no other caves visible under the trees to give him the idea. He was moving fast, probably scanning the ground level and between the trees. His passage was fitful; he paused often as he crackled through the trees, occasionally grunting probably from a low-lying branch. But he was moving away, in the direction of the lake.

Priya figured from what the American had said they needed to get out before Reyna and Catherine got back. So the two women were not at risk from him. Which meant if she could just remain unseen for the next hour or so, the men would have no choice but to leave. She thought this time they might kill her. Strange how she didn't want to die now, considering the long nights over the last few years when she had.

As she lay there, the cold seeping into her heart, the reasons to live came trickling. Reyna's face smiling at her as they sat on a timeless rock and watched a timeless river flow by. Priya's futile well-buried dreams of a family, and belonging. But most of all, the surfacing desperate wish to hold her father's hand and say that she was sorry. To convince him of her regret and shame. To make him believe that she hadn't meant what she'd screamed at him in her helpless rage beside her breathless mother.

That he had killed her mother.

Like his eyes, that died twice in the two seconds that circled the space of a minute. The one second it took to nod at a nurse because he could not speak the words, to permit her to switch off the life of his everyday partner of forty-six years, followed by the 60 seconds of rasping, grasping breaths that withered into silence, followed by the one second in which his only daughter turned away from the silence and screamed his guilt.

Then the minutes and hours and days and months of seconds in which he and she flailed uselessly lost without their oars, drowning in tears yet too guilty to cry.

Yes. She wanted to live. If only to see if life could live in their eyes again.

31 CHAPTER THIRTY-ONE

The footsteps were running and the noise startled Priya out of the trance into which she had crept. The noise stopped.

"Priya!"

The questioning voice was Reyna's and fear filled it. Priya's heart jumped at the sound. She heard Catherine's voice too, calling her name, calmer but with an edge of anxiety, and Priya realized time had passed and the men had left.

Priya crawled out of her haven. The rain had dried out and the sun broke through the tops of the trees in bright silver shards that hung in the air and lost their intensity by the time they reached the forest floor. The sweatshirt was damp and heavy with mud and the moss crumbled off as she swiped her jeans.

"Priya?"

Reyna's voice was reaching into panic. Priya moved as fast as she could through the undergrowth and blinked in the sunshine at the bottom of the slope up to the clearing where the women stood. She tried to speak but her voice failed her. She raised her arms and Reyna saw her and rushed over to the edge. Reyna slid down the short distance, grabbed Priya, and hugged her, tight, close.

"What happened? When you weren't in the house, I thought…" Reyna's voice was shaking.

Priya raised her head, saw, over Reyna's shoulder, Catherine sink onto the edge of the slope, and sit there with a look of relief in her eyes.

Priya stayed in Reyna's arms. She related what had happened. She felt Reyna's arms tighten slightly when Priya described the American, at least the impression of him she had gotten from her hiding place.

Priya said, "They didn't want to be here when you got back. They're looking for me. I don't know if they knew I was here or if they were just searching in case."

"Let's go back into the house." Catherine's voice had regained its strength. Reyna looked as if she didn't trust herself to speak. She took Priya's hand but it was Priya who helped her up the slope and into the house.

∞

Priya took a shower and joined them in the living room. Catherine had lit a fire and the flames were dancing, the occasional spark lighting and fading as a fiber of turf burnt bright then burnt out. Reyna was standing looking out of the window; Catherine was sitting on the couch. The cold had eaten its way into Priya and she tried to warm herself by the fireplace, holding her palms out to the heat for a few seconds. When she turned from the fire, Catherine patted the couch beside her. There was a cup of tea steaming on the little table beside the couch.

Michael handing her a coffee like he had done so many times. The knife from his kitchen sticking out of his chest.

Priya's legs buckled and she sank onto the couch.

"Drink up, get some warmth into you." Catherine said.

Reyna turned from the window. She looked startled out of her thoughts and her eyes were lost in worry. She smiled when she saw Priya, but then seemed to draw a veil over her eyes, the usual control back in place.

"The phone is not working. Don't know if they cut the line or it's just a temporary glitch. Seems too much of a coincidence though." Reyna's voice had also regained its control.

Priya swallowed a gulp of tea and welcomed the heat that burned her throat and stomach. Her voice was shaky when she spoke.

"I get the feeling that they are not going to come back while you two are here. The American guy went back to the house instead of looking for me with the other guy. We need to see if anything is missing."

Reyna shook her head.

"I don't think anything is gone. The papers from the Research Company are all spread out on my bed but there seems to be the same amount. I can't be sure of course. Not yet. And your papers and Daniel's were with us."

Priya said, "So, they were looking for the stuff Daniel sent us."

"Why not your stuff?"

"Because they are probably the ones who searched my house and they would have seen the papers on the Controller Mark II, which they left behind. They also left the financials today. That leaves Daniel's envelope." She paused. "Actually, the only other things are the Excel sheets from my original PhD."

Priya put down the cup of tea and got up.

She said, "Have you got them? We need to figure out what the hell they are looking for?"

Catherine asked, "Priya, are you sure you're okay to do this right now?" Reyna was already at the door and she disappeared into the kitchen, appearing a moment later with Priya's tightly stuffed briefcase.

Priya said, "Right now it feels like I'm never going to be okay to do anything again. But I'm going to find out what those bastards think is worth killing Michael for."

Reyna said, "And Daniel."

Priya sat down on the floor and pulled out the folders with her PhD work. She took out the printouts. One set of Excel sheets had the voltage readings and the other had the battery readings. She had obviously transcribed these figures while she was at the research company. She didn't remember. She grabbed a pen and starting highlighting every voltage or battery reading that was low.

Michael's foot encased in his brown shoe, its laces undone, sticking out from behind the couch.

Priya caught her breath as the image flashed into her head. She pushed it away and tried to concentrate.

Three hours passed in a daze of figures. Priya had drawn out a graphical representation of the figures she had questioned before. Reyna had dragged down the box of financials and joined her on the floor. She was studying every sheet of paper, every brochure, every file contained in it and was and was scribbling notes in an A4 notepad.

They could hear Catherine in the kitchen and she came in every few minutes to check if they had found anything. The radio was on in the kitchen and they had put on the small television in the living room. There were no news programs on the TV but it was coming up to 6 p.m. and Priya knew that most Irish stations showed the news at that time. Catherine came in and sat on the couch.

The reception was terrible and they had to switch off the sound but they all gasped when the picture of Priya flashed onto the screen. It was the picture she had taken nine years before when she'd renewed her driving license. She had just met Kathy and the face that laughed out of the square box looked younger than 27 years even with the white lines of interference. That youthful innocence so pronounced that she had often been carded going into the discos whose age of entry, and age for drinking, was 18. She still looked younger than her 35 years but the last two years had reduced the gap in perception from a decade to a couple.

The footage showed Quay Street, the alleyway leading to Michael's apartment, the activity at the door, a female garda standing at the door, her hands behind her back, the blue peaked cap pointing straight at the crumbling stone wall across the alley. The yellow tape with blue writing stretched across the entrance to the alley, the white van with the stark blue writing, Garda Technical Bureau. The men in their white cotton spacesuits. There were shots of the clinic; but only exterior shots, the clinic lay deserted for the weekend.

"I wonder what the guys at the clinic are thinking. I wonder if they think I went mad and killed Michael. They thought I was with Daniel, well, some of them did. The gossips. The ones I never told I was gay. Now they'll know I'm gay and they'll think that I was fooling around with Daniel for…, God knows what?"

Reyna looked away from the TV and looked at her.

Priya said, "I didn't mean you."

Reyna frowned. She said, "I know, though I was as guilty of that."

Priya sighed. "Okay." She paused then asked, "Why are they targeting me? And not you?"

Reyna said, "They must think that Daniel gave you the information that he actually posted here to the house. He did give you some of the other papers. Who would have known about that?"

"Well, James knew, but that was when I told him after my house was searched. Some people at the clinic thought I had a thing going with Daniel so maybe they thought he had shared information during our pillow talk. Except Tara, she knew there was nothing going between us. And Valerie and Gerry might have known but they also knew Daniel was very security-conscious and any information I was given by the Research Company was restricted to what I needed to know to help with the coding and clinical side."

Reyna started to pace again. She said, "We have got to work it out before they decide to come after you even when we are here. And I can't call off the use of the Controller in every clinic, not physically, and I have to speak to James and Gerry and Valerie. Which I'm going to have to do first thing tomorrow." She pulled her phone out of her pocket and looked at it. "Blasted signal!" She threw the phone on the armchair.

Reyna looked at Priya and said quietly, "I think the safest thing would be to go to the cops. Tell them everything. Get them to protect you while they investigate."

Priya said, "Why would they believe me? They'll probably think I killed Daniel as well as Michael. Surely I would be a prime suspect considering my background. That we were in some kind of abusive relationship that I got my revenge, and then with my mum dying, I went crazy and killed Michael. I mean I *know* I didn't but looking at everything that happened I'm beginning to wonder myself." Priya continued in a quieter voice, "You know, all I did for years was try and remain on the sidelines, private. I didn't want anyone to know anything about me. And now, everything about my life plastered over the news. And in the worst possible way, as a killer, a crazy woman. And I can't even get angry about that because I *feel* crazy now, I *feel* like I could kill."

Catherine turned off the TV. She said, "I've always been a pacifist but if I find out that Daniel was killed…" Her face twisted up and then relaxed and she asked, "We can't hide out here for much longer though. I think you're both right. We need more to protect Priya, more proof. But we also need to make contact with the police. Try to find out what they are thinking. Have you found anything?"

Priya said, "I've highlighted all the dips in voltages and I'm putting them together with the low battery readings."

She sat back and thought.

What would cause the lithium battery in the pacemaker to kick into action?

If the main source of energy dried up.

The main source of energy was the electrical activity around the natural pacemaker. Actually, it was the electrical activity from the heart cells that self-fired. The voltage readings were low from some patients between 2003 and 2006. But those had been blips in the vast sea of readings.

She needed to see the battery readings from the patients who were undergoing the checks when the technicians had died or had a heart attack. If they were low...

She said, "The figures in my Excel sheets didn't have times and dates but the figures Daniel gave me on the Controller II and the ones he sent you on the Controller I do have dates and times. From the figures, it looks like there were more incidents than there should have been. The problem is that there are so many readings. And the battery ones don't show up as low until they go below 95%. But obviously, in some patients the unexpected reduction in electrical activity which would have been used to power the pacemaker led to the utilization of the lithium battery."

She pointed at the sheets of notes on the coding and said, "The algorithms I wrote seem to have been used in the development of the software patch. But I can't be certain because I had to leave the copies in the clinic; I'm just going on my notes. If they were used, it would have been to provide a shield of some sort against stray frequency patterns, as a kind of jamming signal. It makes sense that my algorithms were used, they were obviously needed otherwise I wouldn't have been requested to write them. But the specification I got wasn't clear about the application just the frequencies."

Both Reyna and Catherine looked confused.

Priya said, "I was handed a detailed spec that basically said 'if a frequency pattern emitted within a certain distance by a transmitter is detected then transmit a jamming signal'. That's a real simplification. I wrote the code but it was complicated by the type of signal, the pattern of frequencies and distance. And Gerry kept pushing me to go further and try different things. It was actually quite inspiring." She looked embarrassed for a moment. "For me, anyway. It was a challenge and I guess I thrived on it. Gerry is incredibly smart and had been trained in the States and had all that experience and the fact that he couldn't code that bit and I could, well, it was a sort of validation."

Priya smiled but there was a look of loss in her eyes. She shook her head. "I guess I'm a prime example of the heart screwing up the head. Anyway, I wrote the code and if it was used as a software patch for the Controller II and if the attacks stopped after that, then…" Priya chewed her lip as she thought.

"What?" Reyna leant forward.

Priya spoke slowly as she drew it out on her notepad. "It means that the Controller I and II emitted some kind of stray frequency pattern that caused heart attacks in people on certain occasions. Actually, it caused the attacks in people who were within a certain distance at the time. And the software patch based on my work was applied in 2008 to jam that frequency pattern."

Reyna said, "So, both the patient and the technician were subjected to this frequency thing? Why didn't the patient have a heart attack?"

Priya said, with a note of excitement, "Because they had a pacemaker. So it has to be some kind of damage to the heart and that damage must be able to be circumvented by the pacemaker. The pacemaker keeps the heart rhythm going in the patient while the technician, or Liam, suffers a heart attack brought on by loss of the pacing, by a loss of electrical activity."

Priya was pulling out sheets of paper as she spoke. Her voice was strong, with the occasional tremble of agitation. "That's why Jacintha's battery readings are low now! Her lithium battery is kicking in because she must have no self-firing electrical activity to run the main battery. It must have started being utilized since December, which would correlate with the current reading now. Damn! If we could match up the exact times and dates of the low voltage and battery readings in patients to frequency emissions we could be sure. I'd say the patients who were undergoing their checks at the times when the frequency was emitted are the ones whose readings are low. Looking at the numbers of low readings, the frequency emission happened on rare enough occasions and there are only three incidents, no, four, that we know of since 2003 where it caused heart attacks in technicians or bystanders.. So it doesn't happen in every routine check therefore either it occurs as a very rare and completely random thing or it happens when a specific function is being carried out. And it makes sense that it only affects the person without the pacemaker who is within a certain distance, like John Landon and Liam, really close."

Reyna asked, "Close to the pacemaker or to the Controller?"

Priya sat back, her forehead furrowed, then nodded. "You're right. I assumed it was the Controllers, but it could be the pacemaker."

Catherine asked, "Would the technicians have followed the same procedure? What else is similar between what happened when John and Liam had their attacks?"

Priya found the descriptions of the checks and compared them.

She pointed to a line in Tara's handwritten description. Tara had finished the routine check and just started a programmer test when she had been interrupted. Priya examined the email printout from John Landon. She found the line where it stated that John had commenced the programmer test when the patient had complained of discomfort and John had leaned over her with the wand in his hand and over her chest.

"The programmer test." Reyna and Priya spoke at the same time.

Priya said, "There are a few test routines on the controllers. But they are not used very often, some I've never even used. A stray frequency pattern might have been generated on the very rare occasions that these tests were used. It would explain the rarity of the attacks considering the number of pacemaker checks that are carried out every day in clinics around the world."

The three women were silent for a few minutes. Priya started to gather up the sheaves of paper that she had scattered around her on the floor. The rush of discovery had washed through her and her arms now felt like they were made of lead.

Priya said, "You know that this points to somebody at TechMed Devices or the Research Company. Whatever I may think of Valerie, and I have a deep admiration for Gerry, I can't see them being involved, not knowingly." She shook her head. "They're like Daniel; they worked all their lives to find better ways of helping people. Not killing them."

"People change when money is involved." Reyna's voice was harsh.

Priya said, "Gerry was never motivated by money. I spent a lot of time with him. He had no interest in cars or houses or the trappings. He really did live for his work. And for Valerie." She paused. "Who *did* enjoy the trappings. And she enjoyed playing games with people."

Priya smacked her palm against her forehead. "And someone else… Tara was talking about Aidan being a toy boy. For an older woman who would have a problem with them getting together. Aidan came back from London where he wasn't doing very well at all. That's what Tara said. And she couldn't figure out how he could afford the very expensive car and watch and other stuff. We all assumed Aidan got his job at the clinic because he was Gerry's brother, but what if it was Valerie all along. And Aidan was there that night at Massimo and saw you putting me into your car. He didn't know at the time who you were but he might have told Valerie and she could have put two and two together."

Catherine leant forward on the couch and asked Priya. "Are you sure you're not letting your history with Valerie cloud your judgment?" Her voice was gentle.

Reyna said thoughtfully, "It's possible. Looking at their financials, they made a lot of money and then they seem to have had quite a dip in the last two years. Didn't Gerry say they'd bought at the height of the boom and now they were struggling? They did seem a bit stressed at dinner. I really wanted to see where they lived and get an idea of their lifestyle but Gerry said he had to work late."

Priya suddenly remembered where Reyna had been Saturday evening. And where she had been. The images clamored for her attention again and she closed her eyes and forced them away.

Priya said, "Valerie came on to me just after I solved their coding problem which we think is what prevented further attacks. I was on such a high and she provided such a validation for me. She played me and obviously played Kathy as well. Whatever happened between them drove Kathy to kill herself sending me off the rails and far away from the work I was doing. I can't say for sure she knew what she was doing when this happened. And I don't know if it was deliberate when she flirted with Daniel in front of me the night of my birthday. I thought that her hold on me was gone, after what happened with Kathy and I had not seen Valerie after that till the night of my birthday. I was so disappointed with myself that she could still affect me. I still hadn't dealt with the guilt around Kathy, I had just got news of my mum, I was trying to use drink to wipe out feelings and I'm terrible with alcohol. All added up to one hell of a bad decision that night to try to stop her and Daniel getting together. It wasn't Daniel, I didn't want Valerie, well…I didn't want to want her, a huge part of me hated her but she had this power…" Priya stopped and held her head in her hands.

Reyna said, "Catherine told me what Valerie did with Kathy. Valerie almost pushed you off the edge again when she told you about it, which was just after we asked her about the deaths. And then she gets you suspended, or at least, she may have pushed for it. TechMed stands to lose the most, along with Valerie. Valerie wasn't the one who killed Michael. We know the American man killed Michael and has been looking for you and your PhD papers. They could be linked through TechMed."

Priya swallowed back the image of Michael. And thought of Daniel, lying slumped against the bed, bare-chested.

She whispered, "The way he was lying there with just his trousers on. Like he had been sitting on the bed and when he had his heart attack, he just slid off. So, if someone had been there with him, Daniel was obviously comfortable with the person." Not like Michael. The knife sticking out of his chest. The men had used one of Michael's kitchen knives. To implicate her. No fake heart attacks here.

Fake heart attacks.

The battery readings. The voltage readings. They showed a pattern of failure. Failure of the natural pacemaker in the heart.

Priya had a feeling of horror growing in her mind. She became aware of someone saying her name and she looked up to see Catherine staring at her.

Priya said, "Fake heart attack. Daniel's fake heart attack. What if that stray frequency pattern that killed the technicians could be generated by some thing at will. It would stop his natural pacemaker. And if Daniel had been with a woman that evening like Catherine thought all along, and he was seeing a researcher like he told Reyna and that person was Valerie, and afterwards he's sitting with her, and she uses this thing to kill him..."

32 CHAPTER THIRTY-TWO

They sat in silence for a long time, each trying to put the pieces of the puzzle together in their minds. And whichever way they looked at it, the pieces fit and the answer was Valerie. The darkness outside finally came and found the three women sitting in the trembling light of the fire.

Catherine said, "We need to go to the police with this."

Reyna gestured at the papers. Her hair was loose and scattered around her shoulders from dragging her fingers through. "We have no proof. These are all great theories."

Priya nodded, "And someone could still make a case for me being the one responsible. I mean, we worked it out for Valerie but I was the one who worked with the code, I guess if my code was the basis for this thing, this device that could kill then, if I put my mind to it, I could design it. If I had all the details. And I had been hurt by Daniel and nothing was done. I lost my partner to suicide, my mother just died recently. So I could have designed the thing, killed Daniel, gone crazy and killed Michael. And I ran from both." She looked at the two women and exclaimed, "God! Even *I* think that sounds plausible. Why wouldn't the Guards believe that, over some theory that a well-respected researcher, and she's a doctor too, is in cahoots with a hugely successful medical device manufacturer in the States and could do all those cold and calculating things, for money. I mean no-one knows that side of Valerie, she's very good at games, at hiding what she's really like. How many people have fallen for it?"

Priya looked at Reyna as she asked the last question but Reyna was staring at the fire, a grim look on her face.

Reyna said, "I am going to go in to the Research Company in the morning."

She ignored the protests from Catherine and Priya and continued, "I don't seem to be a target at the moment, and everyone will assume I am as shocked about what happened on Saturday. In fact, I'll encourage that. I'll make them think I think you went off the rails and killed Michael, and that it is all down to you being unstable after Kathy and your mother and then Daniel dying completely pushed you over the edge because you were seeing him as the rumors suggested."

She turned to Priya. "Hopefully I'll be able to find out something that can get you out of the even bigger hole that I'll be digging for you."

Priya said, "I don't care about that. I don't want anything to happen to you."

Priya watched the flames reflected in Reyna's eyes and wished she could stop the world as it hurtled over a cliff.

Catherine got up from the couch and put another load of turf on the fire. She knelt and placed her hand on Reyna's shoulder.

"I don't want to lose you too. I couldn't bear it. You're all I have left."

Reyna hugged her mother.

"You need to stay here with Priya. It wouldn't make sense if you came in with me. It has to be just another day, a normal day. Trust me. All the attention will be focused on Priya. No one is going to know she came here, especially when I go in and pretend I don't even know what happened on Saturday. I have every reason to go in and talk to Valerie; she said she would keep searching. She'll probably come up with some half-baked theory about the deaths of the technicians to put me off. I have to find a way to get some proof though…"

Catherine stayed in the hug. Her silver hair glowed against Reyna's dark sweater. Then she sighed and rubbed Reyna's back and got up.

"I'm going to try and sleep. I'll be awake when you leave in the morning." She gave Priya a tired smile and wandered out of the living room and they heard her slow tread upstairs to her room.

Priya felt a wave of tiredness crash over her. But she couldn't leave the room. And Reyna didn't move either. They sat in the silence without looking at each other. A spark from a loose turf fiber flew out and spiraled to rest on the rug between them. They both reached over to touch out the tiny flame, Priya's fingers landing first. She felt the brief heat of the burning fiber and then the warmth of Reyna's hand on hers. Reyna left her hand there and Priya watched their fingers entwine on the shadow blue rug.

Priya couldn't speak. The fear was overwhelming, the losses of the last three years screaming at her to stop Reyna walking into the lion's den. For her.

Reyna murmured, "I wish I could explain. You deserve to know. But I can't risk losing what I've fought for years to get." She lifted Priya's chin with her fingers and looked into her eyes. "I just need you to know that if I could have given it up, you would be the person I'd have given it up for. I just can't give up. I told you things were complicated. I don't know how long it will take to work it out, but whether I win or lose, I'll come back when it is over. If you will have me."

Priya was confused. "Is it Simone…?" she asked.

Reyna nodded. "She has me where she wants me. Has had me there for years. I can't talk about it; I can't get involved with anyone. If she finds out…"

"Do you still love her?" Priya asked in a shaky voice.

Reyna lowered her face and kissed Priya. Priya let her heart and mind fall into the slow gentle kiss.

33 CHAPTER THIRTY-THREE

Monday, July 25, 2011

She woke up covered in the bedspread. Her eyes and hands took in the empty space beside her where Reyna had slept and Priya felt cold despite the blazing fire. She threw off the cover and scrambled to her feet. There were sounds coming from the kitchen.

Catherine was standing at the sink, gazing out of the window, water running over her hands.

"She didn't wake me. Has she gone?"

Catherine nodded. "About half an hour ago."

Priya sat down at the table. Her limbs felt like they belonged to a stranger, a bigger, heavier person. She checked the clock on the wall; it was 8.15 a.m. Reyna would be at the Fairer Research building at about 9 a.m. depending on the commuter traffic in Galway.

She said her voice sharp with fear, "It was a stupid plan. What were we thinking? Letting her go in on her own."

Catherine said nothing, just turned off the tap and wiped her hands on a dishtowel.

Priya asked, "She took the rental car?"

Catherine nodded.

245

"Can I borrow your car?"

Catherine turned and looked at her. Priya stared back.

"Catherine, I can't let Reyna put herself in danger for me. I agreed with her last night, like you did, but now…" She saw the look in Catherine's eyes and added, "No, I don't want you to come with me. Reyna would never forgive me."

Priya got up. "I'll go to the research building and find Reyna and we'll go together to the guards. I just have to hope that I'm not stopped on the way and that Valerie will be happy enough to let me be taken into custody. It's what she wanted anyway. They must have made sure there's enough evidence to point to me."

Catherine said, "Reyna will be furious with you. And me."

"But she'll be safe."

Priya held out her hand and, after a pause, Catherine took a key ring off the kitchen counter and placed it in Priya's palm. She placed both of her hands against Priya's cheeks and whispered a thank you.

∞

Despite the heavy station wagon she was driving, Priya found the journey over the winding Connemara roads easy compared to the nerve-wracking drive through the traffic in Galway though it was lighter than on a normal working day as many people had time off for the Races. She expected to be stopped at any minute by a white and blue Garda-emblazoned car. Her heart jumped when she saw a Traffic Corps car parked at the side of the road, the blue-uniformed woman writing out a ticket for a trapped driver, her partner watching from the driver's seat, patiently tapping his fingers on the steering wheel. She had a desperate urge to slide down in her seat as she passed the officers, feeling as conscious as she had ever done in Ireland, of her difference, her brown skin in the sea of white. But the woman was engrossed in conversation with her victim who was obviously trying to talk his way out of a ticket and the partner was staring into space.

The area around the clinic was quieter than was usual on a Monday morning, with only a skeleton staff in at work, the rest probably enjoying time off for Race Week. The car park in front of the research building was deserted apart from the rented Mercedes parked in one of the slots reserved for the company staff and one other car. Gerry's Volvo was parked at an angle across one of the slots, not the one with his name on it. Priya had a sudden hope that Valerie wasn't there, but she could have gotten a ride in with Gerry. Priya stared at the two cars and around at the hushed car park. The quiet was only broken by the occasional splash of oars in the river.

Priya crept out of the car and walked into the building as fast as she could without running. Her shoes echoed across the empty lobby. The doors of the lift slid open and the now familiar voice droned its presence. Priya stepped into the small space, her reflected image creeping closer. She hoped whoever was in the building couldn't hear the machinery whispering as the lift ascended the two floors. She thought they might hear the disembodied voice announce her arrival.

The corridor was empty; all the doors leading into the offices and labs were closed except the door to Valerie's office at the end. Despite expecting the voice, her heart jumped when she heard it again. It echoed in her head and she clutched the railing, her hand slipping in sweat and smoothness. She could not see movement in the office and it felt empty even from a distance so she concentrated on the other doors.

The lab in which she had carried out her research was behind the second door and as she gripped the handle and opened the door, she said a silent prayer.

She took in impressions as she scanned the room. The wall of glass behind the counters glared light into the lab. Reyna was sitting upright in a chair in front of the door, her eyes angry. Next to her, was the man Priya had seen at Michael's apartment. This time he wore no yellow gloves but in his right hand was a gun and he pointed it in the direction of Reyna's head. The man stood so that he was not visible to any of the rowers on the river outside the bank of windows. Priya froze. Out of the corner of her eye, she could see Gerry sitting on a stool, bent over equipment laid out on the counter. He was rigid, he hadn't even moved when the door opened.

The man gestured her in with his left hand and Priya walked further into the lab. His eyes were emotionless. The familiar smell of chemicals and cleanliness welcomed her. There was an iron scent in the air and she recognized the smell of blood but she could not see any on Reyna or Gerry. As she moved past the aisle between the freestanding lab counters, she glimpsed a woman, sprawled motionless, a stain of blood leaking onto the crisp white tiles from her blonde head.

The man gestured to Gerry.

"He could do with a hand. And he tells me you're the one who came up with the idea in the first place." He spoke with that same flat confident tone that had terrified her when she was hiding in the hole beneath her tree.

Priya hesitated, confused, and he smiled.

"I know there's no positive reinforcement here, you know, some kind of reward for the brilliant work you're going to do this morning, but maybe you'll both get some weird professional satisfaction. Along with saving your skins. And some pain." He made a jabbing motion with the gun towards Reyna's head and Priya gasped and moved quickly towards Gerry.

"Priya, don't." Reyna's voice was firm but it was cut off with a cry of pain.

Priya turned and clenched her fists as she saw that the man had silenced Reyna by shoving the gun into her mouth. He grinned at Priya's face and nodded towards Gerry.

There were ion study chambers on the counter in front of Gerry. What looked like a handheld controller was hooked up to an oscillometer and a portable keypad. The glow of the readout shone green on his forehead.

Priya sat on the stool beside Gerry. He turned his head and through the grief and fear in his eyes, she saw a subdued madness. Like petrol just thrown on a fire that had been damped down for a long time, licks of flames curling at the edges. She looked behind her and she could see Valerie. The blood moved, a slight but definite movement, which meant she was still alive.

Gerry's hands on the table were shaking.

Priya whispered, "Gerry, you're going to have to pull yourself together. Tell me what's going on."

Gerry glanced at the man and then looked back at Priya.

The man said, from across the room, "Aren't you going to fill her in on what you've accomplished. With her work." He removed the gun from Reyna's mouth and a bead of blood welled up from her upper lip and crept onto her lower lip.

"My work, Gerry? My idea? What is he talking about?" Priya tried to sound completely ignorant, as if she had no idea of what they were working on. She looked again at the equipment on the counter. There was a metal device the size of a matchbox lying against the wall at the back of the counter.

Gerry remained silent, his lips trembled and the man laughed.

"He wasn't so shy when he sold us the idea. Was a good sell actually, had the early stage prototype that he had proved in action; he had the proof of concept for the new device. Everything is set to go. I don't need to convince you of the urgency of my task." He ran a finger along Reyna's lips and smeared the blood into a macabre lipstick. "We have our own little ticking clock here that should be an incentive even if you don't care about my deadlines."

Priya could see the anger clouding Reyna's eyes and before Reyna could say anything, Priya said, keeping her voice as steady as she could, matching his tone,

"I am not going to get any closer to whatever it is you want, and I'm certainly not going to be able to solve any problems if you hurt her again. And I need to do something about Valerie."

Priya moved to Valerie's body. She found a pulse, weak but present. Her hair hid most of the cut on her scalp and the volume of blood was frightening. Priya looked around the room and saw the first aid kit fixed to a bracket in the wall, alongside the emergency defibrillator many of which were now installed in public places around Ireland.

Priya walked over to the first aid kit, ignoring the man, and brought it over to Valerie. Gerry seemed fixed in place, staring down at the blood. Priya used a full roll to bandage Valerie's head. It would hold the bleeding for the moment. She couldn't think of anything else to do for her.

She turned to Gerry.

"I need to know everything. Now."

Gerry rubbed his neck, which was already red. He wasn't wearing a tie and his casual clothes looked like they had been thrown on.

His voice was shaky when he started to speak.

"I used your algorithm to develop something."

He reached over and picked up the matchbox-sized device.

"It works by damaging the natural pacemaker. But it only works at extremely close proximity to the heart. I promised them a device that would work at a distance of 3 feet. And it's almost ready." Gerry shoved the bigger device, the one that looked like a handheld controller, a few inches along on the counter.

His voice had grown stronger with every word and then his shoulders slumped.

"I just can't figure out that one last piece of the code."

Priya stared in puzzlement at the two devices.

She said, "*You* developed something to damage the natural pacemaker? Why?" She felt nauseous.

"Why do you think? I guess I should give you some credit. I had already mostly developed the early version but your research helped me finish it and was crucial in setting me on the longer-range wireless path. You were developing the test scenarios for potential wireless attacks on installed pacemakers but I was able to expand on it to attack the natural pacemaker. It isn't that commercially interesting to attack artificial pacemakers, I mean, what would the target be? Mostly older patients and you'd have to wait around for them to have a pacemaker installed. The first device works at close range to the target so the user doesn't need protection. But with this longer-range one, it will actually be the opposite; anyone without a pacemaker will die. Which, in a way, is a bit of a problem, but one we've been able to solve temporarily."

Priya sank down onto the stool.

Priya turned back to Gerry. "He said you were able to prove the device in action."

Reyna said, "Daniel...?"

Gerry's eyes had been filled with pride as he spoke of his work but now the pride was replaced with pain. He nodded.

Gerry said, "I had to use the close range device." He picked up the smaller device. "The long-range one isn't ready, and I don't have a pacemaker installed anyway." He sighed. "Three wouldn't stop digging, even when I told him his grandfather had sanctioned the development."

"No!" The word came from Reyna.

Priya said, "There is no way that Dr. Fairer would sanction the development of a weapon."

Gerry said, "Three only found out in the last few months about the unfortunate accidents that had occurred with the Controller I. But his grandfather knew as soon as I discovered them but we had already released the Controller II so rather than recalling the Controller I, we made sure that all the Controller I's were returned by offering a hefty discount on the Controller II."

A little more animation crept into Gerry's voice. "The original fault was an aberration, easy enough to fix once we figured out what caused it. But the fault could still theoretically occur with the Controller II so we had to issue the patch, which we developed from your work. But the aberration gave me the idea for the device. And that's really where your algorithm came in. And then when he came along and offered so much money," Gerry shrugged, "well, I needed it. Dr. Fairer couldn't very well say anything about it after he had helped conceal the problems. And he thought he was helping, you know, in the fight."

Reyna shook her head. "You killed Daniel? And grandfather knew?"

"I had no choice with Three. Your grandfather didn't know about it till afterwards. I had to do it. Three wouldn't stop, even when I told him that your grandfather would be destroyed, that we would all be destroyed."

Gerry lowered his voice and whispered to Priya, "Dr. Fairer met him," he gestured with his head to the man, "when he came to collect the plutonium from a decommissioned pacemaker. Supposed to be American government but I don't think what he's doing has anything to do with the war on terror. Seems personal to me."

Priya said, "You were very close with Daniel. And you were able to get close enough to him to use that, that thing." Her eyes widened as the thought came to her. "You're the researcher Daniel had a thing with, not Valerie."

Gerry looked puzzled.

"Me? No. We were friends. Close friends. What do you mean? Valerie?"

Gerry looked at Valerie's prone figure.

"He was a bit agitated to see me that evening. There had been a woman there with him; it was obvious he had been in bed when I arrived." Gerry seemed to be thinking aloud. He shook his head.

"We don't have time for this. They are expecting the device to be ready and working by tomorrow at the latest. It has to be delivered before the 28th."

"Gerry!" Priya felt her voice rise.

The man, who had let them talk, now spoke. "We have had to lose some people to ensure the utmost secrecy. Personally, I don't work this way but we've had to clean up the mess your friend here created when he left his area of expertise. All our work, all our planning, it comes down to this. Whether you can get the long-range device working in the next few hours. Right now, that is what you need to focus on. If I could use the other device I would, but we cannot get closer to the target without suspicion. And that is one thing we cannot afford. Even a hint of suspicion would defeat the purpose, make all our efforts meaningless."

Priya glared at the man. "You killed Michael. Why?"

He grimaced. "It almost worked. Would have been too obvious to kill you then. There can be absolutely no comeback from this. Gerry here suggested a tactic he had successfully used before to throw you off track. You just turned up early. I had an interesting diversion planned so that the cops would have been right outside the door when you found your friend. A little strategic feeding of information into the right ears and you'd have been banged up as a raving lunatic and murderer. We've been searching for your PhD papers. But we have *you* now."

Priya thought she might be sick if she looked at Gerry. "What tactic did he use before?"

Gerry said, "I know you spent the last while blaming yourself for Kathy's death. And I know it was a high price for you to pay for being in the right place at the wrong time."

She looked at him in confusion.

He said, "I couldn't risk you figuring out what you had found. And then when that woman had an affair with Valerie and wouldn't stop calling, it just came to me. I needed a test case for the first device, I needed you to leave that particular field of study, and I needed to punish that woman."

Priya could hear him speaking but the words still made no sense.

"That woman? Kathy?"

He nodded.

"But she killed herself. From what they said, there was a lot of blood, she used razors."

"How many times had she called you before that? What, once every few weeks. I heard her on the phone to Valerie the last few times. Poor Valerie, she didn't want anything to do with that woman. I think it had just been a curiosity thing on Valerie's part you know. I don't think anything really happened but that woman wouldn't let it go. When she called the second time that night I knew you hadn't gone to her. I went in. I'm afraid I had to do the cutting before I used the device. This was one situation I needed it not to look like a heart attack."

Priya turned and retched. She hadn't eaten and nothing came out but a spurt of acid and saliva. She leaned against the counter and held a hand to her mouth. She realized her face was wet with tears. She wondered if she was going to faint and she could hear Reyna's voice calling her through a fog.

Gerry was still talking.

"You went off the rails. Even better result than I could have hoped for." He shook his head. "It was a real pity though, you know, you were the brightest of the lot. God! Priya, think about what we could have done if we could have worked together."

The man said, "Like you're going to do now. If you both are all that bright, it shouldn't take long."

Gerry smiled. "I always liked a challenge."

Gerry patted her hand and her skin crawled. The sun had chased the shadows off the counter and his skin glowed pale against hers.

Priya realized that if he had been crawling at the edge of madness for the last few years, he had just jumped off the cliff.

The man said, "I hate to interrupt but I'm not seeing any progress."

His voice was irritated, the first break in the calm. She needed him to remain calm. She had to forget everything else and focus on getting them out of there alive. She rubbed her face, trying to scrub the thoughts away.

She said, "Considering how I left the study, I don't know if I'm going to be able to add anything. I've spent the last few years trying to forget I had a brain."

Gerry turned to Priya and his voice took on a professorial tone as he pointed out the main elements in front of him. She brought her thoughts into focus as he explained his genius. He took pains to point out where her work had provided him with the answers, or the path to further answers. It seemed like a release for him, after years of not being able to talk about it with anyone, he was suddenly free. Her nausea deepened as she realized he was like a child offering up treasure to his mother, that he seemed to consider Priya as his source, was waiting to drink in her praise.

She closed her eyes. She needed that intellect she had tried so hard to submerge. And she knew in her heart that though her mind had been used to develop a weapon before, she would not let it happen consciously. So as the figures and methods, the frequencies and code, danced in front of her eyes, as she fought to return to a time when that was all she needed to solve her problems, a section of her brain was working on a plan. And her heart was saying goodbye.

She stole a glance around her. She measured the distance from the spot in front of her to the man. To Reyna. To Valerie. She and Gerry were the only two in the room within three feet of where the long-range device would be. She was not going to save Gerry but she needed the man to be closer.

She turned to the man. He had been staring out of the window and she saw him watching the Corrib Princess float by, its upper deck empty. She could hear the commentary in her mind, clearer than when she had sat in its lower deck on the couch seating, proud of her river, proud of her city, showing it off to her parents.

Priya asked him, "If this is going to be used to kill someone, how are you going to protect the person who presses the button? They are going to be within three feet."

He turned his head to look at her.

"He has had a pacemaker installed."

She said, "So when his natural pacemaker is destroyed, the artificial one will kick in and keep his rhythm going. Smart of you. And a huge sacrifice for him."

The man nodded. He said, and for the first time his voice held a trace of emotion, "People have made sacrifices for this. It is necessary."

She tried again, this time desperate with hope that Reyna would pick up the message. "You know, if this device goes off there is still a 3 minute timeframe where your target's heart will stop but the brain will remain alive. It is not a sure thing. If someone were to carry out immediate CPR and keep doing it until help arrived there is a possibility the target could be saved." She kept her eyes fixed on the traces of acne scars on the man's face. She noticed in her peripheral vision that Reyna was staring at her.

"We would be able to distract the help away for a few minutes…" He turned his head and looked back at the window.

Priya focused on what Gerry was doing in his development of the long-range device. The minutes dragged. He was close but he had started just right of center. His calculations were off by a fraction. He had designed the new device to look like a home controller, above suspicion. He had coded it to create the frequency pattern that should have destroyed the particular ion channels in the test set-up. The ones set up to match the ion channels in the heart muscle that controlled the self-generation of the electrical activity. The oscillometer was measuring the frequency that was being emitted. The frequency was being fed into the ion channel study chambers.

She studied the code. And saw it.

He had made a mistake. And the more he looked through it the less chance he had of seeing it. Wasn't that how one of the space shuttles crashed, she thought, a missing comma? This wasn't as simple as punctuation but in the picture in her mind, the error stood out now like a neon sign blinking on an empty motorway.

Priya said, "You're not going to let us go anyway, are you? Once we fix this, assuming we can, what's to stop you killing us then?"

The man turned around. The buttons on his black jacket caught the sunlight and bounced it into her eyes. She knew he couldn't kill them yet. If she fixed the device, he would kill them and leave and someone would die. And there would be a weapon out there that could be used to commit an undetectable murder. What would he do if she refused to fix it?

"Interesting situation we have here. Let me make it more interesting for you. While I don't have a working device, she's expendable." He gestured with the gun at Reyna. "And the other one there. If she's still alive." He nodded in Valerie's direction. "You two 'scientists' are not expendable."

He moved a step closer and pointed at the device. "However, when I have a working device, you will become expendable, I'll probably let him live and I don't really care what happens to her." He pointed to Valerie with his empty hand. Then turned and looked at Reyna. "Ms. Fairer will not be expendable any more. I made a deal, a working device and the daughter and granddaughter live." He smiled. "I see you've already worked it out."

Priya saw that Reyna had been quiet because of the threat to her mother. She didn't know what the exact words would have been but they had been effective.

Reyna's life. That was what it came down to for Priya in this little equation of life. The immediate equation. The extended equation involved other people. She could only see one way to solve both equations.

She nodded at the man and he smiled again. "Waste of a good mind. Maybe we should keep you instead of him. But somehow, I don't think you'd do it for all the money in the world. And I certainly wouldn't want to have to spend the rest of my time holding a gun to her head. Although, if you could convince me that we could work together, you could be well rewarded. And I wouldn't need that." He nodded in Gerry's direction and Priya could see the disgust in the man's eyes.

He turned back to the window. He was now within four feet of the device.

Priya caught Reyna's eye. She stared at Reyna, and then looked at the emergency defibrillator on the wall. She stared back at Reyna and willed her to understand. She saw Reyna's eyes follow hers and she looked back to see that Reyna's eyes had lingered on the red casing. Reyna looked back at Priya and Priya stared at the device on the counter in front of Gerry and back at the defibrillator. She didn't know if the defibrillator would work or if CPR was the answer but she had planted both ideas. She saw the growing awareness and then the horror in Reyna's eyes. Priya took in a deep breath. The message had been received but Priya didn't know if it would be enough. And after she pressed the button, she might never know.

She reached for the new device and took it out of Gerry's hands. She smiled through the glaze over her eyes. She'd used her intellect to win her father's love, had allowed it to be used by Valerie to seduce her, and had spent the time since trying to destroy it. And now, when she'd found someone she could love, who she thought loved her for all the right reasons... She stopped her thoughts from going there.

Her fingers flew over the keypad as she programmed the new weapon. She didn't need to test it. She knew it would work. She looked around again and measured the distance. The man was about 4 feet away. Priya just had to make sure where he ended up was within 3 feet of her and that Reyna was further than 3 feet away. She picked out the spot on the floor. She disconnected the keyboard. Picked up the device. Felt its cold corners as her hands curved around it.

Gerry looked at her and then at the device in her hand.

Priya whispered, "All that money, Gerry, where did it go? I didn't really think that was a great motivator for you."

Gerry glanced at Valerie's inert form on the floor.

Priya continued, "You loved her *that* much?"

She was surprised that Gerry kept his voice to a whisper too. "I love her. She, she…"

"Consumed you?"

He nodded. There was a look of fervor in his eyes. "She didn't know about my work with them. She didn't know where the money came from. She needed all that stuff to be happy, the houses, the car. I didn't, I came from a comfortable background. She came from a poor family you see. We had it all, and then the crash came. She is so beautiful. She doesn't realize how beautiful she is, she thinks she's losing everything as she gets older. She is so innocent."

Priya almost lost control of the train she was driving towards him.

She whispered, almost directly into his ear, "For the last two years, I felt so guilty because of what Valerie and I did behind your back, but you are a monster." She moved her head back and saw first the confusion and then the rage in Gerry's eyes as he processed what she had said.

She moved in again and whispered, "Valerie played games with everyone; she had me, Kathy, Daniel, especially you. She played with all of us but I think she liked your little brother best. Where do you think Aidan got the money to buy all the stuff he has? You gave up all your principles to make money for her and she gave it to him. The good-looking one. The charmer. She couldn't bear the thought of losing her power as she got older, of losing her looks. She loved Aidan, the young man who could keep her feeling young."

She knew she had hit again. She could see in his eyes, recognition, confirmation of his worst suppressed fears. And she could see the mist gather as his mind let go. She braced herself as Gerry lunged at her. She had the new device in her hands, her finger beside the button. She saw the man dart towards them as Gerry's hands gripped her throat.

She saw Reyna start to get up. *No!*

She hoped the man was within 3 feet, he moved fast.

She pressed the button.

She heard falling bodies as her heart stopped. She had thought she'd have 3 minutes before her brain stopped functioning but time flew when you were dying.

34 CHAPTER THIRTY-FOUR

Tuesday, August 2, 2011

The diplomat rubbed under his collarbone where all that remained was a small scar. A part of him was relieved, relieved to be rid of the wires, of the presence in his body. To know that his heart still controlled its own rhythm. But the greater part of him was devastated.

He walked out of the side street clinic and breathed in the morning air. Was there any point in returning to the embassy? If he could, he would still give his life to save his country. But the sacrifice would be pointless if the deed was known. They had known all along that there could be no comeback at all.

He walked down the street towards Massachusetts Avenue. As he turned onto it, he noticed a man standing at the corner, a suit jacket draped over his shoulder. The man was not even looking at him but the diplomat felt a pang of fear. The man reminded him of the American, the neat blue suit, the calm. He wondered again what had happened to him, the man who had been so anxious to prevent the destruction of a foreign economy. Desperate enough to kill a fellow American. He wondered whether the man had acted on his own or whether there had been others in the shadows. The complete lack of communication for the last few days told him the American was dead.

He'd had no choice. He had gone to the meeting. Pretended that everything was fine. Smiled at the woman's jokes. Shook her hand, the hand that would kill his country. Now all he could do was wait and watch as it died.

EPILOGUE

March 2012

Reyna stepped out of the terminal building at Shannon and stopped to breath in the Irish air. She wondered if its silk smoothness felt like home because of what Priya had said. Or whether she had just missed it so much as the last seven months had dragged through the nightmare landscape left after the bomb had exploded in her life. She looked down at the boy gripping onto her fingers, his face wiped clean but still sleepy after the overnight flight. She had wrapped Skyler in as many layers as she could get away with, not knowing what climate she would find in March in Ireland.

She had rented the same Mercedes and this time the heating was not necessary. Skyler was almost five and if he hadn't been so tired, he would have chatted the whole way but instead he snuggled into the passenger seat and slept. Reyna put the radio on low and listened to the debate that had raged over the destruction of a few smaller economies when America had changed its foreign policy. Reyna had listened to the same debate in America, though it had been less heated, had heard the soothing tones of the politician who had signed the changes into law in August, the media loved the attractive, charismatic politician and she had had more than the usual fifteen minutes of fame, but not much more.

As Reyna drove, she occasionally glanced over at Skyler's thin chest, reassuring herself with its movements. The three-year battle was over. And there was no clear victor except, she hoped, Skyler himself. Simone had teased her often enough about her name and had then gone and named the child… But Reyna liked it. Maybe because she loved him with an intensity that accepted every part of him, including the fact that he was Simone's flesh and blood whose fine features and dark eyes and hair he had inherited. And that his father had been an 18-year-old waiter who wanted nothing to do with him or the 'crazy French chef' as he had referred to Simone when she had told him she was pregnant.

And Simone hadn't wanted anything to do with the baby either; there wouldn't have been a baby if Reyna hadn't insisted that Simone listen to the doctor who had told them it was too late for a termination, that she would care for the baby. And Reyna had put up with the screaming, the ranting, the hitting. She had loved that baby from the first breath he took. And in doing so, Reyna had handed Simone the deadliest weapon to use against her. Which Simone had done. For two long years after Reyna, not able to put up with the abuse anymore, had left her. Simone had always made it clear she did not want Skyler so Reyna had never imagined Simone would restrict Reyna's contact with the child to monthly visits, but Simone's spite had been stronger than any vestige of maternal feeling. She used the threat of never seeing the boy again to make sure Reyna could never break free of her. .

Reyna drove slowly. She was too late anyway; the memorial service would be over by the time she got to Connemara. She had always been too late for Priya. Too late to realize what she felt, too late to realize that Priya was not like Simone, could never have been like Simone. Too late for everything, the words cycled by riding on the broken white line of the motorway.

She drove through Galway, barely able to look at the green glass walls of the buildings she could see from the Quincentennial Bridge as she paused in its traffic. There would be enough time to visit the clinic later. The Fairer Research Company was gone but the Fairer Clinic was still there. It supported the patients with implanted Fairer pacemakers but now the pacemakers that were installed were those manufactured by other companies. No company could survive the deaths of the two Daniel Fairers and Gerry Lynch, especially when one of them was the owner of TechMed Devices.

Her insides hurt when she thought of her grandfather, still convinced he had done everything for the right reasons. Until Daniel had been killed. Reyna had watched the agony in his eyes when Catherine had screamed over and over again at him for her lost son, for all the losses. Reyna couldn't bear the pain in the study and walked out to sit outside on the steps of the mansion, melting in the heat of a New York August. Catherine joined her and they had gotten into the car but her mother had run back into the mansion emerging a few minutes later with the wooden rocking horse. Reyna looked at Skyler and knew he would love the carved horse that Catherine had brought back to Connemara. Catherine had flown from New York to Shannon later that day so had missed the discovery of her father's body that evening, slumped at his desk. Age, grief, and guilt too high a toll for his 86-year-old body. Catherine had not come back for the funeral.

The road past Priya's house was edged with traffic so Reyna was forced to sit for a few minutes outside its driveway. The grass was neat, the new paint gleaming and she wondered why Tara and Aidan kept it so well when they were only renting it until they found somewhere else. Or that's what they said but Reyna knew the house was now their home. She envied their ability to put the past behind them. But she wondered whether Tara looked over at Aidan every now and then and wondered.

At least they didn't have to see Valerie. Valerie who had fought on that awful day to hide the truth from Gerry even when threatened with a gun. The surprise at Reyna's sudden arrival that morning and the terror of Reyna disclosing anything about her had pushed Valerie into an attack that the American man had stopped with a vicious blow. Valerie's injury and the resulting brain damage, though slight, had forced her to retire. She now lived in London in the flat she had bought for Aidan and where she had visited him whenever she could in the six years since she'd met him at her wedding to his brother. She had not done anything illegal; she'd eventually been allowed to leave Galway after the police had dredged through her past. Valerie would not talk about the details of the games she had played, or the reasons. Reyna had the feeling Valerie's future would be very different to the one she had planned, that the fear of growing old alone was now a real one.

Skyler mumbled in his sleep. He woke up as they approached Spiddal and demanded the toilet. Reyna pulled in at a hotel in Spiddal and waited for him outside the toilets. She was getting used to having him around again. They came out of the hotel and she decided to stretch her legs. They wandered hand in hand down the main street stopping every few yards as she pointed out places and objects. He took it all in with a serious look on his face. She leaned down to kiss his cheek.

The painting stared out at her from the gallery window. She straightened up and took in the painted words branded across the top of the window.

Catherine Turner Art Gallery.

Reyna stared at the painting and felt her heart break again. She could still taste the salt on her lips. She peered through the glass. Many of the paintings were Priya's. She could see the scrawled signature 'PJ' but she didn't need that to recognize the hand that had painted them. She touched her hand to the warm glass over the seascape she had picked up in Priya's living room and through the wetness in her eye, she noticed the reflection below her; Skyler had his hand pressed up against a portrait of a sheepdog, its lolling tongue almost sticking through the glass to lick his palm. Reyna took his other hand and then picked him up and hugged him tight to her. He chuckled and she rested her forehead against his for a minute before carrying him back to the car.

∞

The potholes in the back road to the house had been filled in and the car glided through the trees. Reyna pulled in at the back door and sat for a minutes taking in the familiar and the new. The skeleton of the building at the side had been renovated and extended towards the back creating a courtyard between the two buildings. The simple lines of the extension matched the old farmhouse. The window boxes on both buildings spilt out a profusion of blue and red and pink, the younger annex sporting even more, with yellow and orange added in to the mix.

Skyler had already scrambled out and Reyna followed slowly. He headed towards the gap between the houses and disappeared around the corner. Reyna heard him giggle and walked around the corner to find him sitting on the cream stones. Sitting facing him was a sheepdog looking as surprised to bump into a little boy. The dog looked up as Reyna appeared and she felt a momentary dart of fear for Skyler but the boy giggled again as the dog ignored Reyna and licked Skyler's face. It got to its feet and Reyna realized it only had three legs. She reached down to rub its head and noticed that the purple bone-shaped tag on its collar read 'Trio'. Reyna laughed as she took Skyler's hand and helped him up.

The extension had large sliding glass doors that were unlocked and Reyna stepped into a light-filled white-walled living room with oversized couches and armchairs spread around a huge fireplace. The early spring sunlight streamed through the skylights. There were photos and paintings hung on the walls, the splashes of sea-green waves and the layers of earth-brown bog inside competing in the battle of colors outside.

Skyler and Trio were getting acquainted outside and the boy's squeals of laughter trickled into the room and then faded as Reyna wandered through it. She stopped at a painting that hung in the corner, feeling a physical ache in her chest as she stared at the portrait. The light brown eyes, the smooth skin, the midnight black hair. She had dreamed this face for months and she was lost in it again.

"Did no-one tell you it was rude to stare?"

Reyna jerked back from the painting and turned to the door.

Priya walked over to the mantelpiece and placed a wreath of lilies on it, the cream flowers resting their heads against the walls. She was thinner, the black suit hung on her slight frame. But she looked healthier than the last time Reyna had seen her lying in the clinic recovery room the day the pacemaker was installed.

Reyna took a deep breath and tried to slow her sprinting heart. She gestured to her own collarbone and asked, "How are you doing?"

Priya patted the slight rise of skin. "Most of the time I forget it is there." She smiled. "Other times I panic when I think I can't generate my own heart beat and I need this thing to keep working."

I miss you. "They miss you at the clinic." Reyna managed to keep her voice business-like.

"I use a home controller to transmit the pacemaker information to the clinic. Still have to do it under a false name. Mostly as a record and a double-check; I pretty much do the checks here."

Reyna nodded. "It's safer this way. We can't be sure whether he acted on his own. Whether there are others looking for that technology. The only place it is now is in your head. I brought everything back here and destroyed the device you used. And all the papers. I can't be sure though. It was chaotic for a while, but I think I covered everything.

Valerie had no idea what Gerry had been doing. She was just used over those last two days to put more pressure on him. She was too busy playing her own games."

They stood facing each other across the room. The silence was broken by the bark of a dog and Priya called out for Trio. She looked back in surprise at Reyna when the dog arrived followed by a little boy.

Reyna walked over to Skyler and took his hand. She drew in a deep breath and turned to Priya.

"This is my son, Skyler Turner. Skyler, this is Priya."

Priya hid her shock well apart from the slight widening of her eyes. She knelt with a smile and held out a hand to Skyler who took it shyly.

"I see you've met Trio already. He was rescued off a calendar." Priya smiled as Skyler looked in puzzlement at the dog who nudged him and headed back out looking over its shoulder.

Priya said, "Go on out with him, he won't let us rest if you don't."

Skyler raced Trio out of the door, the three-legged dog almost as agile as the boy.

Reyna asked, "Is my mother back too?"

Priya got to her feet and gestured at the farmhouse. "Powli dropped us off. He's been another unusual but welcome addition to our lives. Catherine went in to change."

"I'm sorry I didn't make it to Michael's memorial."

Priya said, "I guess there are a lot of things that didn't happen as we thought." She turned away and walked towards the kitchen.

Reyna tried to figure out the trace of anger in Priya's voice. It had been Priya's decision not to call her on the date and at the time they had agreed. Six months. February 1st 2012, 6 p.m. If she had wanted Reyna to come back. Reyna had told Simone about Priya and Simone had finally realized that Reyna would never let Simone hold her captive again. But Priya hadn't called. Reyna had obtained custody on that day, Simone handing over the boy she had used to get what she could out of Reyna. And Reyna had waited for her other love to call her home, brimming with excitement and the freedom finally to tell Priya about Skyler and the hold that Simone had had over her.

Priya said, "He's a beautiful boy. Why didn't you tell me about him?" She was not looking at Reyna.

"At the time I couldn't risk Simone finding anything out about me. And I didn't want to feel anything for anybody else. To give her anything else she could use to control me. I didn't want to lose him. And, I didn't want him to lose me. His mother didn't really want him; she just needed a way to get to me. And to my grandfather's money."

Priya frowned.

Reyna burst out, "I need to take Skyler in to his grandmother. She'll be anxious to see him." She ignored the confusion on Priya's face and strode out into the courtyard calling for Skyler. The boy and dog followed her as she went to the back door of the farmhouse.

Catherine was standing at the kitchen door watching a lime green van leave. The horn beeped and a hand waved from the driver's window as the van passed under the canopy of trees. She beamed as she hugged Reyna and then Skyler and hustled all of them into the kitchen.

∞

Reyna slumped down at the kitchen table and put her face in her hands. Skyler had agreed that Trio needed sleep as much as he did and was now asleep on the couch in the living room. The dog had jumped onto the couch and waited on the boy's feet until he slept, then hopped out of the house.

Catherine made them tea and sat down at the table with Reyna.

"I'm sorry I haven't been in touch in the last month." Reyna's voice was muffled in her palms. "After Priya's decision, I just took off with Skyler. Did you try to get in touch?"

Catherine said nothing and Reyna looked at her through her parted fingers. The look of confusion on Catherine's face matched Priya's face earlier.

Catherine said, "You asked us not to contact you." She shook her head. "I thought you and Simone didn't want contact with me."

"What?" Reyna stared at Catherine. "What the hell would Simone have to do with it?"

Catherine sighed. "I knew I should have called you to check. But Priya was so upset and so sure."

"Priya? Mother, you are going to have to tell me what the hell is going on."

"From your reaction, I gather Simone is what is going on. I think that woman has managed to mess you up again." Catherine patted Reyna's hand. "Priya spent the six months healing. After the last few years, she needed that. And so did you. I didn't protest at the time when you both decided to wait the six months. I knew you both needed to sort your own messes out and to heal. But I hated the idea that it would come down to one phone call."

"Which she didn't make." Reyna said bitterly.

"Yes she did. She called you at 6 p.m. on February 1st as you both agreed."

Reyna said, "No, she didn't. I waited by the phone."

Catherine paused, and then said, "You know I wonder sometimes how you two managed to agree on anything. Did you forget the time difference?"

Reyna leaned back in the chair. A sheepish look wandered onto her face.

"I guess there was so much going on…No, we didn't clarify that bit." She paused and thought back. "So Priya must have called at noon New York time when Simone was dropping Skyler off at the house. I left them there when I collected the papers from the lawyer's office."

"Well, it was Simone who answered the phone. Which upset Priya anyway, but not as much as what Simone told her. Which was that you two were back together, that you had never stopped loving your wife and that no bit of fluff could ever come between you."

Reyna felt the familiar rage at Simone creep into her.

Catherine continued, "It was devastating for Priya. She had moved out here soon after her surgery. She got to spend a lot of time with her father when he lived with us for a few months. She adopted Trio, finished her Art Therapy course. She started painting again and we set up the therapy room in Spiddal at the gallery. I was starting to heal as well; I spent a lot of time with her dad, Joe. We were all doing really well, coming to terms with all that loss and grief. You should see the portrait Priya did of you if you really want to know what she feels about you. Or felt. I've had to keep it in my room since that phone call. And then she calls you to ask you to come back and hears this from the woman she thinks is your wife. And I have to hear that you don't want anything to do with us because I had tried to separate you again." Catherine's voice had risen as she spoke.

Reyna couldn't speak.

Catherine lowered her voice. "After what happened with your grandfather, I think I hid away from you as well. I was scared you would never forgive me if you found out. I don't know if I can forgive myself but it was his choice in the end. I just gave him the means."

It was Reyna's turn to be confused.

Catherine got up and dragged a chair over to the kitchen cupboard. She climbed up, felt around the top of the cupboards, and retrieved an object that she carefully placed on the table in front of Reyna.

The matchbox-sized device lay on the table winking silver in the light of the sun.

Catherine whispered, "I hope you can forgive me." She took the device in her hands and walked out onto the patio. She put the device down, grabbed one of the curbstones from the edge of the patio, and brought it down hard, smashing the device. The slivers of metal spread in a circle, wires and miniature circuits curling at their centre. Catherine gathered up what she could, dumped the pieces in the trash, her movements slow and tired.

Reyna still couldn't speak and Catherine laid a hand on her shoulder and said, "I'm going to lie down with Sky. I think there is somebody you need to talk to." She wandered out of the room to join the boy before Reyna could correct her.

∞

Priya wasn't in the extension and there was no sign of Trio either. Reyna heard the sound of barking from the direction of the lake and walked down the path through the forest.

Priya was sitting on the grass where they had lain. She was throwing stones for Trio who dashed into the shallow water after every stone. He barked as he stared at each stone under water and then looked back at Priya for the next one.

"Are you being cruel to the poor thing?" Reyna sat beside Priya. "Throwing things to him that he can't get."

"I'm not the one who makes an art form of that. Besides, he goes in for them after I throw a few. He gathers them up in a little pile on the shore. He's just delaying, and possibly showing off for you."

Priya threw another stone and Trio chased it, grabbing it in his mouth and hopping to the grass bank where he dropped it. He splashed off again and stuck his head in the water emerging drenched but triumphant with his prize, which he deposited beside the other stone before repeating the process.

"Priya, there is so much I need to tell you." Reyna caught her breath as Priya turned those eyes on her. She hurried on. "There was so much to deal with. I closed down the Research Company and sold TechMed and settled with the families of the technicians who died and with John Landon and also with Liam Whelan. I'm still going to run the Fairer Foundation but I'm going to do it from here as I keep an eye on the clinic. I sorted out the divorce and custody."

She smiled as Priya's mouth fell open.

"Yes, Priya, my divorce. I have not been married in any sense of the word since Simone had the affair with that kid and got pregnant. I stayed with her because of Skyler, because she threatened to take him away. And I knew he needed me. She didn't want him. When we finally reached an agreement, she came to the house to drop him off. I hear she spoke to you."

Priya nodded.

Reyna said, "When I didn't hear from you, I thought… But I couldn't let it go like that. I figured that if I moved over and hung around, you might feel something for me again. I had a speech all ready for you and it was a really good one where I could finally tell what I felt. But then I see you and all the planning goes out of the window. I just know that you make me feel alive again, make me trust, make me laugh. I keep remembering your smile, your gentleness, your courage, your kiss. The cute way you misquote stuff and don't even know you're doing it. I didn't expect to find out you had called."

She stopped speaking as Priya leant over and kissed her.

They laughed as Trio interrupted a few minutes later with a shake and a spray of muddy water over them. He rested his head on Priya's lap. His wet fur was sticking out in every direction.

Priya said, as she smiled back at the dog, "I know he's a mutt but he's beautiful to me."

Reyna pulled her close. "The way you'd say it, beauty is in the heart of the beholder."

THE END

ABOUT THE AUTHOR

R J Samuel is the pen name of the author, who lives and works in Galway, Ireland. She was born in 1967 in Nigeria to Indian parents. She left Nigeria in 1984 to study in Galway, Ireland and has remained in Galway since then, apart from a 3-year episode in the southwest of France. She is an Irish citizen and now considers herself almost Irish as well as almost Indian.

She has been writing creatively for 6 years, excluding her period in France where she wrote nothing creative, probably because she was running a restaurant\bar despite having a background in Medicine (she is a qualified medical doctor) and IT (she has a Masters in IT) and absolutely no background in restaurants, apart from eating in them.

Her story 'Helmets' was shortlisted for the 2011 Over the Edge 'New Writer of the Year Competition' and she was the only entrant to have both her fiction and her poetry long-listed for the Doire Press '1st Annual International Fiction and Poetry Chapbook Competition' in January 2012. Her short story 'Vision Painter' went on to be short-listed for this competition.

She is currently writing her second novel, 'FALLING COLOURS – The Misadventures of a Vision Painter', which is also set in Galway and which is based on the short story 'Vision Painter'.

www.RJSamuel.com
Twitter: @R_J_Samuel

Made in the USA
Middletown, DE
03 March 2015